CYBORG AND THE SINGLE MOM

OTHERWORLDLY MEN # 3

SUSAN GRANT

Cover art by Biserka Design

ABOUT CYBORG AND THE SINGLE MOM

*Can a single mom who is afraid to lose her
heart find love with a fugitive cyborg who
has forgotten he has one?*

Evie hasn't forgiven Reef for invading her home and terrorizing her chihuahua, but agrees to a temporary stay to help Earth avoid an alien invasion. But does the suburban mom really want to shelter the alien hit man who almost offed her sister and future brother-in-law?

Reef can't understand why these humans care about him, and has no memory of his life before he was conscripted and turned into a bio-engineered super solder. But as his computers fail, the man he once was emerges, and soon he's determined to figure out how to navigate this thing called love.

Read the hot and heartwarming conclusion to the Other-Worldly Men series today!

(Based on the title How to Lose an Extraterrestrial in 10 Days)

PROLOGUE

Planet Sandreem
> *Twenty-five years ago*

Silent and determined adversaries, the boy and his father were locked in battle. Their foreheads nearly touched as they sat hunched over a Sech board, scrutinizing several dozen game pieces carved to resemble soldiers. The bustle and laughter of the rest of the family filled the cottage, while filets of fresh-caught river eel sizzled on the grill. A few raindrops splashed against the windows of the cottage, the last of an early evening squall.

Eriff tried to predict the result of his father's confident moves across the game board. Some endings had him invading his father's Holy Keep, but others had Eriff's goddess falling to his father's onslaught. Which would be the best move? The right move.

His father's quiet voice broke his concentration. "Life or death...so it always is for you, boy."

Eriff glanced up into amused blue eyes that looked just like his, according to his mother. *"As vivid as the noon sky on High Sun Day,"* she'd say. *"With hair as black as soot and eyes like those, my fair Eriff, you'll snare your lady's heart with a glance, just as your father won mine."*

His father's chair creaked as he leaned back. He pretended to work stiffness out of his limbs. "I fear I'll grow old waiting for you to make a decision."

His father's teasing left him puzzled. Time sped by when he was stalking his prey—outside in the woods hunting, or here in a game of Sech. "Have I taken too long?"

"Let me say this. It seems the goddesses gifted you with infinite patience. With life so slow on this backwater planet, it'll serve you well, I think." Under his breath, he added, "Move your archer...there."

"But that will open my quadrex to your warriors!"

"Take a chance." His father's eyes sparkled.

"But, Papa, my archer, it's not *logical*."

"Not everything in life can be logically thought out, Eriff. Often, taking a risk brings the sweetest reward of all."

Often, but not *always*. And that was the part Eriff didn't like about his father's advice. As soon as a player's goddess piece was taken, the game was over. But in Sech, even the lowliest soldier could topple an empire.

Eriff moved his scout, planning to inch it forward and breach his father's Holy Keep.

His father gave a shrug and captured one of Eriff's commanders, dropping the piece into a worn leather pouch.

Eriff lowered his head.

Chuckling, his father reached across the table to ruffle his hair. "So serious...an old soul your grandmother says. I wish for you the chance to leave this world and find your fortune, but alas, the chances of that are next to none."

Eriff perked up. "You had that chance, Papa." Maybe this time his father would tell him of the years he'd spent fighting the Drakken. There were stories, oh so many stories—Eriff could see them in his eyes. But no matter how much he pleaded, the man never shared them. All Eriff knew was that his father joined the Coalition Space Force as a teenager and went off to see the galaxy.

At least he'd come back. A great-uncle on his mother's side hadn't. Mangus Slipstream left to become a scientist long before Eriff was born and no one ever heard from him again.

Well, Eriff was staying put. Even if he wanted to leave, how would he? It was rare for ships to pass this way. Commerce required wormholes for the ships to speed through vast distances that would normally take months and likely years. There were no wormholes near Sandreem.

It was quiet here, and that's the way Eriff liked it. No one wasted much thought about the rest of the galaxy or the war. Why should they when nothing happened here to remind them of it?

Eriff might have doubted there *was* a "somewhere else" if he hadn't seen the evidence with his own eyes: a deep-space cargo transport. But he'd been little more than a babe and remembered nothing of the crew except for the stink of their craft.

His father did, however, bring home one treasure from

the far-off lands: the Sech board. It was a revered family possession. As soon as Eriff could hold a game piece in his hand, his father taught him how to play.

Just then, a double crack of thunder echoed down from the mountains. The table vibrated, rattling the game pieces out of position. Eriff gasped in dismay, trying to put the pieces back in order. His father's hand covered his much smaller one, stopping him. "The game's over."

Thunder rumbled on and on. Eriff joined his sisters at the windows. "I never heard a storm like this before," Sayree said.

"Me, either!" Karah sang out.

Eriff threw open the window and peeked outside. Clouds raced across a clearing sky. Thunder boomed again, roaring. *Screeching.*

The small house shook on its very foundation. It sounded as if the sky was tearing open. Eriff's heart bounced with the thrill of it. Then a shadow passed over the house.

"Look!" He came up on his toes as an enormous, gleaming starship descended toward the horizon. Ribbons of white clouds trailed behind it. It was going to land! "Father! Is it a Coalition ship?"

"Yes."

Eriff wasn't sure what they'd have done if the answer had been otherwise. If the Drakken had come, it would be to slaughter them all. They had no mercy, no religion. While the Coalition worshipped the Goddess and all Her descendants, the Drakken were nonbelievers. His mother told him it was why they'd split from the Coalition long ago. His father said the Drakken Empire had spent nearly every year since trying to invade the Holy Keep on Sakka and take the goddess-queen in a real-life game of Sech.

Eriff's mother answered a banging at the front door. Rion, chief of the planetary watch, stormed in. "Visitors, Deklan. We're mobilizing!"

Eriff's father was already pulling on his boots. "Who are they, where are they headed and what do they want?"

"Coalition deep-space patrol ship. Eastern quadrex. Don't know yet. They stopped answering questions after we exchanged the basics." Rion shrugged. "Or maybe our radios just weren't too good."

"Are they ever? We'd better cobble together a welcome delegation and hightail it out to the landing site. Otherwise they'll think we're a bunch of backward rimmers."

"We *are* backward rimmers," Eriff's mother pointed out.

His father pulled her close for a quick kiss. "No need to shout that fact." He tucked a hunting knife into his belt, and a flashlight. Then he forked a slab of grilled eel into a piece of flatbread, splashed on some hot sauce, rolled it all up and stuck it in his hip pouch. "I'll be back later with all the news."

Eriff grabbed his bow and arrows and ran to the door.

"Where are you going?"

"I'm off to hunt." And hunt he would. He'd hunt the off-worlders. He wanted to see what they were made of, these ship-dwellers, these folk from the central worlds. *The land of Sech and goddesses.* And he'd do it all without their knowing. No one on Sandreem could move through the forest as silently as he could.

"You haven't eaten dinner." Suppressing a smile, his mother set a plate of food under his nose. With one whiff of the aroma, all thoughts of starships vanished. He sat down hard and dug in.

There was only one thing Eriff loved more than Sech, and that was food. Each bite was its own wonder—the contrasting tang of the spices and the textures; the crunch of cuttle-squash, the moist, smoky flesh of the grilled eel; the sweetness of grass ale with the sour aftertaste that made his cheeks ache.

When he was finished, he made the sign of the goddess over his heart, thanking Her. "And you too, Mama." Then he grabbed his gear and ran outside.

This time of year the sun hung low in the sky all night. Everything was bathed in soft, pink-orange light. Eriff's feet bounced soundlessly off the spongy forest floor as he raced along narrow, shadowy paths secret to everyone else but him. Drowsy tree barrets chirruped. Water left over from the rains fell from huge, furry icquit leaves high above, landing with a *plop, plop, plop* sound that soon drowned in the noise coming from the spaceship in the clearing.

He stopped short. The craft was huge—bigger than twenty or thirty cottages. Impossible that it could get off the ground! But he'd seen it fly. It was white, blinding white, and triangular: heavy-looking with stubby wings. But in the air it had looked so graceful. It reminded him of the ancient rays that glided below the waves of the inland sea but that flopped clumsily when stranded on the beach.

Something stank—metallic and hot. The cooling engines. A sneeze pushed up his nose but he swallowed it, his eyes watering. To get a better view, he shimmied up the trunk of a tree, springing from branch to branch like a whip-tailed conifox. Crouched low, he waited for the ship's crew to greet the group of Sandreemers just now arriving at the ship.

His father and the others nervously smoothed their clothing, running fingers through their hair. The ship's hatch opened and a tall, strong man with short, bright orange hair, a tall fair-haired woman, and a bald, dark-skinned man strode down the ramp, looking impressive in their crisp uniforms and gleaming insignia.

The groups greeted each other. "My apologies for intruding," the orange-haired man said. He seemed to be in charge. Probably the captain. "A balky fusion drive necessitated we put down for some repairs." He stopped himself. "Engine... working bad," he said, explaining with gestures and simpler words, as if Eriff's father and the other Sandreem party were stupid rather than technologically backward compared to the rest of the galaxy. "We won't be here long, a few standard hours. My crew will remain onboard."

"Then please accept these blessings of our planet." The disappointed Sandreemers presented the off-worlders with baskets of fruits, nuts, vegetables and ready-to-cook game. Another basket contained local handicrafts.

As soon as Eriff's father and the rest left, the fiery-haired captain reached into a basket and pulled out a thick, limp, skinned eel. He showed it to the crew, and they all burst into laughter. He threw it into the underbrush with obvious distaste.

The fools! That was a female river eel, prized for its tender meat. One that size would have made rich, sweet filets for a dozen people or more.

Anger simmered in Eriff's belly. The strangers thought

they were better than the Sandreemers. Better than his father. Nothing was more important to Eriff than his family. To insult his world and his people was to insult him!

"Stay onboard," the captain told his companions. He checked for a weapon on his belt. "I'll have a look around."

"I don't recommend it, sir," the bald man said. "I saw a few small life forms around the perimeter. I don't think there's anything dangerous, but better not to take a chance."

"The only thing dangerous around here is the natives' idea of fine cuisine. Did you see that thing? Goddess, a snake!"

"Sir, I believe it was an eel."

"Whatever. It's not going in my mouth. But *this* is." He showed them a lumpy pouch. Eriff couldn't see what was inside.

The bald man's brow went up. "Picnic, sir?"

"You could call it that. I've been on this ship too damned long. Give me a secured perimeter, say one click, all the way around. That way you're happy and I'm happy."

"Yes, sir."

The captain strolled away from the ship like he owned every square inch of ground. For a long time, Eriff mirrored his exploration from high in the trees. At several points during the man's stroll, Eriff took aim with his bow. *Stupid off-worlder, don't you know I've got you in my sights?*

By the stream, the captain stopped, closing his eyes and inhaling, as if Sandreem was the most beautiful place he'd even seen.

It is. No place in the galaxy equaled Sandreem in beauty; of that Eriff was sure.

The captain prowled more than walked, listening, smelling, seeing, but still he didn't sense Eriff's presence. He crouched by the stream, letting the water run over his hand to test the temperature. Coward. A Sandreemer would have jumped in with no hesitation.

The man stripped naked. This was no soft-bodied freight hauler; he was as fit as Eriff's father. Soon the captain was floating on his back in a deep pool under a canopy of willows. His uniform fluttered from the gnarled branch of an ancient ebbe-apple tree. Under it was the pouch he'd brought along from the ship. "Picnic," the bald man had said.

There was food in that box. Off-worlder food.

Eriff slid down the tree. Covered in shadows, he was a shadow himself as he sneaked up to the captain's gear. A brush of his fingers over the man's uniform and his amazing pistol sent a frisson of excitement up his arm. What would it be like, using a weapon like that to hunt?

A splash sounded from the pool. Eriff froze, his heart slamming against his rib cage. Thankfully the captain was still floating, unaware he'd soon be walking back to his ship hungry.

Eriff snatched the pouch and took it with him into the woods. He lifted the lid. The food had been kept warm somehow. It seemed to be a dish of layers of meat, pungent white cheese and vegetables, flat and brown and unfamiliar. He inhaled the aroma and shuddered in pleasure. Then he squished a finger into the food and brought a morsel to his mouth for a taste.

"Goddess," he whispered. It was spiced with flavors he

didn't recognize. He dug in and scooped up mouthfuls until not a speck of sauce remained.

The off-worlder waded to shore and shook water from his hair. He'd dressed before he appeared to notice that his meal was missing. "Where the...?" Eyes narrowed, his mouth thinning to a furious slash, he peered into the woods as he turned in a full circle. "Who's there?"

Eriff scampered away, leaping from tree to tree. The captain followed, surprisingly soundless, but Eriff evaded him, knowing every hiding place, every twist of branch of the ancient trees. His blood sang with the thrill of the game. It was like Sech, only real.

Gulping air, Eriff paused above an obvious path where he lifted his bow and arrow. He'd show this intruder what Sandreemers were made of.

He waited until the captain passed under an ebbe tree laden with large fist-size fruit before he let the arrow fly. It snipped the stems of several ebbes. The falling fruit bounced off the captain's head.

Eriff expected the off-worlder to be furious, but he threw back his head and laughed, shoulders rocking. "To my impressive and invisible adversary," he said, lifting an ebbe in a toast to the trees where Eriff crouched unseen.

Silently, Eriff drew back the bowstring. Before the captain had a chance to take a bite from the ebbe, Eriff loosed the arrow.

The fruit exploded in the captain's hand.

His face darkened, and his narrowed eyes turned frighteningly cold. "That was close, rimmer. A little too close, in fact. Are you tiring of your game, then, and wish to make it real? We can make it so, if you wish." He drew his pistol, sighting through the scanner. "We can make this as real as you want."

Eriff pressed flat against the tree trunk as the muzzle tracked past him. And stopped. *He sees you!*

Eriff's knees shook. Pure terror gripped his chest.

The captain lowered the pistol. "Goddess be, it's only a child. Come down from that tree! Are you hungry, little rimmer? I have more food." The off-worlder made a show of rooting around in his pocket. "But you'll have to come down and get it."

He thinks you're as stupid as he thought Papa was. Something in Eriff just had to prove the off-worlder wrong.

Sweat trickled down Eriff's jaw. He raised the bow one last time. As steady as he could, he brought the arrow around to his target and fired. It caught the captain's right epaulet and sheared it off. *Thwack!* The captain's Coalition rank and a large piece of his uniform shirt was now pinned to the tree.

Thwack! The captain's left epaulet joined the right. Eriff caught the briefest glimpse of the captain standing there, his shirt in shreds, before he took advantage of the captain's distraction and fled.

Tree to tree he leaped until he was far enough away to descend safely to the paths. And then he ran like the wind in the direction of home—

Something slammed him in the face. It felt like a stone wall made of light and heat.

He landed hard on his back, his head swimming. *Run!* He scrambled to his feet and charged forward. Again, lightning flashed behind his eyes, and he was thrown to the ground.

Whatever was there, he couldn't see it, but it was as impenetrable as any wall.

The captain's footsteps were getting closer. *Run!*

Eriff's skin tingled and stung. He managed to get his knees under him, using his bow as a crutch. *Hurry.* Twigs snapped and crunched behind him much closer now. The captain was almost there.

Fear flared, sharp and hot, driving him to his feet.

Something slammed into his back with the force of a mighty kick. He was thrown face-first into the dirt.

An explosion of pain stole his ability to move. A second later, it took his consciousness.

Eriff woke to nausea and the sight of the ground careening back and forth below him. Someone held him by the waist-belt like a sack of grain, swinging him as he walked.

Nausea surged. Sweat needled his body. His stomach balled up, spilling its contents on the forest floor.

He heard groans and laughter through the sounds of his retching. Male voices. "So you steal my food, little rimmer," one said, "and have the nerve to vomit it up on my boots."

It was the off-worlder captain. Eriff had shot arrows at him. He'd be furious. He peddled his legs, trying to free himself.

The captain gave him a hard shake. "Be still. You're in enough trouble as it is. Read the charges against him, Major Atir."

The bald officer cleared his throat. "Charge number one

—following the captain for a goodly amount of time without him detecting your presence."

"Guilty!" the captain sang out.

"Charge two—stealing the captain's dinner from literally behind his back."

"Guilty!"

"And—the most heinous of the lot—stripping the captain of his rightfully earned Coalition rank in a most humiliating fashion."

"Guilty!"

They were going to punish him. Maybe kill him. Eriff swiped his knuckles across his nose, trying hard not to cry.

"No one's ever bested the captain like that," the officer said.

"Need you remind me, Major Atir?"

Eriff sensed the men were smiling at the captain's dramatic, wounded tone, but he was too sick and scared to be sure.

"You'd better remember how to walk really quick, little rimmer. For a scrap of a thing, you sure are heavy." He dropped him to his feet. Eriff's legs wobbled like overcooked kristalks, but the man propelled him along. "When I ordered the force-field around the ship, it was to keep wild things out, not to keep them in. But if not for that perimeter, you'd have escaped me. No one escapes me. Until now, that is. You have a gift, a natural-born talent. I know of a school for special boys like you. In fact, I helped found the school."

A school? After hearing the charges against him, he was sure they planned to execute him. Now it sounded as if they meant to draft him. Forced conscriptions were legal—it was wartime; it had *always* been wartime—but in the Rim it was the stuff of fireside stories, not anything that actually happened to anybody. And not to kids.

His boots hit the gangway of the ship. Eriff's blood chilled. The men were bringing him on board.

"No!" He dug in his heels. "I want to stay here. I don't need a school." Especially not an off-worlder school.

He was a Sandreemer. He could never leave the woods and the inland sea, the midnight sun in summer and the smell of his mother's cooking in the dead of winter when the sun stayed down all day. If these men took him, it would be like tearing out a vital organ. He'd be as good as dead. "Please!"

A hand spun him around. In a second, the captain's face had filled his vision. "Enough!" The intensity of his piercing green gaze and the deadliness of his tone struck icy fear deep in Eriff's chest. "I serve the Coalition in many ways, but what I loved most was working as an assassin. Do you know what assassins do?"

Sniffling, Eriff shook his head. "K-kill people?"

"On command. And sometimes when we feel like it." He gave Eriff another hard shake, choking him by the collar. Eriff's stomach protested but he was too terrified to throw up.

"Soon men like me will be obsolete. Mere humans will be no match for the super soldiers of the future. Biomechatronic components integrated into the human body on the cellular level. A REEF—Robotically Engineered Enemy Fighter. When I return to base, I will begin gathering candidates for the program. But it looks like my side trip through the Rim rewarded me with an early recruit."

Only now did the captain's hand loose its hold on Eriff's collar. He wheezed air into his starved lungs.

"A reward indeed. Your talents are undeniable, little rimmer. With bioengineered enhancements, you'll be unstoppable."

An officer called down from inside the ship. "We're ready to launch, Captain."

"*No!* You can't take me! My parents will never let you!"

"Hell, boy, they'll thank me. I just gave you a future beyond their wildest dreams."

His father's words came back to haunt him: *"I wish for you the chance to leave this world and find your fortune, but alas, the chances of that are next to none."*

Eriff grabbed hold of the hatchway as the captain tried to push him through it. He held on to the rim of the hatch for all he was worth.

Anger tightened the man's voice. "You might be the ideal age, size and temperament for the REEF program, little rimmer, but as for intelligence? The way you're hanging on to that hatch I'm having my doubts. Let go of the goddess-be-damned door!"

Eriff hung on with all his might. "Papa!" he yelled. "Mama!"

Other crew members gathered around, drawn by the commotion. Finally, Major Atir crouched to peel his fingers off the hatchway frame, one at a time.

"No!" Eriff scrabbled for a handhold as he was dragged away. Once more he swung from the captain's hand, which was looped through his waist-belt. "Mama! Papa!" His finger-nails scraped over the deck of the starship.

The hatch slammed shut. Eriff stopped screaming for his parents and simply screamed, until his throat was in danger of shredding raw. Someone would hear him before his voice gave out. Someone would come.

"Quiet!" A stinging slap across his face brought his attention back to the captain. Eriff shook, gasping and sobbing. "That is enough, little rimmer," he warned in a low growl. "With luck, you'll be a REEF. Start acting like one." He threw Eriff into a small room and locked the door.

Sunshine poured through a single porthole on the far wall. Eriff crawled to it, clinging to the rim throughout the launch of the mighty starship.

The effects of the pistol's paralyzing blast lingered. His stomach rolled; his arms and legs trembled. Humiliated and afraid, he dashed away a stray tear.

I am weak.

Weakness had kept him from preventing what happened to him. But what if his body was made so strong by machines that he never again had to worry about it failing him? What if no matter what kind of trouble he got into, he'd be strong enough to get out of it?

What would it be like, he thought, to be *unstoppable?*

The huge ship trembled and shook, but Eriff's shivers slowly stopped, as if he'd grown too cold for even that. The farther he was taken from home, the colder he got, until he felt nothing at all. He stayed at the porthole long after Sandreem shrank to a blue-green star and disappeared, staring outside until his tears had dried to tracks of salt on his cheeks and his heart was as hollow as the void of space outside.

The door slid open. The captain sauntered in and leaned a shoulder against the wall. With those miss-nothing eyes, he studied Eriff. "I was right about you," he said finally.

Eriff recoiled. This off-worlder knew nothing about him. *Nothing.* Hatred welled up in his throat, almost choking him. He gathered every last bit of it and concentrated it in a glare he wished could be as deadly as he felt.

A slow, satisfied smile curved the captain's lips. "Yes, indeed. Once we get those emotions under control, you're going to be one cold son of a bitch."

ONE

Present day

EARTH CELEBRATES TRIUMPH OVER ALIEN FLEET

Off-duty Patrolman Relates Personal Terror in Encounter with Extraterrestrial Killer

SACRAMENTO, California—With the entire world at the edge of their seats, U.S. President Laurel Ramos announced that the alien invasion force threatening Earth had been turned away. "Today we have two new heroes—California State Senator Jana Jasper and her extraordinary extraterrestrial friend, Cavin Caydinn. I hereby rescind the state of emergency and declare this day a national holiday. Senator Jasper, Major Caydinn, today we celebrate your courage and vision as one world newly united by a common cause. A very grateful world, indeed."

Over the weekend, Jasper, 32, and Caydinn, 34 (est.), were taken by officials to an undisclosed location in the western United States where the pair were successful in deterring the invasion.

The tale of terror and daring had a romantic beginning. Jasper, the youngest child of U.S. congressman John Jasper and former Soviet ballet dancer Larisa Porizkova, met Caydinn when they were children. Caydinn's father, a scientist, traveled to Earth to determine its suitability for acquisition, a fact not immediately known by Caydinn at the time. Sources close to the couple say that after landing in the invisible spacecraft on the Jasper family ranch, young Caydinn sneaked away to explore on his own and encountered the girl. "It was love at first sight," enthuses Evie Holloway, thirty-five, Jasper's sister.

Despite the passage of over two decades, the pair never forgot each other. According to sources close to the couple, Caydinn abandoned his post as a high-ranking military officer to warn Jasper that plans were underway for a takeover of Earth. Despite several attempts on his life by a biomechatronic assassin (popularly known as a cyborg), Caydinn seems to have triumphed, Jasper at his side.

The Jasper family is a political dynasty with roots dating back to California's earliest days. The clan laid claim to a permanent place in world history with their highly visible role in the invasion crisis—a role they are likely to continue. The family remains in seclusion following the death of legendary patriarch and former California governor Jake Jasper from complications of a stroke.

Recovering in the same hospital, Patrolman Greg Rowe,

46, spoke for the first time on battling the enemy in our own backyard. After being treated for second-degree burns to his right hand, the veteran of the force offered a gripping account of his encounter with Caydinn's would-be assassin: "He melted my weapon—turned it to molten metal so I'd drop it. Then he floated me twenty feet in the air and stuck me there. I thought it was over. I thought I was going to die. I'll tell you what, twenty-seven years on the force and I never saw anyone like him. He was one cold son of a [expletive deleted]."

Tonight, the "outer space killer" remains at large.

Evie Jasper Holloway peered past the open front door to her house, searching for signs of an alien invasion. A very personal invasion. The REEF was dead, but the fact that an extraterrestrial killer had paid her home a visit at all continued to unsettle her. He'd broken into her home, rifled through her things and traumatized her dog!

Barking, Sadie gazed at her with luminous dark brown eyes, her wet nose twitching. The Chihuahua's heart beat furiously as shivers wracked her little body.

"Such a powerful heart." Evie kissed a silken ear. "That's the heart of a lion, not a little dog. Yes, it is. You're my brave girl, fighting off that monster."

A piece of fabric torn off the alien's pant leg was the only evidence of the confrontation when she'd left Sadie in care of a pet-sitter at home while she took the kids to Disneyland for Easter break. No one was sure of the details, but when the police arrived at the house, Sadie dropped from the ceiling onto their heads. The dog hadn't been the same since.

Then again, neither had the rest of the world. Jana and Cavin had spent the weekend holed up in a secret bunker in the desert hacking into the long-ago crashed Roswell saucer. They'd used its aged software to trick the aliens into believing Earth owned a powerful space fleet. It was the ultimate scam, the kind of crazy scheme that shouldn't have worked but somehow did. On the downside, if the aliens ever found out they'd been duped by a bunch of low-tech Terrans, they'd turn around and come right back. No one but the president, a few select officials, and the Jasper family knew about the trick —and only because they'd been part of the masquerade.

"Aren't you coming in, Mom?" Evie's two teens strode past without a care, running upstairs to pack suitcases to bring to the family ranch, where the entire Jasper family would gather to mourn the loss of their patriarch, "Grandpa Jake."

From the top of the stairs, her son John shook his head at her. Her unease baffled him. "An assassin from outer space was in our house, Mom. Our house. Think of it, a real Terminator. So cool."

Cool? The kid was insane. This house was her safe haven, a small slice of sanctuary in a world where privacy was a commodity. She'd grown up on the campaign trail; she knew how to handle herself in public before she learned to walk. But unlike the rest of the Jaspers, she hadn't a single ounce of desire to be around government in any shape or form, nor did she want the responsibility of public service.

Except when one of the family members hit a milestone

like an election victory, placing her in the reflected glare of their spotlights, she'd gotten her wish. Now her perfect suburban anonymity had gone *poof*.

It shouldn't have come as a surprise. Prophetically, not too long ago over a couple of margaritas, her brother, Jared, compared their desire to live a private life to selling one's soul to the devil: sooner or later your debt would come due.

He was right. Their family's role in saving the planet had dragged all of them back into the public eye—and an interstellar killer to her door. An alien "terminator".

Warily, Evie inspected her dining room table and the newspapers the assassin had left scattered. The only things that mattered to her were home and family—her children. Cavin's would-be murderer would have stolen it all without a blink of an ice-blue cyborg eye.

You were disposable to him, a means to an end.

That was the root of what upset her, she realized. Not mattering. It was a sore point, and getting more so as time passed. She was the black sheep of the family, the perennial underachiever.

Yet she was happy. Deep down, she knew she'd eventually find her calling, her true purpose in life. But she wasn't disposable; she knew that. To her ex-husband, maybe, and to the press. Even her own family—her sister, her parents—made decisions involving her without always taking her opinions into account. And now a hitman from across the galaxy thought he could treat her that way too? Screw that.

Evie almost tripped over a pair of cleats and a baseball cap left in the middle of the landing. "Can you put this stuff away, please?"

She slowed as she passed the dining table, swiping at dust that had accumulated on the dark, glossy wood during their absence. The assassin had sat in that exact spot, coldly hunting through her things, snooping through her personal items and old mail, and—her gaze shifted to a grouping of family photos—looking at her.

She'd come home to find one of the photos moved out of position, as if it had been lifted and put down a few feet away. *Her* portrait.

Her mouth twisted. *You can't catch the eye of the average Joe in the produce aisle of the supermarket, but alien villains? Oh, yeah.*

A man who was more machine than human...whose perfect body could commit perfect crimes; a man who was focused, relentless, emotionless; whose every move was weighed in advance. *And yet who took a moment to look at you anyway.*

A shiver ran through her that wasn't entirely unpleasant.

"Oh, Mom. Don't be scared." Ellen returned to throw her arms around her. "It's okay."

Evie let her daughter think she was comforting her. Thank God the kid misread her tremble. It was sick, sick, sick! She'd had enough experience with cold, uncaring bastards from Earth—starting and ending with her ex-husband—that she didn't need to import any from other worlds.

Evie handed Sadie to her daughter and escaped to the kitchen. Immediately, the room soothed her frayed nerves. From the counters of speckled brown granite to the groups of scented candles in white chocolate, raspberry truffle and chocolate chip, chocolate was the theme in the kitchen and throughout the home Reese Pierce Holloway III had abandoned when he left her for his business partner.

Two years and the pain of Pierce's infidelity still stung. It wasn't as if she loved him anymore, but home and family were the essence of her existence. Living through the breakup had been devastating. But she'd recently turned the corner. The extra pounds she'd added to her life-long full-figured body had started to come off with yoga and long walks. She was almost back to her usual curvy size twelve, feeling better about life, better about herself.

She threw open the refrigerator door to the seriously disappointing sight of every spare inch of shelf space crammed solid with boxes of strawberries. Spoiling strawberries.

"Uh oh," Ellen said from behind her. The sinking tone in her daughter's voice matched her suddenly deflated mood. "Weren't those for the swim fund-raiser?"

"Yup." Evie sighed, wanting to wallow in self-pity, but shrugged it off and assumed her usual cheery can-do attitude. "What's done is done. Let's see what we can salvage and bring to the ranch. The rest will have to be thrown away."

She'd turned her hobby of making chocolate-covered strawberries into donations for various functions and charities. People loved the berries. No one else did them like she could. Several businesses actually wanted to *pay her* to make them so they could sell them retail. The thought of being compensated to do what she loved was exciting—and frightening. Her brother, Jared, convinced her that the idea had real potential. Then Ellen jumped in, surprising her by designing a Web site for a ninth-grade class project, titling it: "Evie's Eden: a Garden of Berries."

Then the world turned upside-down, aliens showed up, and her dream died in a storm of outside interference.

Evie wasn't surprised. She was used to other things taking priority. Other people. Now she was back to where she'd started—her traditional role of looking out for everyone else.

She should be happy about that, right? People needed her.

Ellen helped her collect the salvaged berries and some groceries for cooking meals at the ranch, cramming it all in two shopping bags. With the bags and Sadie, they returned to the front door.

Fishing for her keys, Evie swallowed the lump in her throat. What was wrong with her? Why was she feeling so low? She had no right to be sad about losing her chance for independence. With Earth's future so dangerous and uncertain, she'd be selfish to mourn Evie's Eden and what could have been. Call it one more thing she could blame on the REEF and the rest of his evil empire!

"It's a good thing I wasn't home when that brute walked in here," she grumbled, shoving the key in the lock. "I'd have taken a chunk out of him. I swear it, if I ever get another chance, I will."

Sadie snarled in agreement.

"Mom, he's dead," Ellen reminded her. "Aunt Jana said so."

"D-e-a-d," John spelled out.

"Proof that there is a God," Evie said. With a sense of finality, she slammed and locked the door behind her.

The REEF wasn't sure how long he'd been unconscious, but when he woke, a single question pounded inside his aching skull: why was he still alive? He shouldn't be breathing. His heart shouldn't be beating.

Something had gone very wrong.

His senses came back one by one: the air was cool, and the ground under his back was hard. Dry...barren...a desert. He'd been left for dead in this arid place. A high desert—he remembered that much. Nevada, the Terrans called it.

You're fucked, he thought, using a newly acquired Terran expression. Not only had he failed to take out his target, he was badly injured, his internal bio-hardware was failing and his only means back home was sitting in a charred heap on a ranch near Sacramento, California.

Situation: Grim.

A rock dug into his spine—a wake-up call back to a life he no longer wanted, had tried to terminate, actually, but apparently he'd had no more luck ending his own life than that of the man he'd been hired to kill.

What kind of super soldier are you?

Why, he was the best. No one came close to his track record. With a 100% success rate, he'd been the no-arguments, number-one choice when shadowy figures high in the Coalition government decided to terminate a man identified as Prime-Major Caydinn, a fast-rising officer in the military who'd gone AWOL. REEF had tracked him all the way to this out-of-the-way little world the locals called "Earth."

How was the REEF to know that Earth was next on the

Coalition acquisition list, and that Caydinn had traveled here to save the female Terran who was now his lover, despite having been favored to marry the Coalition's queen? Or that Caydinn would try to evade him in his desperation to warn the woman and their orbital scuffle would cause both of their ships to crash, stranding them here?

It wasn't as if REEF could inform his anonymous employers that he'd botched the mission and would they please come pick him up on their next swing past the planet? Who'd want to waste time retrieving an assassin who could not kill?

An assassin who'd begged his quarry to end his life.

Caydinn had refused to accomplish that task, so REEF took over, shutting down his systems one by one. It hadn't worked. A malfunction of the worst sort. Now here he was, stuck on this laughably primitive backwater planet.

Without warning, his body convulsed. Lightning flickered behind his eyes, and tingling in his scalp told him that his short black hair stood on end—both signs of an impending seizure. He attempted to use his master command center to control the erratic impulses, but to no avail: his body went rigid as the seizure came on full force.

Whiplashes of pain alternated between fiery hot and freezing cold, depending which confused nerve ending was making the call. Agony compressed every cell in his body, squeezing the breath from him until it felt as if he were being crushed between two heavy metal plates.

When he came to, the sun had moved significantly across the sky. The seizure left him trembling and exhausted and certain of the reason behind his inexplicable deterioration: his employers wanted him dead.

Before, he had merely suspected it. Now, convulsing and half-paralyzed, he was certain the kill order he'd downloaded with the information on Caydinn had contained an embedded malicious code written to cause him to self-destruct.

And he knew why. The order to assassinate such a high-ranking, important officer as Caydinn had been so heinous and irregular that there could be no witnesses. Easy solution: kill the REEF and erase all links to the crime. However, now there *was no* crime because REEF had failed in his mission.

Too bad no one told his bio-hardware that, he thought with a wince. He was going to self-destruct anyway.

A piercing screech from above wrenched his attention to the sky. Spots swam before his eyes. He blinked to clear his vision and the spots coalesced into birds, large birds, circling overhead with only an occasional flap of their sweeping wings.

He used the telephoto lens in his balky but still-operational retina implants to zoom closer. The birds were brown-black with featherless, red heads, white bills and yellow feet. Data scrolled behind his eyes: *Earth species: Cathartes aura. Weight: 5.1 lbs. Length: 27.4 in. Wing span: 6 feet. Description: The Turkey Vulture is one of North America's largest birds of prey. Best known for their practice of feeding on dead animal carcasses, but will occasionally attack young and helpless animals, as well.*

Young? He was in his prime! And helpless? Bah. He was a REEF-01A, a Robotically Engineered Enemy Fighter—

human-looking to the casual observer, but with enough engineered enhancements to earn him the official classification of "deadly weapon." He was one of the galaxy's most-feared super soldiers, raised since boyhood to kill. Not to *be killed*.

He'd extricate himself from this situation somehow, even with half his systems offline. REEF assassins never gave up. Not even death ended a REEF's single-minded determination to complete a mission. Legend told of a fellow REEF whose bloodied and broken human body continued to slither behind its target *after death,* its inner components still whirring as they dragged the mutilated body toward the intended kill.

A shadow whooshed across his vision, interrupting his reverie. Something heavy thumped onto his chest. REEF shifted his gaze downward and made eye contact with one of the ugliest creatures he'd ever seen. To add insult to injury, the vulture tipped its head and looked him over with slight distaste as if disappointed he wasn't dead yet.

Another scavenger landed nearby with a swishing of feathers and wind. It walked over to REEF and pecked his forearm. A little taste before the feast began? Goddess, they were going to eat him alive.

No! Dying on his own terms was acceptable, but he refused to be picked apart by a repellent, feathered, garbage-consuming Earth creature.

REEF tried to get up, but the impulses wouldn't travel from his brain to his arms and legs. His body, once always at his command, refused to obey him.

You can end it all another way. With his tongue, he felt for the self-destruct cap hidden in a recessed compartment behind his rearmost left molar. He'd been fitted with the apparatus in case he was apprehended by Earth authorities and could not escape. It would prevent Coalition technology from getting into Terran hands. One brief flash of plasma, and there'd be nothing left of him to pick through.

No one will miss you. A broken piece of machinery, he no longer was of use to anyone. The realization left him feeling hollow inside. Lonely.

REEF made a hiss of displeasure. He didn't like feeling lonely; he didn't like feeling anything. It had always been the job of his command center to dispense nanomeds into his bloodstream as needed to suppress emotion. Now that command center was malfunctioning.

A professional killer cannot afford to feel.... REEF made fists on the dirt as visions of the kills he'd accomplished over the years flickered through his mind. The vast majority of the hits had been quick, even instant, but there had been a few that hadn't gone as planned. In his mind's eye, he saw the stares of shock before he administered the final blow; he heard the futile pleas for clemency....

Stop! Feelings kept coming, and he could not shut them off. He didn't know how. How did humans cope? The pointed tip of his tongue hovered over the explosive device behind his molar. One press and it'd be all over....

But a distant rumbling grabbed his attention. With his acute senses, he homed in on the sound and analyzed it. It was an Earth vehicle. *Designation: Truck.*

Annoyed, he pulled his tongue away from the explosives. Killing a Terran along with himself would be sloppy.

Pebbles and grit popped under tires as the truck pulled

off the road and onto the shoulder and stopped. A tall male jumped down from the old truck. He wore jeans, a plaid shirt and cowboy boots. His skin was browned and wrinkled from a lifetime spent outside in this harsh climate. Mirrored sunglasses covered his eyes. His silver hair was cropped close to his head and styled to look flat on top. He was older, in his seventies, at least, but he was lean and muscled, in excellent shape.

A former military man—REEF knew the look.

A large, black plastic bag swung from his hand as he sauntered over. "Shoo," he said to the vultures congregating nearby. He shook open the plastic bag—the body-size plastic bag. Then he froze, seeing REEF conscious. "You're alive."

"Disappointed, Terran?" REEF sneered, his voice hoarse and despicably faint.

"Are you in pain? Can you walk?"

"No and no." REEF knew his answering glare was startlingly blue and cold as ice. Even this military man, whom he suspected was a lot tougher than he appeared, flinched at his infamous stare.

The Terran glanced around, as if unsure what to do. "I came here expecting road kill."

"Obviously."

"Major Caydinn said you'd died."

"And here I am. Alive." Goddess knew he'd tried not to be. "State your identity, Terran."

The man crouched next to him. "I'm called the Handyman. The missus—she's the Gatekeeper."

The Gatekeeper? The Handyman? Codenames.

"Best to get you back to the farm right away. There, me

and the missus will patch you up, and do what we can for you, technology permitting."

Terran charity—bah! But his options were few. He weighed allowing Caydinn's Terran minion to rescue him versus being picked apart like carrion by oversize, flea-bitten birds.

Or maybe he'd just vaporize himself.

If you terminate yourself, won't that give the people who want you dead exactly what they desire?

A valid point, that. Perhaps he'd leave his fate up to the goddess. Let them sort out his destiny, for he wanted no more to do with it.

The Handyman sauntered to his truck, unlocked the back, and returned, tugging on a pair of gloves. "We'd better get going. Don't want our nosy government friends to find you. They wanted to get their hands on Caydinn, you know, but he's off-limits. He's a hero. You, on the other hand, are fair game. The Men in Black are looking for your corpse as we speak."

REEF downloaded the term from his intermittent data-bank: *Men in Black: English. Colloquial term for secret government officials assigned to investigate the presence of extraterrestrials. Definition refers to the dark hue of the suits and sunglasses worn. Often employ unconventional and unauthorized methods of arrest and detention.*

REEF managed a snort. "Maltreatment at the hands of rogue Earth bureaucrats? I think not." He struggled to get up and sparks erupted in his eyes, agony slicing through his brain. He choked back a cry as the metal-plate sensation squeezed, crushing him.

The Terran was at his side in an instant, shoving something in his mouth and behind his head to cushion his skull. "Hang on, son. Hang on. There's help for you back at the farm."

REEF's hands contracted into fists, knuckles scraping over the coarse sand as he rode waves of agony. This time, he decided, he really was dying.

When the seizure passed, he was in far worse shape than after the one before. Another and he probably wouldn't wake up, he thought hopefully.

Caydinn's minion slid gloved hands under his shoulders and dragged him to the truck. He was stronger than he looked and finally wrestled REEF's limp body into the vehicle.

With one final thud, REEF, the most feared assassin in the galaxy, bred to kill from boyhood, half man, half machine, the apex of Coalition technology, landed on his back in the rear of a Terran's battered old pickup truck.

Evie carried a tray of berries out to the back patio at the ranch where her parents were hosting a gathering in honor of her grandfather's passing. Jana and Cavin were back in Nevada, hundreds of miles away in a secret bunker sheltering the being who'd tried to kill them.

The thing survived. Ugh. Although the last she'd heard, the assassin was barely clinging to life. If there was any justice in the world, he wouldn't cling too hard. It had been enough of a shock learning he was alive.

Evie set the platter of treats down on the table, smoothing

the table cloth and tidying up the cold buffet of meats, fruits, vegetables, Russian specialties and, of course, desserts. She and her mother had worked since sunrise putting it all together. In some ways she was grateful for the nonstop schedule of mourners passing through the ranch house. It kept them all from thinking too hard on their loss.

Evie's father walked past her, pausing long enough to press an affectionate hand on her shoulder and leave a kiss on her cheek. Immediately, he was swallowed up by a group of journalists the family had known for decades. In the space of a month the congressman had battled false accusations of campaign finance crimes, seen the near-invasion of Earth, the death of his father and the almost-death of his youngest daughter. Now he smiled, wearing the perfect brave face he saved for the public.

"Evie brought her berries," the word went around.

Evie slapped away her father's press secretary's hand before he snatched a white-chocolate-dipped berry. "They're for the guests, Arnie."

"Just one," he pleaded.

"One," she relented. She replaced a few almond slivers on one berry and re-sprinkled some miniature white chocolate chips on another. Wiping her hands, she backed away from the table.

"You're not planning to do another Cinderella, are you?"

"You mean run off before this ball's ended? That's exactly what I'm going to do. Except I won't be leaving any glass slippers behind." She took a step backward. "My pumpkin carriage awaits."

Warm arms and a cloud of rose-scented perfume

enveloped her. "You will stay a little longer," a husky, Russian-accented voice said.

"Hey, Mama." Larisa Porizkova Jasper wore a black silk tunic over slim black pants, cinched by a multicolored belt that was a work of art on its own. Her thick, honey-blond hair was tied in a knot at the base of her long neck, making obvious her beginnings as a legendary Russian ballerina. Long-limbed and slender, she was glamorous, a classic beauty. Heads never failed to turn when she entered a room.

Evie was nothing like her.

Yet that was okay. Her mother had made sure both Evie and Jana grew up confident, celebrating their individuality.

Somewhere along the way, Evie's confidence had taken a beating.

Evie lowered her voice. "I can't stay, Mama. The press is here." After her rebellious teenage years and her aborted education at a local, second-string junior college, the press had dismissed her as Jasper deadwood. In turn she'd dismissed them, avoiding them at all cost. Her lack of academic and professional achievement was obvious enough without having to see it reflected in their eyes.

"The press is on their best behavior today. They fear the wrath of your grandfather's ghost." Mama took her by the hand. "I have someone who wants to see your creations with fruit. I told her they are as unique as they are beautiful, just like you!" She kissed Evie on each cheek then beckoned to an exotically gorgeous woman dressed in a fuchsia and gold sari. "This is Leila Jones of the International Labor Organization, a U.N. agency."

Evie fell instantly into daughter-of-politician mode as her mother introduced them.

"I have heard so much about you, Mrs. Holloway." Leila held fast to Evie's hand. She wore a gold stud in her nose, crimson lipstick and a pair of black nerd eyeglasses that were wildly out of place and yet humanized her. "Your desserts are to die for. I have an event coming up—several events—and these berries would be perfect. May I have your card?"

"But I—"

"My daughter caters all our events," her mother bragged.

Stunned by her mother's exaggeration, Evie made a speedy amendment. "Just the desserts. I don't cater—"

"My daughter is humble, is she not?" Her mother gave her hand a warning squeeze before she walked away.

Evie clenched her teeth. It wasn't that she didn't want to start a business; she wanted the freedom to do it in her own time. Now her mother was pimping catering opportunities. It made saying no awkward. The familiar pressure to give in to family demands and expectations gnawed at her. "What sort of event did you have in mind, Ms. Jones?" she asked tactfully, hoping the woman wasn't serious about hiring her to cater it and was only buttering up a congressman's immediate family.

"Organizing events is not my favorite chore. It is a necessary part of my work now when I am not overseas."

"What sort of work do you do?"

"I am investigating the terrible problem of child trafficking in Asia, Africa and the Middle East. Over a million a year are forced into servitude, some who are as young as five."

"Five!" Evie thought of John and Ellen in that situation

and shuddered. "That's kidnapping on a mass scale. Why isn't there more of an outcry? How can we continue to allow this to happen?"

"Traffickers take advantage of parents who believe their offers of work will give the children a chance for an education and more opportunity. This is why my role is so important. People must be educated. These youngsters are forced into sexual exploitation, begging and plantation work—everywhere an adult would not want to labor so hard and so cheaply. I have just returned from Nigeria. There, I witnessed the rescue of several hundred malnourished children from a quarry. Many more had died. Many more around the world die each day. Lives ruined, childhoods beyond repair. It is all very sad."

"Very sad," Evie whispered. Her grief over her grandfather's death was so close to the surface that she started tearing up at the anguish in the woman's dark eyes. "I'll tell you straight up that I don't cater events outside the ones my family organizes. It's just a hobby. But, if I can help you help those kids, I'll gladly do it."

Leila slipped Evie her card. "You'll call me and tell me what you charge."

"I won't accept anything over the cost of my supplies."

"How generous of you! I will list you as one of our donors for the event, and—"

"Please don't. I just want to help. But anonymously."

The woman clasped Evie's hands, squeezing. Then her smile faltered. "Of course, with our own planet living under the threat of a takeover, all of us are in danger of becoming slaves ourselves, yes?"

"My family is leading the fight to make sure that doesn't happen," Evie said with confidence. "You need to stay focused on your work here, Leila. Here on Earth. It's so vital."

But she couldn't stop the small tremor that went through her with Leila's words. Adults profiting from children's suffering—it made her sick. Surely out of all the planets in the galaxy, Earth wasn't the sole source of such depraved, unscrupulous bastards. With a sudden chill and a new perspective, Evie Holloway found herself praying that was in fact the case.

Coalition Headquarters, above the planet Sakka

His temper boiling, the Headmaster strode into the office of the Minister of Coalition Intelligence located deep within a huge orbiting structure called The Ring. Minister Vemekk's cronies trailed him, trying to slow his pace and calm him, but he had no time for protocol today. When he got this angry, he wanted to hurt someone. But those days were long over. He was no longer a paid killer. He created them.

"Where is my REEF? I demand an answer." The Headmaster slammed a fist on Vemekk's desk. "Now!"

The minister eyed him with a coldness he rarely saw in a career-minded politician. The two ministers who had preceded her had died under mysterious circumstances. Some whispered assassination. But this bitch looked like she could take care of herself. "You will not," she said evenly, "do that again."

The Headmaster acceded to her rank with a curt nod. His REEFs worked for Vemekk and her ministry. He needed her. But she needed him too, by the goddess. As the founder of the REEF Academy, he'd taken what had amounted to an experimental program and turned it into a permanent institution that each year chose the finest youngsters in the Coalition and gave them the opportunity to become their civilization's finest warriors—a growing army of super soldiers.

In the early days before his duties as headmaster tied him to an office, he'd handpicked them, most from backward Rim worlds where such an honor would have otherwise remained an unfulfilled dream.

"Better than human," he said, quieter. "Better than machine, my REEFs are unstoppable."

"Yes, yes. Of course. However, at this point, Headmaster, the case is closed."

"Minister—"

Her voice chilled further. "The REEF is gone. Killed in action like so many of our soldiers are each day we battle the Drakken Empire. You must accept this. Now go. I have much work to do."

How dare she dismiss him so readily? A failure on the part of a REEF made him look bad. If the Headmaster lost the trust of the Ministry, they'd find someone else to run the REEF Academy. He would not let that happen. He'd grown fond of playing God.

"Headmaster?"

"Yes, Minister Vemekk. I thank you for your time." He

clenched one hand into a fist and slammed it crosswise across his chest in salute. Then he took a step backward, turned on his heel and left.

Fuming, he strode back to his office. His top assassin was missing, and no one could tell him why! It was a REEF o1A, his *first* REEF o1A, and the first to have true bio-regenerative properties integrated successfully into his hardware. If an implant was damaged or missing, nano-threads grew until the gap was bridged. And yet the REEF had vanished without a trace.

What had happened to him? Was it a malfunction? Death in the line of duty?

Initial reports theorized the REEF may have been forced to activate his self-destruct device. Every REEF had such a suicide device implanted as ordered by the ministry, but the Headmaster never made a single one operational. If the Coalition found out, he'd be executed for treason.

How could they have expected him to provide his REEFs, his treasures, the means with which to destroy themselves after he'd given them life? Instead, the self-destruct caps bore the exact time and day of the insertion of each REEF's main command implant, and the name of its creator: him. It assured the Headmaster that each of his rare and wonderful REEFs remained irrevocably tethered to him. His precious children. In this way, he'd never had to relinquish all the control that handing his creations over to the Coalition would have required.

He'd get to the bottom of this, despite the Ministry of Intelligence's lack of motivation to investigate. They were too distracted by an encounter with a powerful, unaligned world at the edge of civilized space to give the issue the attention it deserved. Earth, the rogue planet was called. But the REEF program was *his* program, and the 01A the assassin that had started it all.

The models prior to "Oh-One" had proved unstable, but that boy had grown into his best. Oh-One would not go out on a mission and simply not return. The Headmaster would do whatever it took to prove it.

He settled in front of his computer. A review of the REEF's recent missions revealed no patterns other than extreme efficiency. In the end, an exhaustive search for the assassin's whereabouts indicated only what the Headmaster already knew to be true: Oh-One had been dispatched on an ultra-secret assignment. It might take days or it might take months or even years, but he'd find Oh-One and bring him home. Dead or alive.

TWO

The REEF-01A stood in the center of a stage as the curtains slid fully open. The audience's conversations turned to gasps and nervous murmurs at the sight of him.

"Look at his eyes. They chill you to the bone."

"Don't make eye contact."

"He—I mean, it—isn't going to shoot you for looking. It kills only on order."

"You'd better hope so."

The REEF's enhanced hearing picked up every word of the mostly useless chatter. Anything of possible use was stored away in his bio-implants, which were integrated irrevocably with his brain on the cellular level. The convulsions and nausea of the early days were long gone, as was the clumsiness of learning to use his improved limbs. Drugs had helped his body and mind accept the improvements. Now he couldn't imagine living without the enhancements. Without them, he wouldn't be able to do the job for which he was designed.

The Minister of Intelligence began the briefing from a podium. REEF cared little for public relations, but the ministry occasionally pulled in a REEF to show off. "Better than man, better than machine," the minister said. "The REEF are our most reliable and deadliest fighters." He waved a hand. "Behold. The first humanoid bioengineered to kill."

Applause sounded. REEF lowered the audio for that input. With infinite patience, he used his laser-sharp gaze to scan the audience, mostly military members, high-ranking government officials and spies. His bioengineered-enhanced senses picked up everything from the vibration of accelerated heartbeats to the telltale scent of recent sex. The flood of information was analyzed, partitioned and stored or discarded as necessary as he continued to scan for threats near and far.

"He may look human, but given the kill order, he'd end your life without a flicker of remorse. Emotion in a REEF is a serious malfunction detected automatically and corrected —immediately."

More nervous murmurs from the audience, and a question-and-answer session ensued. Detached and obedient, REEF demonstrated a series of fight moves using weaponry both built-in and external. As he whirled around in a powerful roundhouse kick, a KILL order scrolled across his vision, blocking out all other, extraneous inputs.

His target was sitting in the audience.

REEF narrowed his eyes, found him. The man's gaze

sharpened with the alarm all quarry displayed with the initial realization of being centered in the sights of their killer.

REEF's prediction hardware advanced the scene to its next logical steps: *The target pushes to his feet to escape you; you hear the shouts of others in the audience as you take aim with your laser-guided pistol; their fear scent fills your nose. You fire; the bullet pierces his forehead, dead-center and so silently that not even those closest to him know he's been hit. Already lifeless, the eyes stare at you as a thread of blood exits the left nostril.*

Any feelings about his actions would be deadened, compartmentalized and analyzed by his systems, allowing REEF to view the instance objectively. Killing was an administrative detail, nothing more. But, standing there on the dais, he couldn't do it; he could not pull the trigger in front of all these people.

KILL.

Can't...

REEF stared down his extended arm to the weapon he'd pointed into the audience. He gripped his pistol, his skin sweating under his black glove as the conflicting order wreaked havoc with his systems.

MALFUNCTION DETECTED.

He lowered his arm and immediately assumed a ready position. Three point eight seconds had ticked by according to the elapsed time on his internal clock, but no recollection existed as to what occurred during those moments.

The audience applauded. All were still seated except for a single man hurrying down one of the aisles, excusing himself from the briefing room.

REEF calculated a reason for his premature departure—*Needs to urinate: probability 81.1%*—and dismissed the incident.

His command center alerted him to an incoming message: *REPORT TO MALFUNCTION ANALYSIS BAY IMMEDIATELY*

He stepped down from the dais and left the stage. A retina scan, two DNA scans and an image confirmation later, he entered the familiar quarters of the REEF lab.

Dutifully, he reclined on the table. Attendants clamped metal cuffs around his wrists, ankles and waist. As he submitted to the diagnostic, he tried his own analysis of what had happened on the stage. Instead of answers, he experienced a sensation of loss. The diagnostic would detect the emotions. They'd be labeled a malfunction and corrected.

As he anticipated, one of the scientists approached him with a faceguard designed to keep REEF from biting his tongue during convulsions. It meant they planned to do major repairs on his systems. "You need to be stabilized before we begin," the scientist said.

REEF turned his gaze to the ceiling and waited patiently for the procedure to begin. An apparatus resembling a hollowed-out head descended.

Fear sparked, and a sense of violation, before his command bio-implant stamped both emotions out. He did not want to feel anyway. It confused him. Unbalanced him.

Fix me, he thought.

The device locked in place over his face, plunging him into darkness. His respiration and heartbeat accelerated. He couldn't slow his reaction. A white-hot flash of blinding light erupted in his head. It shot down his spinal cord. Searing pain. He strained against the imprisoning cuffs.

Fix me, he screamed in his head.

"He's coming around again!" a woman shouted.

"Fix me!" he roared out loud.

"Put him under and keep him there!" A man's voice this time. "Do it, or we'll lose him."

Someone was pulling on REEF's right arm. Pain lanced from his wrist to his shoulder. He jerked away in surprise.

"Knock him out—now!"

Warmth began at a pinpoint in his other arm and spread quickly throughout his body. When it reached his head he spun into blackness.

The blackness splintered into trees...so many trees. He was running through the woods that he somehow knew by heart. A cottage appeared. He dashed through the door and stopped to stare at a table laden with plates of food. Others were already seated there: a man and woman and two little girls, one a toddler and the other not much older. Everyone smiled.

They are happy to see me, he thought. The sensation of belonging was so powerful it took his breath away.

Water dripped from his hair to the floor. He stared confused at the droplets hitting the floor. The wood planks were glossy enough to reflect the firelight from a nearby hearth. He knew that hearth. He knew it just as he knew this table and the woman with warm brown eyes and a bright smile. She laughed and shook her head. "Late for dinner? You? I don't believe it. Where were you, swimming in the stream?"

He shook his head. Something heavy hung from his hand. He stared at his fist he raised it high. Several heavy, large, dripping eels dangled from an iron hook.

The woman clapped her hands in delight. "Beautiful!" She was so pleased with him. He felt her love warm every bone in his small body as she drew him tight to her chest. "He's barely five circuits and he's already as good a provider as you, Deklan," she told a grinning man with black hair and bright blue eyes who looked somehow familiar too.

"Now go dry off," the woman ordered him, taking the eels. "I'll not feed wet boys at my table no matter how much I love them and no matter how hungry they may be...."

REEF was loath to turn away. He belonged with these people. Who are they?

Who are you?

I am REEF.

The answer somehow felt wrong.

Cavin Caydinn paced the length of the small room, impatient for the REEF to awaken. "It has been two days since the surgery. Surely by now he can tolerate a short conversation."

"He needs to sleep," the Gatekeeper warned sharply.

At that, Cavin hid a smile. The REEF was fortunate to have such good caretakers, recovering under the watchful eyes of the Gatekeeper and the Handyman. For a half century, the couple had been the guardians of the "Roswell saucer," the little scout ship Cavin had rigged to trick the Coalition fleet into believing Earth possessed a major space force. Now they'd been tasked with protecting an extraterrestrial whose existence needed to be kept secret at all cost.

Surely they'd do just as good of a job with the REEF as they had the *CSS Shakree* all these years.

A mass of curly auburn hair almost overwhelmed the Gatekeeper's small body as she adjusted the IV drip on the REEF's medication. She wore an apron tied around a floral dress. Flawless skin disguised the fact she was approximately seventy in Earth years. But her delicate appearance was deceiving. She was a covert government agent with a license to kill anyone who threatened her ability to protect the secret hidden in the basement below the house—and now the one lying helpless in a guest bedroom with a floral pattered quilt pulled up to his chest.

Not how Cavin ever imagined seeing the REEF.

"He'll wake shortly," she said, turning, her mouth stretched thin with disapproval.

"I must learn what he knows," Cavin explained gravely— and rather apologetically, for the woman had clearly bonded to her patient. "The fate of your entire planet depends on it."

"The fate of this planet depends on many things," she said cryptically. "In the meantime, I'll fetch some refreshments." With a swish of apron strings, she left Cavin alone with his former archenemy.

REEF peeled open his eyes only for a moment before squeezing them shut again. "Still here," he muttered. He was still alive. *Blast it.* He'd left his fate up to the goddesses and this is what they chose for him? He couldn't tell if it was cruelty or humor that drove them to torture him so.

The aroma of something delicious enticed him to open his eyes a second time. He inhaled, his mouth watering. After a few moments, his hazy vision cleared. He was in a Terran-style bedroom. The bed was small with a soft pillow for his head. One square window punctuated the wall to his left. Curtains covered it, but they were flimsy and white, more for decoration than for keeping out the sun that streamed into the room, giving it a cheery demeanor he had no intention of sharing.

The meddling Terrans had brought him here, he remembered. They were friends Caydinn's, the man he was supposed to have killed.

State coordinates of my current location. He made the demand of his internal command center but there was only silence in response. *Where am I?*

Silence. His systems must have suffered a complete breakdown.

Grimacing, he used his depressingly average, un-bioengineered-assisted senses to analyze his environment. Tubing ran from a bottle suspended on a stick to the assassin's arm, transporting a clear liquid into his bloodstream: nutrients and perhaps medication. For Terrans, it was advanced technology. To anyone else, the items were relics of a far more primitive time.

His old clothes had been removed, replaced with an outfit of pale green fabric, thin and soft. The clothes were comfortable like the bed. He brushed his knuckles across his chin. The bristles indicated he'd been here several days. An ache in his raised hand drew his focus to his forearm. A long scar ran the length from the heel of his palm to his inner elbow. Goddess. His master command center—the controls for his entire system—the blasted Terrans had disabled it!

He could hardly fathom the implications. Without operational internal hardware, he was neither fully human nor fully robot. He was...nothing.

"It feels strange, I know. I'm not quite used to it myself."

REEF swerved his focus across the room. A man sat in a chair, studying him. "Caydinn," he growled.

"We couldn't stop the seizures," he said in their native language, the Queen's Tongue. "If we hadn't disconnected the command implant, you'd have died." He gestured to REEF's forearm. A thin and neat scar took the place of the gauntlet he used to wear.

REEF felt for the destruct device buried in his molar.

"It's gone too," Caydinn said.

REEF let his head fall to the pillow. "It's all over for me."

"Quite the opposite. You're just beginning." Caydinn leaned forward. His voice grew quieter. Almost gentle. "You have a chance at a new life. Whether you ultimately decide you want this life or not is up to you, but it will be offered nonetheless."

For a long moment REEF gazed at the man he would have killed had they not come to this maddeningly primitive world. He saw no trickery in his eyes, no spite. "Why are you being kind to me? You have every reason not to be."

"I need you healthy and alive to answer my questions."

"Ask fast, because I plan to shut down my systems —permanently."

"I'm afraid you're too human for that now," a female voice trilled in the Terran tongue called English.

A delicate-looking older woman carried a tray into the room. With her was the man who'd rescued REEF in the desert. "You fought too hard to live these past few days for me to believe you honestly want to die." She set the tray on the bedside table. "Here we are—milk and cookies!"

The tray contained a dish and two glasses of white liquid: the milk of four-legged grazing creatures. The cookies were light brown dotted with darker brown spots. He inhaled. They were the source of the tantalizing aroma he'd detected before.

The small woman fussed around his bed, adjusting his pillow, making tsking sounds about the bruises on his face and arms. Her gaze held genuine concern. He wasn't certain what to do.

Kindness was foreign to him.

She reached across the bed to tuck in his quilt. He grabbed her wrist. She shot upright, shock registering in her eyes. Then one reddish brow went up. *She'll kill you.* Regardless of age, she was healthy, he was not.

REEF opened his hand and released her. *Goddess, what happened?* In the past, his command center implant would have calculated and accomplished the appropriate response. Now he was doing it alone. Clearly not so well.

But the woman took his reaction in stride, as did Caydinn, showing patience and understanding rather than censure. "This woman is known as the Gatekeeper," Caydinn explained. "She guards the scout ship that crashed here many years ago in the initial exploration of this planet. She and her partner the Handyman will help you recover."

The Gatekeeper's face was kind as she scrutinized him. REEF managed a slight smile in return but it was more of a grimace. His facial muscles weren't accustomed to expressions of happiness.

As REEF turned to Caydinn, his mouth formed even more easily into a frown. "Of what service can I possibly be to you?"

"Let me start from the beginning." What followed was a complicated explanation as to Caydinn's reason for coming to Earth. Finally REEF understood why the former officer had been targeted for termination. "They didn't want you to marry Queen Keira."

"Or they didn't want the queen marrying at all. It doesn't matter which. Both point to turmoil in the Coalition. I aim to exploit it to save Earth. Who are they? Who was behind the attempt to kill me?"

"I don't know. The order came via the Ministry of Intelligence, inserted anonymously into my internal command center."

"We powered up your ship."

REEF's heart sank. "But that viewer was programmed for automatic two-way!"

"We found that out," Caydinn said dryly.

"They saw you, then. They know you're alive." *And they'll know for certain that I failed.* He'd known his employers wanted him dead, but he'd clung to the hope that he was wrong and that he'd be able to return to life as he knew it.

With Caydinn's news, he knew he'd forever lost that chance. A REEF who bungled such an important mission would be discarded and terminated, even if sabotage was the cause of it.

He couldn't go home, and the only people he knew on Earth were the ones he'd tried to kill.

Caydinn continued. "A woman appeared on the screen. Not the minister of intelligence—the description Jared gave me doesn't fit her or any other females in high positions in the government—but she was strong, very fit and wielded one or more daggers. She lost her temper not once but several times. Does that resemble any REEFs you know?"

"No. None would be that undisciplined."

"It remains a puzzle, then." The officer let out a disappointed sigh. "I want to know who she is."

"As do I, Caydinn."

"I, on the other hand, have ordered chocolate chip cookies," the Gatekeeper said, her eyes twinkling. "Go on. Try one."

Drawn by the delicious aroma, REEF turned his gaze back to the tray. When was the last time he'd eaten real food? Too long, he thought and grabbed a confection. His hand trembled less than before. A good sign, that. "I'll be walking by the end of the day," he boasted. "I know how to drive Earth vehicles. I will leave this place and make my own way."

"Oh, no you won't," the Gatekeeper argued.

"You're in no condition to leave here yet," the Handyman chimed in, joining them.

Caydinn nodded. "Your internal components can no longer accelerate your healing processes. Moreover, you're in danger. The Gatekeeper fears that if certain secretive elements in Earth's government learn of your existence they may try to kidnap you. If you fall under their control, there'll be little we could do to stop them from opening your body to view the bioengineering that remains inside you. If you think you feel subhuman now, wait until you are lying helpless in their hands in a lab."

A lab. REEF suppressed a shudder. "Yet *you* walk free because you are Earth's hero," he pointed out mockingly, irritated by the prospect of his restricted freedom.

"I walk free because everyone knows who I am. No one could abduct me without a lot of people noticing, including the leaders of this world. You, on the other hand, don't have the same advantage. They don't know who you are."

"Then tell them. As soon as everyone knows who I am, the problem is solved and I can leave. Why has this not been done already?"

"Namely because of the charges against you. Robbery. Assault. Assault with a deadly weapon. Criminal mischief. Harassment and trespassing. Trespassing on government property. Attempted murder." Caydinn turned his hands up. "To name a few."

REEF made a dismissive sound in his throat. "Minor complications. Use your status amongst the Terrans to drop the charges."

"We're working on it. But understand that should you be arrested, at the very least you'd be deported—off-world."

"Excellent!"

Caydinn frowned at him. "Which would be a disaster. The political situation is delicate, trust is fragile. It's better to keep you someplace where you can be protected until I'm sure the situation is safe. I won't risk the repercussions of moving prematurely. Too much is at stake, globally. *Galactically.*"

Caydinn's face radiated passion for his cause. REEF realized how much the officer had risked coming here to save his lover and her people. REEF had been alone for as long as he could remember; he couldn't fathom making that kind of sacrifice for a woman—or anyone.

Not that he didn't want to. He simply wouldn't know how.

People loved you once. A family.

He'd not been loved as a REEF, however. Reviled and feared, yes, but never loved. Yet, long ago, he'd been part of a family. A family he couldn't recall.

Well, if they loved him so much then why did they let him go? As a child! Why didn't they try to contact him just once in all these years?

REEF made a fist as a different kind of pain gripped his chest. Emotions, he thought darkly. They were getting in the way more and more often. Did they just come and go with no warning? Is this what he was doomed to suffer for now on? He pitied poor humans more than ever.

And what are you now, if not human?

Not human. Not robot. *Nothing.*

REEF twisted his fist on the quilt in a desperate bid to keep his emotions in check. He couldn't see the point in having feelings. Life was so much easier without them. Perhaps something could be done to eradicate his before they took hold permanently.

The Gatekeeper glanced down at his clenched fist but

didn't comment on it, though her eyes were soft with compassion. "What's your name, young man?"

"REEF."

"Not your model designation," Caydinn said. "Your given name."

"REEF," he said, his chin coming up. It was all he'd ever called himself.

"Didn't your parents name you?"

"The memory of it was erased during training," he explained stiffly. The process of using drugs and mind control to create a REEF was not well known.

"We'll have to come up with a surname and an alternate identity for him," Caydinn said, thoughtfully rubbing his chin. "At least he's fluent in English."

The Gatekeeper and Caydinn contemplated REEF as if he were a scientific specimen. "The accent will have to be explained, though," she said. "It's unusual and rather thick— more so than yours."

REEF's mood soured. "I have no desire to polish my Terran words." He had no desire to be on this planet, period. It reminded him too much of his failures and his new dependence on others. "And I will choose my own name."

Locked inside his mind was his birth name. Images of a lost boyhood flickered in the back of his mind, the thinnest shreds of recollection. "Sanders," he murmured. "Sand... Sander..." Sand Dream? The information was there, just beyond his reach.

"Sanders," Caydinn agreed. "It's a fairly common surname on Earth. How about Joseph Sanders? Or Donald—"

"*Eric* Sanders," REEF blurted out. The Earth name was

somehow familiar, but it wasn't exactly what he was looking for. He focused, trying to discern the significance of the name, but the harder he tried to see into his past, the more pressure it put on his frayed systems and his head began to ache.

The Gatekeeper nodded. "Eric Sanders, it is." Her hand landed on Caydinn's shoulder. "You must let him rest now. He's not out of danger yet."

"Good," REEF said. "There's still a chance I won't make it."

The Gatekeeper pursed her lips, her eyes shining. "No more of that. When you leave here, it's going to be out that front door on your way to a new life."

"A Terran life," REEF scoffed.

"It's not so bad." Caydinn's eyes belied his nonchalant words. It was obvious the former officer found aspects of his new life very satisfying indeed. "You'll adjust. And where I plan to hide you, no one will question who you are."

"Hide me? Where?"

This time Caydinn smiled fully. REEF couldn't decide if it was a good or a bad thing, for clearly the officer had already made a decision regarding his relocation. "This place," Caydinn said, "is called suburbia."

THREE

Washington (AP)—Jared Jasper marries Queen of Galaxy in a move claimed as a victory by both sides.

President Ramos declared today Jared Jasper Day, a national holiday celebrating Jasper's marriage to Queen Keira. "A more selfless, brave and amazing man does not exist on this planet," the president said. "Although it is difficult to do, we must let him go off to a faraway world where I have no doubt he'll positively impact his new society with his unmatched heroism."

"Your sister is dating an alien," Evie's ex-husband accused after dropping the children off after his twice-monthly court-ordered visitation.

"And my brother just married one, Pierce. It's old news."

Pierce nodded grimly. Evie knew what he was thinking

—Jared, the poor bastard. Queen Keira was a galaxy-class diva. Evie had seen her in action the day Jared had argued with the queen via the display in the REEF's spaceship. They didn't learn until later who she was, and by then it was too late. Thanks to Jared's boasting, the queen and the rest of the Coalition thought he was the Prince of Earth and quite the catch. The offer of a marriage alliance as a peace treaty was an offer Earth couldn't refuse. It was just one more scam for Earth to try to pull off. And one more sacrifice for the Jaspers to make.

"But your brother's on another planet," Pierce argued. "Jana's dating that alien here."

"'That alien' has a name. It's Cavin. *Cavin.* And he's more than just dating her. They're moving in together."

He reared back slightly. "They're having relations?"

Was he for real? "It's called sex, Pierce. *Sex.*" Evie remembered sex. Fondly. "They're adults and in love. You do the math."

"But he's...an *extraterrestrial.*" The word squeezed past Pierce's straight, perfectly white clenched teeth like dough through a cookie press. Except if his voice were to be made into cookies, they'd be inedible, bitter and burned.

Evie clenched her jaw. "There was a time I'd have been right there with you. But who cares if he's an alien? He saved our planet. At this point, he could be a golden retriever and I wouldn't care."

Snarling and barking, Sadie burst through her doggie door, nails clattering on the gleaming hardwood. She skidded down the hallway and into the foyer, stopping at Pierce's size ten, beige Italian designer slip-ons, where she waited hopefully for some sign of acknowledgment from their owner. Pierce ignored Sadie every time he came over, yet the loyal little dog did everything she could to win his favor.

It was a parody of their entire marriage.

Evie stopped to scoop up the Chihuahua. The dog yipped and squirmed nervously—more nervously than usual, that was. It was almost as if Sadie understood that the REEF had survived. For the entire week the monster had clung to life, Evie had kept her fingers crossed he wouldn't make it. Unfortunately, he'd pulled through. On the plus side, she didn't have to worry about him setting foot in her house again. Too many people were watching him.

Pierce knew few details of the assassin's visit to the house. As jumpy as Pierce was with everything alien, she planned to keep it that way.

Pierce persisted. "No matter how you look at it, Cavin's an alien."

"I thought you celebrated cultural diversity."

"Evie, that's irrelevant. He's a different species!"

"No, he's *human*. Just like us. We're all technically humans, them and us, with a few DNA differences. Haven't you been keeping up with the news?"

"He's intermingling with our children."

"Of course Cavin's been around them—with Jana. I'd think mutually committed love was something you'd want John and Ellen to see. Or maybe it's too far outside your prism of experience to imagine."

Pierce frowned. "I loved you, Evie."

"Well, you had a funny way of showing it. Screwing that..." Evie choked up. *Damn it.* Trying to compose herself, she stared hard at the ceramic planter of lavender sitting next to the open front door. Even after two years, even though she no longer loved Pierce, she still couldn't get Angela's name up and out of her throat. "...that home-wrecker."

She blushed hard. *Way to go, Evie.* Now she sounded like the 1950s housewife Pierce accused her of being, which was everything gorgeous, high-powered, go-getter, athletic, Harvard-educated-MBA Angela wasn't.

"Gotta go, Pierce. I have some orders to fill." Spinning on her heel, she left Pierce standing by the open door in the entryway.

She winced and almost snorted hearing Pierce trip over the swim-team duffel bag Ellen had dropped by the door. She scooped up a cup half full of melting ice left on the hall table and sniffed the contents. Root beer. John's. She made a mental note to have both kids make a sweep through the house and clean up after Pierce left.

"Orders?" Pierce followed her into the kitchen. His eyes widened at cookware on the island and the stacked-up fruit. The finished berries were an impressive sight, she had to admit.

"For my chocolate strawberries. I've been donating them to charity, anonymously, but word's gotten around. I've been inundated with requests from all over. That gift warehouse, Ka-bloom, keeps e-mailing, the place that makes those giant balloon bouquets. They wanted twenty dozen of my berries for their summer gift special. I said no, of course. I'm happy doing what I'm doing. It's exciting, though. People actually want to buy my berries."

"But you're giving them away for free. That's a lot of work to get nothing in return."

Nothing? Her face grew hot. "I get a lot in return. Like satisfaction, tremendous satisfaction. I'm helping the fight to end human trafficking."

"Like drug smugglers?"

"No, *people* smugglers. Slavery, specifically child slavery. It's sick, and needs to be stopped."

"Ah, I get it. This is your family's newest crusade."

His statement deflated her instantly. He made it sound like she was a robot who operated only on family orders. Or that she was too stupid to think independently.

Maybe she was, and always had been. The issue of her intelligence was a tender spot. At times, she'd felt inferior intellectually to the high achievers in her family, and Pierce knew it. Over the years, he'd never hesitated to exploit that vulnerability if he felt it served his interests.

She set down Sadie and yanked a pallet of strawberries from the fridge. Then she found her best baking sheets, slamming them one by one on the granite counter.

"Evie, I want to finish talking about the children's situation."

"There is no *situation*." Evie yanked aluminum mixing bowls from the cupboard and clanged them on the countertop.

"Don't fight, you guys." Ellen swished into the kitchen in fuzzy socks to snatch something from the fridge.

"We're not fighting, sweetie. We're talking."

"You're banging pans, Mom. That's what you do when you're mad. Can you bring me over to Katie's house?"

"After I make this one last batch. And tell your brother to lower the volume. It sounds like World War Three is taking place in my living room."

Simultaneously with the emotionally charged skirmish taking place in her kitchen, she thought.

"Your family is in the spotlight," Pierce said once Ellen had gone.

"They saved the world!"

"But no one else on Earth has aliens coming over for dinner, getting cozy with relatives. Your family's involvement isn't good for the kids. It's too much pressure on my family."

Pulling out aluminum measuring cups, she slammed them onto the counter. "So, we're *your* family again? It sure didn't feel like it when you filed for divorce and didn't ask for custody."

"The court order can be revisited at any time the home environment becomes detrimental to the children."

Her blood went ice cold as heat rushed to her face, a reaction she was certain Pierce didn't miss. This was more than an argument. This was life-altering. Living without Ellen and John? She couldn't imagine it. The idea was too painful. *Breathe. In through the nose, out through the mouth.* Or was it the other way around?

She pulled a cook pot from under the stove, her voice much quieter. "You can't be serious."

"As a heart attack, Evie. See, it's win-win. More of the children with me, and less of my money going to support the only Jasper without a college degree so she can sit home eating bonbons."

Evie contemplated the pot in her hand and then her ex-husband's head. But she took the high road and dropped the pot on the burner instead of on his skull.

Pierce appeared oblivious to how close he'd come to death —or at least a lingering vegetative state.

"Bonbons?" she practically squeaked. "That's what you think I do all day? Seriously?"

His gaze tracked down her fitted T-shirt to her jeans. She'd never hidden her curves, but his expression of distaste made her want to cover up. "Just an educated guess."

"Out." She grabbed a wooden spoon and jabbed it at his chest. "Out now." Pushing him with the spoon, she backed him out of the kitchen and down the hallway until he bumped up against the front door.

"I'm going to be keeping a close eye on how this is affecting Ellen and John," he warned. "If the situation becomes too much for the kids, I'll go back to court for custody."

Evie pushed down on the door handle, opening it. Pierce stumbled backward over John's cleats and she slammed the door in his face.

She whirled away from the door, sweeping her bangs off her forehead as she returned to the kitchen. Her sanctuary. There she spread her hands on the cold granite counter and breathed deep, her hair falling over her face. *You're not married to him anymore. You don't have to tolerate this.* True, but he still had power over her, the power to take away what meant the most to her—her kids.

Being a mother was something that came naturally. It was the one area of her life not impeded by self-doubt. One look at the way Ellen and John had turned out gave her all the reassurance she needed.

But had she been blind? Was her family's role in the crisis really that much of a strain on the kids? Had she grown so used to being in the public eye over the years that she failed to see the harm it was doing to her own children?

She picked up a strawberry and admired its lush perfection. Soon it would be a work of art, dressed in chocolate. And the taste? Divine. Even better than it looked. But the fact that it would indirectly help a child escape forced servitude was the "icing" by far.

"This is your family's newest crusade, I take it," Pierce had said.

No, it was hers. Hers!

She thought about the e-mail from Ka-bloom. Her late grandfather had earmarked trust-fund money so she could use her hobby to launch her own business. So far, she hadn't touched a cent. But if she went commercial and donated every dollar over the cost of doing business to her cause, she could really make a difference.

Evie Holloway, entrepreneur, philanthropist.

Maybe, just maybe...

Shaking, she grabbed her phone and opened up Ka-bloom's e-mail. Doubts crept in but she tried not to listen. *We can do the berries for you,* she typed, closing the note with, "Evie's Eden." Before she changed her mind, and she had about a million reasons to do so, she centered her shaking finger over the Send button, held her breath and brought her finger down. The e-mail was on its way.

Weeks had passed with no further mention of "suburbia." REEF knew efforts to move him to a new location hadn't died, but with the world's attention—and the Jaspers'—diverted by the royal marriage, REEF and his situation had settled to the bottom of the priority list.

Just as well. His aim was to get well again, to get strong, and he was slowly closing in on both goals.

At least the Terran couple at the farmhouse dispensed their charity without making him feel too pathetic. He wasn't so sure about his next caretaker, but now that preparations for the royal marriage were finished, he had the strong feeling he'd find out soon.

In fact, Caydinn and Senator Jasper were due to arrive at the farmhouse that evening. It was their first visit in weeks. REEF was certain that the subject of where to place him for the remainder of his so-called rehabilitation would top the agenda. Oh, joy.

With a stifled sigh, he returned his attention to the book of glossy photos spread out on the table before him. Morning sunshine streamed through the living room windows. He sat with his weight balanced on his elbows, his hands flat together and two fingers propped under his chin as the Gatekeeper leafed through another one of her picture books.

"How about these?" the woman asked patiently, showing him page after page of fruits, cross-sectioned and whole and in all stages of growth.

His head ached from concentration. Nothing looked familiar. Perhaps he was trying too hard. Perhaps he wasn't trying hard enough. The Gate-keeper never tired of showing him book after book in hopes that if a photo struck the right chord, his memories would return all at once like a dam breaking. So far it had been more like a pitiful trickle.

His muscles ached from exertion as he leaned back in the chair and stretched out kinks. His dawn workout had taken its usual toll. His reduced strength at first was a frustration, but over the weeks spent in the care of the couple, he'd learned to view his weakness as a challenge. Running, weights, pushups, sit-ups —he'd come a long way from the afternoon the Handyman stood by to catch him as he tried his first steps unassisted.

He was less certain of his emotions. Sometimes he experienced them so powerfully that he skated on the razor's edge of control. It was normal, the couple assured him time after time.

"Normal" was an easy enough term for someone who hadn't had their insides reconstructed to resemble a machine, who hadn't been mind-wiped to accommodate a massive knowledge databank now mostly useless to him. Some of it he remembered, including most of the English language he'd memorized, thanks to the phenomenon Caydinn had explained called neural pathway grooving. If a thought or action had been performed often enough, the human brain learned it, much like a vehicle's tires wore a rut in a road after traveling it time and time again. Reading the printed word, however, remained a source of frustration.

As did efforts to recover his memories. When the Gate-keeper turned the last page, he shoved away from the table, defeated.

"It will come," she assured him. "Give it time."

"Time." He made a sound of disdain in the back of his throat. Time was the one thing he had plenty of and didn't want. It wasn't that he was unhappy at the farmhouse. The couple had been kind to him, but here he felt as trapped and useless as a once-valuable but now-broken piece of equipment stored in a dusty closet because no one knew quite how to dispose of it.

Not human. Not machine. Nothing.

He blocked despair before it took hold. So far his efforts to get rid of his emotions had met with failure. He wouldn't stop trying. Strong feelings caused nothing but problems. They clouded his judgment and distracted him. He was, however, becoming better at blunting emotions. If that wasn't considered "normal," so be it.

The Gatekeeper observed him with compassionate eyes. She treated him as he imagined a woman would treat a son. Likewise, the Handyman had taken the role of a father. They were the closest thing to family he'd ever had.

No, better. They didn't abandon him when he was vulnerable like his real family had.

He thought about resting his hand on hers briefly to convey his gratitude, but without the guidance of his command center implant to tell him if the gesture was right or wrong, he didn't dare take the risk.

"That too will come in time," she said in a gentle tone as if she'd read his mind. "You're not sure how to give and receive affection. The ability is there, inside you, but locked away. Just as a picture, a taste, or even a random scent will open the floodgates of your past, someone you meet will provide the key to unlock your heart."

He snorted. "Bah!" Terrans and their fairy tales. Unlock *his* heart? REEF pitied the poor soul who went through the trouble only to find it empty.

The phone in Evie's kitchen rang, shattering her concentration. Her fingers were coated with chocolate. She sucked a few on her right hand clean—never waste good chocolate by rinsing it down the sink—and took a peek at her phone. It was Jana.

She stood there, her index finger in her mouth, as a powerful sense of obligation to pick up the phone warred with her increasing desire to carve out a more independent life. Phone calls meant complications, usually in the form of favors needed by the family, who had careers and enormous responsibilities: "Evie, can you take care of this, Evie, can you pick up that, or write, check on, call, stop by..."

She ran errands while they saved the world. It had always been that way. Normally, she embraced the role. Now, for the first time in her life, it chafed. Freedom, her freedom, had suddenly become very important.

The ringing stopped, then started again. Jana must really want to reach her. Sadie pranced around her ankles, barking something that sounded like, *"Answer! Answer!"*

Evie reached for two large blocks of solid chocolate, one white, one dark, and pretended she heard nothing. It was a test of her newfound emancipation.

A text came in: *Evie answer the phone!!! :)*

The phone rang a third time.

Jana could leave a message if she wanted her so badly. If it were an emergency, if something bad had happened, she wouldn't have added emojis.

Humming loudly to drown out the sound, Evie rinsed a basket of plump berries and dropped a pound of grated white chocolate to melt in a double boiler. In another pot she added dark chocolate as she prepared to make a batch of her famous black and white strawberries. The trick was to keep her hands busy. Then she wouldn't pick up the phone to see what Jana wanted.

A double chime told her that voicemail had taken the call. Finally!

Relieved, Evie grabbed a block of dark chocolate and a grater and worked up a sweat filling a bowl. The fragrance of chocolate filled her nose, and she inhaled as if it were a drug.

The phone rang again.

Jana, you little shit.

"*Answer! Answer!*" Sadie's nails pitter-pattered across the hardwood floor.

"No, Sadie. Not this time."

Jana texted: *Evie, please. Answer. I know you're there.*

"No, you don't," Evie said.

"Yes, she does, Mom." Ellen peeked into the kitchen. "Aunt Jana called my cell and I told her." She hesitated at Evie's expression of dismay. "Oops. Was I not supposed to?"

Evie gripped the grater. "I'll call her later."

"She says it's really important."

Evie rolled her eyes and tossed the grater in the sink.

Ellen hung around and to Evie's shock actually started putting away the clean dishes in the dishwasher without her asking.

"Clever, honey, but it might be private," Evie said and shooed her disappointed daughter out of the kitchen with a quick, apologetic kiss.

She waited until Ellen was out of earshot before she called Jana. The woman could be in Washington, D.C., Area 51 or, for all Evie knew, on another planet.

"This had better be good," she warned when her sister answered on half a ring. She bit into a strawberry and leaned back against the counter. "I'm all ears."

FOUR

Evie was frozen. She expected Jana wanted something, but never anything like this. Surely she'd misunderstood. She yelled, "You want me to harbor a depressed, suicidal fugitive assassin—an *interstellar* fugitive cyborg—IN MY HOUSE?"

She caught herself and lowered her voice in case the kids' ears were tuned in. "Jana, I have children here."

Maybe Pierce was right: her family really *was* dangerous.

"He hasn't tried to kill himself in weeks."

"I take it that's supposed to be good news."

"God, Evie, that doesn't sound anything like you. All your cats are from the ASPCA, and Sadie was from Chihuahua rescue."

"We're talking about an adult male, not a lost puppy!" Evie ground her palm against her throbbing forehead and tried to follow along as her brilliant, social crusader little sister campaigned on behalf of the killer, the killer who invaded her house, who tried to murder Cavin, who sliced an

SUV car in two, who'd left a motel riddled with holes from his outer space ray gun. "He has a long history of violence, and that's just the stuff we know about."

"He was under the influence of his bio-hardware implants. They've been deactivated. He's just like us now. It's why he needs protection."

"May I suggest a nice state-run institution? Or maximum-security prison, perhaps? You mentioned strays—drop him off at the pound, for Pete's sake. You've got connections, Jana. Use them! I bet the CIA could point you to some really jammin' places in third-world countries."

Evie bit into another strawberry as Jana gave her a long sob story about the REEF's miraculous rehabilitation, the Men in Black, and why her saying yes to this screwed-up scheme would prove a worthy sacrifice for humanity. Jana expected her to crumble the way she always crumbled.

Evie turned around and took in the sight of the berries, the melting chocolate, the boxes. With a little luck and courage, the Ka-bloom order would lead to more orders, and her business would be off and running.

Not unless she freed herself from Jasper obligations first.

It wasn't that she'd stop being there for them; she just wanted some veto power for once. That meant getting them to understand she'd no longer be available round the clock, and that they shouldn't expect her to say yes to every damn thing, either. It was high time Evie Jasper Holloway set some limits.

"There's another reason this plan won't work, Jana. I've decided to go back to work." There. She'd said it. It was official. She'd taken the fantasy and made it reality. "I'm starting my own business making gourmet chocolate strawberries. It means I may not be here all day everyday like always." Her heart slammed against her ribs. She felt suddenly energized, almost dizzy. She'd never taken such a daring step all on her own.

"REEF can help you!"

Evie's spirits plunged in the face of her sister's relentless Jasper optimism. If she wasn't careful, the undertow of her sister's persuasion would pull her under. "I don't get it. Doesn't a single man living in the house with me, a single woman, concern you? Or are you too focused on my playing mommy to a semi-reformed murderer to see how this might be a problem?"

"I've gotten to know him. So has Cavin. He's safe."

Jana meant *she* was safe. "You know, it's damn depressing knowing everyone, even my own sister, views me as the ultimate nurturer instead of passionate and sexy and..."

"Evie," Jana pleaded.

"...it would serve you right if I ended up having a totally erotic, scorching affair with an extraterrestrial hitman!"

Sadie growled, her hackles coming up.

"Don't worry, baby, Mommy's not that crazy. But your plan is, Jana. Have you asked the REEF what *he* thinks about all this? Maybe he doesn't want to be shipped off to California. Maybe he doesn't want to do time in the suburbs." If the REEF said no, she realized with a burst of hope, *she* wouldn't have to. "The pets, the kids. The chaos. Have you told him?"

She punched a finger at the kitchen, at the food piled on the island, the pots on the stove, sports gear left where you were most likely to trip over it, cat toys, Sadie's water bowl on the floor, a pair of swim goggles on the table, the T-shirt tossed over the back of the couch, the dogs barking in the backyard, the screams and bomb blasts from John's video game. "I don't have to give you gory details. You already know. Oh! And the driving, don't forget the driving. Summer's the worst. I'd have to drag him to football camp and swim practice, the kids' friends' houses, the store, the cleaners, the gas station—and that's just before lunch. Weekends are worse. You want to send him? Go ahead. But he won't last a week. Tell ET to phone home. No, better yet, tell ET to *go home*."

"I don't believe it," Senator Jasper said. "My sister hung up on me."

REEF stood in the farmhouse kitchen, drinking water to hydrate after a long run. The abode was not large, and his hearing was still acute, making it doubly hard to escape listening to the tail end of the phone conversation that had taken place in the next room and Jana Jasper's gasp of surprise.

He had a very good idea what it had been about too—the plans for his relocation—and he was quite tired of being kept in the dark. It was his future, after all. It might not be the future he desired, or expected, but it was his nonetheless and, by the goddess, he'd have a say in it.

He sauntered into the living room, a towel slung over his neck. The black T-shirt he wore clung damply to his skin. In this clime, it would be one hundred Earth degrees by noon.

In the living room, the Gatekeeper and her mate shared a couch while Caydinn and his lover stood near the window looking quite unhappy. Everyone had been privy to the ill-fated phone call except him, it seemed.

"She said he won't last a week," Jana complained. "It *is* chaos at her place sometimes. But it's part of the charm, part of what makes the best kind of loving home in my opinion. I think it's just what he needs while we figure out what to do with him. But maybe I'm wrong and Evie's right. What if we send him there and it proves to be too much?"

"Nothing on this miserable planet could possibly be, as you say, Senator, 'too much.'"

At the sound of his voice, everyone spun around to look. REEF folded his arms over his chest and leaned a shoulder against the door frame. "Perhaps it is time to share what you plan to 'do' with me, since I am the one to whom you will be *doing* it."

He realized he'd uttered the demand with his teeth gnashing together. Anger was the emotion he was least able to harness, but he tried to do his best and would do so now—although that wasn't so easy since he'd discovered it took a quorum of Terrans and a Coalition Space Force deserter to decide his fate.

"Well?" he prompted, his stomach churning. "Who is this Terran who thinks me a coward? I demand to know his name."

Jana glanced to Caydinn, who sent a questioning gaze to the Gatekeeper, who whispered something to her mate. Then Jana approached him, her hands clasped together under her breast as if in prayer. "It's my sister, Evie. And she doesn't think you're a coward. In fact, she sounds a little afraid of you."

"Smart woman." He sneered out of old habit. "REEFs are feared throughout the galaxy."

The Gatekeeper looked disappointed in his reaction. "Tsk, tsk. She's a young mother of two."

Guilt was another, unaccustomed emotion. REEF expelled a long breath and along with it quite a bit of his outrage. "I do not wish for her to be afraid of me," he muttered. Then he stood up straight. "Nor do I want her Terran pity!"

"She doesn't pity you, trust me on that," Caydinn commented.

She feared him, however. It came as no surprise. *Not human. Not machine.* A man like him would be an aberration to a woman like her. He was everything she was not. He destroyed; she nurtured. He was a loner; she was the center of a family. He'd lived in a barracks, and she in a home filled with warmth.

Months had passed, and he hadn't yet forgotten the immediate and almost overwhelming sense of calm that had stolen over him the day he'd entered her dwelling. Rich hues reminded him of gourmet delights, the earthy color of ebbe bark, and the furry underside of icquit leaves. And the scent... a sweet fragrance he hadn't been able to identify had made him breathe deep in pleasure—a reaction his command implant would have controlled had he not already begun to malfunction. Those failing systems were why, he supposed, he'd let Evie Holloway's maddening creature live.

He could hear the annoying pet's yapping noise even

now. The blasted thing had been relentless, sinking its needle-sharp teeth into his pant leg, but the thought of permanently silencing the Chihuahua in front of the photo of the woman who owned it had been curiously unpalatable.

Not only did that photo save her dog, it had stopped him mid-hunt. Inexplicably. She was just a woman, after all... captured mid-laugh with her head tipped to the side, luxuriant dark brown hair spilling over one shoulder. But her eyes seemed to hold mischievous secrets that all but begged the joy of discovery. And her body...it was as lush as her hair, full, creamy breasts peeking over the low-cut neckline of her shirt.

A man could lose himself in a woman like her.

A fleeting fantasy of her soft and naked in his arms brought a bolt of raw heat to his groin. He immediately tried to control his reaction and succeeded—but only barely. That he'd reacted at all was the clearest sign yet that he was fundamentally changed from the broken REEF carried here months ago. He was fundamentally changed from the REEF he'd been for nearly all his life!

Sweat tingled on his forehead. He swallowed thickly, making a fist on the door frame. When he glanced up, everyone watched him worriedly. "Do you feel ill?" the Gatekeeper asked.

"No," REEF assured her tightly. He felt many things in that moment, but ill wasn't one of them.

At a loss for appropriate parting words, he left the room to pace the length of the front porch in the heat.

The Handyman joined him, boots scuffing on the weathered planks. He wedged the tips of his fingers in his jeans pockets and stood next to REEF, squinting out at the shimmering horizon.

"I'm sexually attracted to her," REEF admitted. "I saw only her photo, of course. But, just now, I reacted when my imagination filled in some details." He opened and closed a fist against his thigh. "What do you do when...that happens?"

The Handyman chuckled. "It's been a while since it's taken me by surprise, but I find mind over matter works best. It's all you can do. Focus elsewhere. If all else fails, take a cold shower."

REEF lifted a brow.

"Or a cold swim. Anything cold. Or, of course, you can take advantage of opportunity if the lady is available and willing."

They both thought of Jana's sister and went awkwardly silent.

"You've never...?" the Handyman asked after a moment or two.

REEF pushed all expression from his face. He squared his shoulders, clasping his hands at the small of his back. "Physical desire interferes with a REEF's duties. Thus, it is suppressed by nano-meds." The dosage had ebbed and flowed with the hormonal changes in his physical body all his adult life. Now no such firewall was in place. For the first time, he was fully functional sexually. He could experience the heat of desire like any other full-blooded male.

It was one more reason Evie Holloway—or any other female—would be wise to stay at a safe distance until he mastered the many complications of being human.

KILL.

The order scrolled across his vision, blocking out all other, extraneous inputs. His target was in his grasp. It was dark; he could not see. His infrared vision systems seemed to be down, but his other sense heightened to compensate. And his weapons...where were they? No matter. His bare hands could bring death with equal swiftness. The only inconvenience was the need for proximity.

KILL.

Ever patient, he waited for his prey to move closer. A human's pulse made a tapping noise, barely perceptible; the respiration was even and soft. Relaxed. His presence had not been detected. Yet, an occasional grunt told him his target was in a state of low-level pain or perhaps overexerted.

He waited. When the sounds and scents were at their peak, he sprang.

"REEF!"

He snatched his target. So easy. It tensed but did not struggle. Smart, that. Struggles would only speed its demise. *KILL.* The order was all-consuming, directing his every thought, his every action. He could have no peace until he'd accomplished his mission.

"REEF, wake up!"

Clarity and bright daylight exploded in his vision, stamping out the shadows. He jerked backward to find his hand was clamped around the Gatekeeper's delicate wrist. His other hand was already halfway to her throat.

Goddess. He released her, almost throwing her away. She

stumbled, and he reached out from the bed to catch her, righting her. "Please accept my apologies," he managed. "I do not know what happened."

"There you are..." Rubbing her arm, she searched his face as she sat down on the edge of the bed. "A minute ago your eyes were so cold, I almost didn't recognize you."

"My eyes were open? But I was sleeping. Dreaming." Shaky and sweating, he rubbed a hand over his face. "A nightmare, actually." Of the old days, the suffocating control, the lack of free will. As difficult as his transition to being human was, he already knew he'd never trade it to go back to his existence as a REEF.

Did his subconscious feel differently? The thought made the dream even more disturbing.

"Did I hurt you?" he asked.

The old woman laughed off his concern. "It would take a lot more than that, young man." Her reddening wrist told him otherwise, but he knew he'd not hear a complaint from her.

She sprang off the bed and threw open the curtains. "Ah, a beautiful day. You had better get ready."

Ah, yes. The time of his departure was upon him. Perhaps that was why his sleep had been so disturbed: odd dreams, thrashing out in his sleep. Squinting in the too-bright sunshine, REEF threw his arm over his eyes. All his senses seemed heightened compared to a few hours ago. The dream had been that strong; it had him remembering what it was like being a REEF.

"Oh, now, now." The Gatekeeper clicked her tongue. "What kind of face is that? Rise and shine. You have a big day ahead of you, Mr. Eric Sanders."

REEF muttered a soft sound of distaste hearing his assumed names. His mood sank further now that he'd been reminded of his departure for California.

And Evie Jasper Holloway's house.

She doesn't want you there. He'd told Jana Jasper as much the day the decision was made. "She never said yes," he'd pointed out, somewhat wary of the unfolding plan.

"She didn't say no," the senator had assured him.

"That can be implied by her ending of the call," he argued. Could she not see the logic?

But the senator had dismissed his argument with a simple "Oh, that's just Evie."

REEF wasn't so sure. Well, if nothing else, he and Evie could agree on one thing: he didn't like the plan, either.

Perhaps he'd make his way over to where his old spaceship was crashed on Jasper property. He'd been an excellent pilot. If neural pathway grooving worked as it was supposed to, he'd still remember how. *If* the blasted ship was still flyable, that was. The last he'd seen it, its nose was buried in springtime mud....

"*Tsk, tsk.* I see that mind of yours at work, plotting and planning. Don't you be thinking of ways to escape this. It's for the best. You know that. Now, hurry and get ready."

The Gatekeeper paused by the bedroom door to add in her singsong voice, "I prepared a special breakfast."

When she'd gone, he swung his legs off the bed and checked through his brown leather wallet one last time. It contained money, credit cards, a California license that bore his photo and a Secret Service ID card. Ironically, Agent Eric

Sanders was gainfully employed by the government and licensed to carry a concealed weapon.

He smoothed two fingers over the weapon he'd wear on his person at all times. A primitive piece, but one well suited for the cover story for the initial part of his journey as a single, white Terran visiting "friends" in California.

REEF made a soft snort as he stripped and headed into the shower. He wasn't certain what awaited him in California, but he was quite certain it wasn't friendship.

After breakfast, REEF hoisted the strap of a suitcase bag over his shoulder and turned to the couple who had sheltered him for so long. He was at a loss as to what to say or do in farewell. Awkwardly, he attempted to express his thanks. "I should be dead. But for your kindness, I would be."

"Oh, come here." The Gatekeeper pulled him into a hug. The body contact shocked him. And somehow soothed him. He realized then how little voluntary human touch he'd experienced over the years and how much he hungered for it.

She moved him back so he could see the tears glittering in her eyes. "You've become like a son to me, REEF."

Feelings swelled in his chest, uncomfortable and unfamiliar. "You have been like a mother to me," he said. Except this one hadn't wanted to give him away like his real mother had.

Not trusting the emotions churning inside him, he turned away only to be pulled into yet another surprise embrace, this time by the Handyman, whose awkward and honest affection matched his own.

"I'll miss you, son," he said, thumping him on the back.

REEF submitted to the hug, trying to convey his gratitude through the brief body contact. Then he stepped back and led the way out the same door through which he'd been carried less than two months ago.

His thick-soled leather shoes clomped down the wooden steps. The new wallet pressed reassuringly against the rear pocket of his jeans. A black T-shirt completed his Terran attire.

The Gatekeeper stayed behind as she had for fifty years, while the Handyman drove him to a remote stretch of road and stopped.

REEF got out. The heat was intense. It was completely silent. High above, buzzards rode the wind. He aimed a glare in their direction. *Not this time.*

The creatures were soon joined by a different kind of "bird." A black, unmarked helicopter descended. Its blades kicked up a tornado of dust and pebbles. They pinged off REEF's sunglasses as he jogged to the open door and climbed in.

The pilot tipped his sunglasses up to scrutinize him. "Agent Eric Sanders?" he yelled above the noise.

With a deadpan expression, REEF nodded and accepted an offered headset.

"I'm Colonel Connick. Call me Tom. You don't know who I am, I don't know who you are, and to the public, neither of us exists. We'll keep it at that, right? As for conversation, everything else—sports, women—it's all fair game."

It was going to be a quiet ride, REEF thought, slipping on the headset, as he knew little of either.

The helicopter lifted off and turned west toward California. Toward the unknown.

REEF had journeyed into the unknown before, only this time he'd be forced to rely on instinct, on hope, rather than indisputable data relayed to his brain via a bioengineered device. An odd feeling of exhilaration filled him at the prospect.

He'd never experienced freedom before. If this is what it tasted like, he had to say he liked it.

"He won't last," Evie Holloway believed. He folded his arms over his chest and settled back in the seat. He wouldn't last, eh? By the goddess, he couldn't wait to prove her wrong.

FIVE

REEF parked in front of Evie's house in the brand-new Hummer that had been waiting for him on arrival in Sacramento. He sat there, the engine idling, as he went over in his head what to say or do when he showed up at her front door.

He ran through scenarios in his mind. *Greetings. I am Eric Sanders. Your sister sent me.*

No, don't say "Greetings." Say "Hello."

Hello. I am Eric Sanders...You know why I'm here. Shall we make the best of it?

He shook his head.

Hello. I'm REEF. I almost killed your sister. I almost killed your dog. May I come in?

He gripped the steering wheel, cursing his blasted ineptness in everyday affairs. Which scenario was the right one? He plotted each course of action, predicting each to a logical conclusion.

"I fear I'll grow old waiting for you to make a decision..."

REEF went absolutely still with the sudden memory.

"It seems the goddess gifted you with infinite patience. With life so slow on this backwater planet, it'll serve you well, I think..."

In his mind he saw a Sech board and a smiling, handsome man...

His father. The realization sparked as much pain as curiosity about the man who had coldheartedly given him away. His own sire. But the memory evaporated as all the others had.

REEF wanted to know more! When would the blasted floodgates open? Would he always be a stranger to himself? How could he get to know others if he didn't know himself?

Evie Holloway's garage door opened, diverting his thoughts instantly. A white vehicle backed out. On the side door was a sign decorated with fruits and flowers. "Evie's... Ed...Eden." Painstakingly, he sounded out the sign, word by word, slowed down by his near-illiteracy.

Evie's Eden? Was not Eden the land of paradise in a Terran book of deities? Adam and Eve and the Garden of Eden, the Gatekeeper had read him the tale. The female in the story tempted the male with forbidden fruit, resulting in terrible consequences.

It wouldn't be difficult to tempt *him* with food, REEF thought. It was his weakness. Only time would tell if Evie Jasper Holloway would prove to be a weakness, as well.

He glimpsed glossy brown hair tossed over a shoulder as the woman backed into the street and drove off.

Now what? Did she not know of his arrival? Or worse, she knew his arrival time and sought to avoid him.

He silently cursed not being able to contact her himself before arriving, but Caydinn and the senator had assured him all was under control. He should have known better than to trust Terrans. They were nothing but trouble.

Executing a U-turn, he followed Evie's vehicle down the street.

———

Sadie stood up, growling over the top of the driver's seat.

"Stop that." Evie tried to get the dog to sit, but her little body was rock hard. "Sadie, down. Sit!"

Sadie's hackles were up; saliva foamed between her lips. "Oh, for God's sake, Sadie. Not rabies, not today. It's our big day, baby-girl. Our first real berry delivery. We want everything to go smoothly."

She dragged the barking dog away from the seat back and forced her to sit in her lap. Sadie tried to climb back up but Evie snatched her back. She swerved and almost went through a red light.

The car behind her followed so close it almost hit her. Was that why Sadie was barking? She glared at the rearview mirror. Some idiot in a Hummer. A nice-looking idiot, she thought, taking a second, longer glance. Thirties, dark sunglasses, short dark hair, chiseled features—but still following too closely. "The world would be a safer place if people like that drove Mini Coopers, not Hummers," she told Sadie.

Trembling, growling, and intermittently barking, her tail snug between her legs, Sadie perched on Evie's thigh, craning her neck to see past her head to the car behind them.

Evie picked up Sadie and held her close, bringing her nose-to-nose. "We're going to have a little talk. Nothing's wrong. Nothing's going to happen. The bad man's gone. Mommy said he can't come to our house." Which was something she had the feeling Jana was having a hard time accepting, if the missed calls, texts, and voice mails on her cell phone were any indication.

Evie decided to make it easy for both of them and ignore every single one. She was too afraid she'd crumble under the onslaught of Jana's fervent, unrelenting campaigning on the REEF's behalf.

Hot blasts of Chihuahua breath hit her in the face. Shivering, the dog growled and whined at the same time, an indescribable sound that only Sadie seemed to be able to produce. It was as if the dog were trying to tell her something. "I'm going to put you in your doggie bed for a little bit until you calm down."

Sadie spun huge, terrified brown eyes to her. Unmoved, Evie kissed the dog on the head and stuffed her into the dog carrier sitting on the passenger seat, zipping the door closed as the light turned green.

Muffled growling continued from inside the carrier. "I'll take you out for a potty break when we get there—I promise, Sadie-baby."

Evie wound through the streets of old Roseville to Kabloom's. On the side of the warehouse, she pulled up next to an old white delivery truck. A cluster of men gathered at the back of the truck, unloading crates. They looked rough, like hardened dockworkers. Hardened dockworkers in a bad mood, she thought, wriggling her fingers in a friendly wave.

They scowled in response and muttered amongst themselves, almost nervously. What? Did they view her as competition? *Too bad, boys.*

Evie found some shade and parked with the windows open for both Sadie's sake and the pallets of finished berries in the back. A young female clerk met her at the delivery counter with the invoice. Smiling, Evie savored the heady moment. "It's my first real delivery," she said, laying her hand over her heart. "Excuse me for being entirely too excited."

The clerk opened her mouth and screamed. Then she dove behind the counter.

"Drop your weapons! FBI!" Men in dark vests and helmets swarmed into the warehouse lot, aiming semiautomatic weapons at her and everyone else.

Evie stared, frozen. The scene was so far from anything she expected to see that she'd lost all sense of time and place.

"FBI! Get down!" they bellowed. *"Get down!"*

Something in the urgency of their voices got her moving. Hands over her head, she bolted for the shelter of her SUV— and Sadie.

Shots exploded; bullets zinged.

"Take shelter—*now.*" Someone caught her by the arm and yanked her backward. Bullets clanged against the metal walls of a dumpster. She heard them hit as she went down. It's where she would have been standing if he hadn't grabbed her. The man had saved her life.

There was no time to say thanks. He enveloped her with his body as they rolled. His flesh and bones were all that kept her skull from bouncing off the asphalt as they tumbled into the shadow of the two huge dumpsters.

More shouts. Automatic weapons fire. A shriek of pain. It was chaos.

The man kept his hand pressed firmly to the back of her head, holding her down, but he didn't have to. Quite willingly, she crammed her face against his chest. A heartbeat thumped under her ear, almost as loud as her own. The scents of sweat, hot skin and fabric softener filled her nose as the man crushed his arm over her shoulders. It was almost intimate.

She'd never been so scared in her life. And she'd never felt so sure someone would keep her safe.

After a while the noise subsided. Voices still shouted things like "Stay down!" and "FBI!" but the firefight had ended.

Her rescuer released his hold on her. She sat up, shaking as badly as Sadie usually did.

Oh, God—Sadie! "Where's my dog?" The SUV's rear tires were completely flat. The back window had been shot out. Little pieces of tinted auto glass were everywhere. "My dog is still in there! Sadie!"

Then she heard muffled barking.

Relief shuddered through her. "I need to get her out of there."

The man yanked her back before she had a chance to run. One hand held her near, the other gripped a gun. "I'll get your dog when it is clear," he said in an unusual accent.

South African? Dutch? She twisted around to look at him. As he scanned the parking lot, his gun drawn, she caught his face in profile—hard and unforgiving, not the kind of man for whom giving comfort was second nature. A black T-shirt stretched across his chest and shoulders and disappeared into the waistband of a pair of faded jeans. He was well built with incredible pecs and rounded biceps. Clean-cut, he wore his jet-black hair cropped short. But unlike the other men who'd swarmed in, he wasn't wearing a blue vest emblazoned with FBI and DEA. "Are you an undercover agent?"

He turned his head, dipping his chin to view her over the top of his sunglasses. His eyes were so intensely blue, the purest of sky-blues, that they literally took her breath away. Or maybe it was the pain from all the bruises throbbing to life from her elbows to her knees that did it.

"Or are you one of the bad guys?" she joked, still shaking.

He let out a quick cough of a laugh. Curiously, he didn't smile.

He didn't answer the question, either.

Over by the white truck, it sounded like the group of mean-looking men were getting pulverized by the other agents. Clearly *they* were the bad guys. It reassured her that her rescuer was on the right side. Her side. She didn't exactly snuggle closer, but she definitely sought more body contact. He smelled really good. He was hot and he'd saved her from getting injured. "Thank you."

He turned to her again. Faint beard stubble shadowed his chin and jaw, framing his way-too-serious but very sexy mouth. She wondered what it took to make those yummy lips melt into a smile. A kiss of gratitude?

Evie, you're delirious. "If you didn't stop me, who knows, I might have been shot in the head."

"That assumption is incorrect." He pointed with his gun to the holes. "If you take the trajectory of the bullets and merge their path with your predicted final location, this one would have pierced your neck." He moved the gun to the right and a little lower. "And these two, your chest."

A surge of sheer terror clogged her throat. A cold sweat broke out all over her body as her mouth went dry. "How do you know that?"

"Experience." He took off his sunglasses. His eyes could have filled a book with the stories they knew.

Something about his response jarred her, causing her to pay attention. She took a second, longer look at him—the accent that sounded a lot like Cavin's, the startling blue eyes. She knew where she'd seen his face before...in the police sketch released after the attack on Cavin and Jana.

Her gaze dropped to the scar on the inside of his left arm. A long, thin scar.

Where his gauntlet thingy used to be.

Shit! Her heart rolled over as the realization of who he was plowed into her like a freight train. "You're him—you're the REEF."

She scooted away. She'd been falling all over him like a teenager with a crush. She'd practically climbed in his lap! "That was you in the Hummer. You were following me."

"FBI!" A group of men approached them, guns aimed. "Drop your weapon! Drop it!"

Rather unfortunate timing, REEF thought. Evie's shocked

and angry expression made it obvious that she hadn't been expecting him today—or ever. Now he wouldn't be able to explain that he was here on her sister's orders. It left him in a bit of a pickle, as the Gatekeeper would have said.

He slid his weapon across the ground and lifted his hands. He knew enough of Earth law enforcement procedures from his pre-mission research on the planet—and a few action movies—to say and do the right things. In contrast, Evie meanwhile sat a few feet away, fuming, her green eyes blazing. She reminded him of a plasma grenade ready to blow. Would she turn him in to the Terran officials? Would she scream? Or run? All three?

"This witness is mine," REEF informed the agents.

"Yours?" Evie blurted out.

"Mine," he repeated, leaving her to mull over the note of possession in his tone. Ah, but she deserved as much for her "he won't last a week" comment, did she not? For thinking him weak and a quitter.

"My identification is in my back pocket." He held his hands high as one of the agents pulled out his wallet. "Agent Eric Sanders, secret service, special ops."

Evie shot him a sharp glance at the lie. He answered with a visual shrug, daring her to say something. She knew the risks of revealing his true identity as well as he did.

If he fell into the wrong hands, he could very well "disappear" so he could be "studied." Certainly, Caydinn and the senator would arrive within hours to lobby on his behalf, but by then it might be too late.

Evie's laser stare bored through the side of his head. It

was as if she'd read his thoughts and found the prospect of his capture tempting. Yet she said nothing.

"He checks out," the Terran agent said, handing around the wallet for everyone to take a look. "Who's she?"

"I'm Evie Holloway," she piped up. "Evie *Jasper* Holloway. My purse is in my car."

"You're a Jasper?"

"She's not involved." REEF stood, brushing off his jeans, and slipped his weapon back in the holster under his shirt. "I was surveilling her myself under a separate investigation."

Evie whipped her head around and glared at him. Again, he dared her to speak out. She maintained her silence. It seemed they were more on the same side of this than he or she liked to admit.

He stepped closer and offered her a hand. Her white low-cut shirt was form-fitting. At this angle, he had an unobstructed view of the lacey, flesh-colored bra she wore underneath. Her breasts were full, ready to spill over the cups. *Too bad you cannot be there to catch them in your hands,* he thought. A now-familiar heat hit him down low, but thanks to the Handyman's advice, he knew what to do.

Focus elsewhere. Swallowing, arm extended, he averted his gaze and thought of everything else but Evie's body. She grabbed his hand. He pulled her to her feet, releasing her perhaps a little too quickly, but not before feeling the chill of terror in her grip.

She was in shock. A woman like her would not be used to these circumstances. He, on the other hand, was more than acclimated to battle. Only one thing kept this scene from feeling overly familiar: everyone was still alive.

An ambulance siren wailed in the distance. Or mostly alive, he mentally corrected, seeing a couple of agents tending several bloodied men.

But every minute spent in the scrutiny of law enforcement increased the chance he'd be recognized, arrested and made to answer for his crimes. He didn't want to answer to anyone, least of all Terran wardens. "I'll take her off your hands now, gentlemen."

"I wish you'd done it yesterday, Sanders. Your witness just happened to stroll in on the biggest RICO case in four years. Just sashayed into the middle of a takedown."

"Excuse me," Evie interrupted. "I didn't sashay anywhere. I was making a delivery. I own Evie's Eden. Kabloom's is my biggest customer."

The agent ignored her and spoke only to REEF, whom he clearly saw as one of them. *If only he knew.* "There was a drug shipment in the white truck. We had to move. Then she shows up. We didn't know if she was involved in the money laundering or not. With organized crime—the mob—you've got it all. Drugs, racketeering, executions, you name it. It's an ongoing investigation, can't divulge more, but a word of caution regarding your witness—it's unlikely the syndicate will care she was here, but she'd be wise to keep an eye out for any suspicious or threatening activity."

REEF could almost hear the crash as Evie's accusing glare collided with his.

The agent holstered his weapon. "I'd like to ask the berry lady a few questions."

"Berry lady?" Evie was openly indignant at the agent's

condescending tone. For someone so far out of her comfort zone, she had plenty of pride to spare.

To her further ire, REEF waved a hand in a flourish, granting the agent permission.

A tow truck pulled into the parking lot to take Evie's vehicle away. "I'll salvage her belongings," REEF said.

"And my dog," she called to him.

"I would not dream of abandoning it," he lied.

"How much stuff were they buying?" the agent asked Evie. "Who paid you? Cash? Check? Who are your associates?"

While the agent questioned her, REEF opened the car and gathered Evie's car keys and her purse. The sweet scent of fruit and something else just as delectably sweet wafted out. He breathed deep. Chocolate...it was as if the goddesses had crafted the aroma in heaven itself. It brought fond memories of the Gatekeeper's cookies.

He brushed off broken glass and lifted the boxes out, setting them on the pavement in the shade. The day was hot, but perhaps some of Evie's cargo could be salvaged.

An ominous growling rumbled from inside a pet carrier on the front passenger seat. Ah, yes, REEF thought. He mustn't forget the creature. He lifted the pet carrier by the handle and raised it to his face. Two glistening, unblinking eyes rounded at the sight of him. "So, we meet again. Hello, Sadie."

The growling became more guttural.

"I hope we can make amends, or at least come to some sort of understanding, as I've been sentenced to do some time in your home."

Curiously, the growling stopped. At least one thing had gone right today. He and the emaciated excuse for a canine had made peace.

A splattering sound broke the silence. The pungent scent of urine hit his nose at the same time something hot and wet splashed around his ankles.

"Goddess," he muttered, dropping his gaze from the leaking carrier to the ground. The maddeningly little Earth creature had peed all over his new shoes.

SIX

As tempting as the thought of strangling the dog was, it was fleeting. REEF could no more terminate Evie's exasperating pet now than he could have that day in her home. Then, he'd blamed his mercy on a malfunction. Now his only excuse was the necessity to leave this place without delay. Every minute spent in the scrutiny of law enforcement increased the chance he'd be recognized and caught. He wasn't afraid of the Terrans; he didn't want them complicating his life any more than they had already.

REEF hoisted the carrier with one hand and strode across the parking lot. "I'll take my witness now, gentlemen. Good day." He snatched Evie by the elbow and turned her toward the Hummer parked in the street. Anger radiated off her in red-hot waves, but he couldn't risk explaining why he was here until they were out of earshot of the agents.

She wrinkled her nose. "I smell urine." A stray droplet fell from the bottom of the carrier and splashed onto the pavement. An odd little cough erupted in her throat. Was she laughing at him? "She peed on you."

"It would seem so." He pushed on her arm to hurry her along but she dug in her heels. Now what? The woman was maddening! "It is time to go, Miss Holloway."

Amused, one of the agents called to them. "Do you need some assistance with your witness, Sanders?"

REEF lowered his mouth close to her ear. "Do I?" He intended the question as a dare to goad her into cooperating, but her voice dropped to an equally private tone.

"I'm not driving anywhere with either of you until you rinse off. There's a hose over there. I'll take care of my dog. But as for the assistance—" she let her gaze slide down his body "—if you really think you need help washing, I'll see what I can do."

The thought of her hands moving over his wet skin rendered him speechless as he managed what he was sure was his first blush as an adult male.

Evie grabbed the carrier, leaving him to stand there, arms hanging at his sides, as he tried to figure out how she'd so thoroughly routed him.

Your talents lie in killing, not in repartee with a beautiful woman. *Fool was he to even try.*

Then it hit him: she'd flirted back! Or, at least he assumed her retort was a form of flirting. Bottom line, she'd revealed awareness of him as a man—not as a machine, a cyborg, but as a male. If only his command center was up and running to analyze and make sense of the flood of new data.

He caught up to her at the hose. With Sadie tucked under her arm, she rinsed off the pet carrier. Her hair fell over her face, hiding her expression, but her jerky movements were a good measure of her anger.

Once more REEF found himself quite unintentionally at the precise viewing angle to ponder Evie's cleavage and the lace hiding beneath her shirt. Her skin looked so soft, so smooth.

He swallowed hard. How easily he'd scoffed at her "he won't last a week" remark. Now a week sounded like eternity. How would he ever last that long in close proximity to her? Since Evie Holloway was strictly hands-off, it wouldn't happen without a lot of cold showers.

"Evie Holloway, I'm here because your sister and Caydinn wanted me relocated for my protection." Protection —bah! Goddess, how he hated to admit that. "My sudden appearance shocked you. My apologies. I never intended that. I thought you knew."

A derisive sound came out of her mouth as she scrubbed the carrier far harder than the small amount of urine would have required. "Jana shouldn't have told you to come. I said no."

"Actually, you didn't. But you did say that I wouldn't last a week."

She froze, her face flushing pink as her eyes narrowed. "She told you that?"

"Quite clearly." It seemed he couldn't resist baiting her and then anticipating her reaction, which had so far brought great rewards in the vast range of emotion she was capable of displaying.

She didn't disappoint. "I didn't mean it. She should have known that. I was so tired of my family interfering in my life.

Tired of them always expecting me to drop everything to accommodate their crazy schemes, tired of never sticking up for what I want." She rammed her thumb at her chest. "So instead of a simple no, I told her what basically amounted to 'bring it on.'" She dashed a wet hand across her forehead. "But I guess that's all TMI."

"TMI?" REEF had been doing all he could to follow the storm of colloquial language, but this word puzzled him. He no longer had his database to define the vast amount of English regional slang.

"Too...much...information." She went back to washing, her motions jerky. Her hair fell in a luxurious sweep over her face. He ached to smooth it away, to touch her skin, to see if her lips were as warm and soft as they looked. To kiss her until she forgot all about her anger and redirected that passion to him.

Goddess... His body reacted to the fantasy.

Focus elsewhere.

"Long story short," Evie was saying, "I'm steamed."

"Steamed?"

She jerked her fierce gaze to his. "Angry. Furious. Head-shatteringly irate." She made a soft snarl as if to demonstrate the point. Her sheer range of expression fascinated him. "On top of that, this happens." She waved a still-shaky hand at the crime scene. Sirens wailed in the distance, growing closer. "Fear, carnage, confusion...and it's not even noon."

Barking interrupted them.

Evie lifted her wretched dog to her lips and kissed it on the nose. The creature wriggled, its tail whipping with happiness as Evie climbed to her feet. "She's not scared of you anymore. Peeing on you gave her a sense of power."

"A more likely reason is that my bioengineering is disabled. Animals are often bothered by the vibrations, which I no longer emit."

Evie's attention flicked to the scar on his arm and quickly back to the dog. The idea of his having hardware installed in his body repulsed her. He couldn't blame her for feeling that way. He set his jaw and took the hose to rinse off his shoes.

"But you're totally human now, right?"

"I'm learning to be."

The anger in her face melted into surprise. "Learning?" Blazing with anger only moments ago, her eyes filled suddenly with tears. Goddess, her moods shifted like the tidal currents on Ramakka. "You saved my life. In my opinion, most people could learn something *from you*."

Her gratitude filled his chest with unaccustomed warmth, but he kept his focus firmly on cleaning his shoes. She didn't know the things he had done over the years; he couldn't guarantee his eyes wouldn't reveal some of them and cause her to change her mind.

She touched his arm so he'd look at her. "I mean that. You would have taken those bullets for me. You were willing to die in my place."

To his shock, her bare arms pebbled with tiny bumps.

"It's the most romantic thing that's ever happened to me," she breathed.

The hose fell out of his hand. Evie squealed and ducked as water sprayed everywhere. He snatched the hose off the ground. "My apologies," he said. "Some Earth equipment is unfamiliar."

So were conversations about romance.

"I meant romantic in the classical sense," she explained. "As in knights in shining armor, damsels in distress."

"Of course." The classical sense. *Did you actually think it would be otherwise?* He was acting like a schoolboy around her.

Except, he was definitely not a schoolboy.

"I am glad to have been of assistance," he said stiffly. "Once I see you safely home, I will go. Alternate accommodations have been secured."

"Please." She snorted. "You were a top-secret Coalition operative. That's the best you can do at lying?"

He started to argue then realized she was right. "Apparently so. I never needed to lie. It wasn't necessary. My duties were always quite straightforward."

She reacted to that information with the same expression she had when she viewed his scar—something between fear and revulsion with a little pity mixed in. *You must stop reminding her what you are.* No—what he *was.* "There are no alternate accommodations arranged—but they can be."

A few shouts interrupted them. More officials had arrived on the scene. A maze of yellow crime-scene tape was being used to cordon off the area. Evie peered somewhere over his shoulder and frowned. "Don't turn around," she whispered. "One of the agents keeps looking at you. I think he's suspicious."

Turning, REEF shot his infamously cold glare in the Terran's direction. Immediately, the agent went back to taking notes. It was indeed possible he recognized REEF. There had been a police sketch circulating, but to his knowledge, it had been pulled from public record.

Still, some might remember his face. That would be unfortunate. A curious agent's meddling would only delay the matter of his future getting sorted out, and he wanted it sorted out without delay. He was weary of being dependent on others, weary of being forced to do someone else's bidding. He wanted a say in his life, what there was left of it. "I do not fear the Terrans," he sneered.

"You looked!" Evie's green eyes snapped with anger. The tide of moods had turned once again. A dangerous riptide, if he were to hazard a guess. "Why did you do that? If I were on a foreign planet, and a representative of the indigenous species had just given me critical instructions—I'd listen."

A few furious steps erased what distance remained between them, presumably so she could further scold him outside of the earshot of the agents. She stood impossibly close, clothed only in that distracting, insubstantial shirt and form-fitting jeans. Her scent was sweet and powdery with the faintest hint of musk. He made a fist with one hand, gripping the hose with the other so he wouldn't be tempted to touch her. If it were another time and place, if he were another man, he'd have slid his hand around the small of her back and dragged her close.

He knew exactly what he'd want from her.

In his time of service to the Coalition, he'd hunted prey in palaces and filthy alleys, galaxy-class hotels and third-rate pleasure inns. He'd seen couples kiss—and more. He understood the mechanics required to accomplish a variety of acts.

A lack of hands-on experience made him no less eager to taste this woman, to explore her. To feel her respond to his touch.

His breath caught. He was so hard it hurt.

"You want to spend the night in jail? Is that it?"

Evie's fury brought him crashing back to reality.

"That's what I suggested to Jana in the first place, you know," she ranted, completely unaware of the direction of his thoughts. "Go on. Go over there and turn yourself in. What's stopping you?" Fuming, she cradled Sadie close to her body and waited for his answer.

The exhausted dog was already asleep, a far cry from the vicious, frothing creature of their last encounter. Why? Because it was no longer afraid.

The realization struck a chord. He too transformed his fear into aggression. "It seems your Sadie and I are more alike than I care to admit. We both snarl and snap to disguise our fear. Now that I am aware, I will not do so again."

In the space of a single breath, Evie's expression went from anger to shock, to understanding and, finally, forgiveness. Honesty had paid off. However, he had no intention of making a habit of admitting to weakness.

He further felt Evie's astonished gaze on him as he opened the door to the Hummer, waving her inside.

With relief he shut the door behind her after she'd boarded. He loaded the remainder of her possessions in the rear compartment and slid back into the driver's seat. "Now I will drive you home."

"And then?" she asked.

"And then I inform Caydinn and the senator of their error and await their further instructions."

"No," she said.

He stopped, bracing himself for another complication.

"You're as much of a victim of my family as I am. I don't think we should ask them what to do. We should do what we want to do. They've been moving us around like pawns in a chess game. I say we take our pieces off the board and make our own rules."

"Are you proposing an alliance?"

"I want control of my life back. You want control of yours. I don't know if we can call that an alliance. A cease-fire, maybe." She glanced side to side before leaning closer, as if worried someone would overhear their conversation. "Look, they sent you here for protection. After what happened today, I could use some. With the mob involved, no one would question my hiring a bodyguard. I'd like to offer you the position."

Act as Evie Holloway's bodyguard? Even without his bio-hardware to calculate odds, he knew the probability of failure was high. He'd always taken lives; he'd never preserved them.

Until today.

True, and he did need time to make plans to escape the trap into which he'd fallen.

Turning to her, he proposed, "In exchange for my protection, you will teach me to be a Terran."

"Like alien finishing school."

"Say again?"

"My services for yours," she clarified and offered her hand in the quaint gesture of Earth friendship.

He took her hand in his and nodded. "Your services for mine."

Something passed between them then. The delivery of a dare? A binding verbal contract? Or something in between?

His oddly heightened senses were aware of her all over again. Her flesh seared his palm as her scent filled his nostrils. He could feel her heart beating—he could hear it. Even the rustle of her hair was loud to his newly sensitive ears. He couldn't explain it. It was like the old days when he was out hunting a target, only this was no hunt.

Or was it?

REEF turned away and started the engine. It was time to drive Evie to safety before she drove him to distraction.

SEVEN

Evie stole the opportunity to study the REEF as he merged the Hummer into traffic. He was an enigma. On the outside he was all lean muscle, nothing soft. Efficient, confident, he radiated quiet intensity, like a coiled spring. Or like an ex-con after ten years' hard time in San Quentin.

It made it easy to picture him in his former profession. Yet, she'd made him blush at the hose—blush! A manly blush, a tiny hint of color above each cheekbone, but, still, it was obvious he'd turned red at her teasing. Why?

He'd killed people on his government's orders. He'd run secret missions for the largest military force in the galaxy. There was no way he could have done all that and maintained a sense of innocence.

"Is there something amiss?" he asked, sensing her stare.

"I'm trying to figure out how in the world I made you blush."

He swiveled his head to look at her. Dark sunglasses hid

his eyes and blocked anything she might have read in them. "My emotions have been suppressed for many years. Spurious physiological reactions are to be expected."

"Spurious as in fake?"

"That is correct."

"Oh, no, it's not. I don't know squat about robotics, but I know men. I know men almost as well as I know food—except that I've had much better luck with food. Your blush was genuine and adorable, and most of the women I know would have swooned seeing it."

"This is true?" He seemed much more interested in the conversation now.

"Are you kidding me? The tough bad-boy type with a vulnerable streak is considered the Holy Grail of men."

"Holy Grail." He frowned all over again. "A legendary drinking vessel?"

"That people searched centuries for. It means you're what many women look for and never find."

He made a dismissive sound and returned his attention to the road. Well, he might not want to talk about it, but she had her own theories about that blush. The bioengineered-implants had always controlled his every thought, his every move, but deep down there must have been a part of him left untouched: his humanity, freeze-framed since childhood.

Evie dug through her purse for something to alleviate the sting of her scraped elbow, amazingly, her only injury thanks to the REEF. "You're a lot more human than you give your-self credit for, Eric."

"Use the Sanders identification in the company of others

and REEF at all other times," he said, flinching as she spoke the name.

"But isn't that—"

"My designation, yes. Use it anyway." His voice lost its edge. "I don't remember my real name."

"Is that because of your injuries, or..."

"No." He stiffened. "Upon entering REEF training, my mind was wiped clean of potential distractions."

"Oh God," she murmured. The idea of anyone having the power to do that to another person left her feeling nauseated.

The atmosphere in the car had chilled.

REEF took a hand off the wheel and made a fist on his thigh. "Repulsive, yes?"

"Horribly."

He reacted with his usual frown—his facial screen-saver she'd begin to think of it—which at first glance looked like anger. But, looking deeper, she saw what should have been obvious. Shame. He was either embarrassed by what he'd revealed or by her reaction—or both.

"It's not you that repulses me, REEF." Did he really think that? "It's the people who did that to you."

The alien who had petrified her now pushed every protective button she had. Cavin had told her that REEFs started training between five and eight years old. It tore at her heart. "You were just a kid when they did that to you. A helpless child."

"It is the way it's done," he said.

"They erased your memory. They took your past." And everything he was. "That's...inhumane."

"REEFs are not human."

"Sure they are. They're humans augmented by internal machines."

"And controlled by them. By design, our humanity becomes secondary to the machine." At that, his hand returned to the steering wheel, flexing, hinting at inner tension, but his expression remained stony, his focus on the road.

She was horrified by what he'd revealed. Yet, he acted as if it were no big deal. *This* was the society Earth wanted to align with? A civilization that turned little children into weapons? "I volunteer my time helping relief organizations trying to end child slavery. How the hell are we going to do that if the rest of the galaxy thinks it's okay?"

"I was not a slave," he argued.

She made a soft snort.

"Nor have I have seen current evidence of slavery on Earth," he accused.

"You've only been to the United States, that's why. In many poorer countries it's a big problem. It's why I started my business, Evie's Eden. I want to use the profits to help the people and organizations fighting against the forced servitude of children. Over a million kids a year are trafficked across borders to work in mines, or on plantations. Sometimes they're forced into prostitution or even the military like you were. I saw a photo of a seven-year-old holding a rifle. His eyes still haunt me. They were empty. *Empty,* REEF. He was fighting for some warlord, but he didn't care if he lived or died."

REEF's shoulders stiffened. A muscle thrummed in his

jaw as the tendons of his neck stood out starkly on his smooth, suntanned skin.

"It must have been incredibly traumatic being taken from your family at such a young age."

"It is a great honor to be chosen for the REEF Academy," he said, his chin coming up. "The Headmaster and his staff are some of the Coalition's most celebrated soldiers and scientists. My parents would have wanted me to go."

"Why?" What kind of family volunteered their child to have their humanity gutted and replaced with computers?

"A wish for me to have a better life."

"It doesn't make it right."

REEF's grief-stricken expression told her she'd gone too far. She bit her lip and shut up. Hundreds of thousands of child slaves left parents back in the villages believing they'd given their babies a shot at a better life. Reality told a far different story. But if it caused REEF less pain to believe he'd been honored by his selection as a REEF as opposed to being destroyed by it, then who was she to shatter that illusion?

Lord knew, it was a lot easier believing Pierce walked out on her because he'd felt trapped in his role as family man rather than to accept that his actions reflected a fundamental rejection of everything she was.

And what was she trying to do, anyway? Turn the ex-killer into the poster boy for child servitude?

In the thick silence, Evie fumbled for the packet of disinfectant wipes she'd forgotten about. She'd cleaned the small scrape on her elbow, but REEF had taken the brunt of their fall. "Use a couple of these on your cuts," she said to melt new tension between them. "It'll take away the burn and keep them from getting infected." She reached for REEF's arm. And froze. On the perfection of his suntanned skin, save his old scar, only the slightest of coloration changes marked where there had been bumps and bruises.

"Your scrapes are gone." How...? "That cut on your palm was bleeding." A smudge of dried blood on his faded jeans told her she wasn't crazy. "But you healed."

He glanced down at his arms and took a double take. "I have." He sounded as surprised as she was.

"I know you have microscopic robots in your bloodstream that swim around and do repairs, but Cavin's never worked this fast."

Jana had described the medical miracles that even Cavin's damaged body's defenses could perform, but this... this was like magic. For the first time Evie understood the enormity of the chasm between the Coalition and Earth.

Her brother had sacrificed the life he'd wanted in order to marry their queen and secure a peace treaty between the two sides. But it was more than peace Earth was after. Queen Keira's people possessed the technology to cure cancer, and almost every other known disease. Earth couldn't afford to fight the Coalition, and they couldn't afford to leave them. But was gaining the means to knit spinal cords together overnight or repair retinas in hours worth making peace with people who turned little kids into cyborgs? It was not an easy question to answer.

"A REEF's healing abilities are always accelerated," REEF explained as he drove. "But with my command center hardware gone, the process was degraded—almost nonexistent. I'd lost most, if not all, of the nanomeds, and I had no way to regenerate new ones. I'd seen the signs of that already. At the farmhouse, if I injured myself, I healed almost as slowly as the humans did." Puzzled, he shook his head. "I have no explanation for this healing other than it seems to have returned—" Without warning, he swerved off the street and into the parking lot of a local strip mall that contained a sushi place, a drycleaner and a vet.

"REEF, this is not where we turn."

He didn't seem to hear her. She followed his stare to the restaurant's sign. An eel curled around the letters forming the restaurant's name—Uncle Unagi. "What is this place?" he asked.

"It's a Japanese restaurant."

"They serve serpents here."

"We call them eel. *Unagi* means eel in Japanese. Fresh-water eel."

"Ah...yes..."

What was up with him? He was acting strange.

The hair on the back of her neck prickled. Despite her compassion for him and what he'd been through, he was still an unknown quantity. "The owner keeps them in a tank out front like they do in Japan," she said. "On weekends you can watch him slaughter them. John and Ellen think it's the coolest. Personally, I think it's disgusting. I like eel grilled inside a sushi roll. I just don't want to know how it got there, right?"

Intently focused on the eel tank, REEF opened the car door and climbed down from the Hummer.

"REEF?" He either ignored her or didn't hear her. She grabbed Sadie and went after him.

She found him examining the tank with a strange, almost wistful look. "Do you want to try the *unagi?*" she asked. "I'll order us some."

"Please." He dug in his pants for his wallet and pulled out several fifties and a credit card.

"Whoa, we don't need that much." She chose a ten and made a mental note that money handling would have to go on the lesson plan too. They hadn't taught him too much on the farm. Then again, it had been miles from anything resembling civilization. "Be right back."

The sushi chef took the order. Evie waited next to the counter, clutching Sadie, trying to sort out REEF's strange, impulsive behavior. This was not good. Not good at all. She'd taken comfort in his calm, rational demeanor, his basic predictability. Now he was anything but. No question, she'd have to watch him.

Doubts coursed through her again. The last thing she needed when people were keeping their eyes on *her* was having to keep an eye on REEF.

A couple walked into the restaurant. As they placed an order, Evie peered around them. REEF was still staring into the tank with an embarrassing intensity. The woman seemed to notice too. Evie caught her eye, praying her smile was in fact a smile and not the grimace she feared.

Then, lightening fast, REEF thrust a hand into the fish tank and pulled out a wriggling, dripping-wet eel.

"Holy shit!" Evie dashed outside and ran to him. "What are you doing?"

"Freshwater. Male." REEF slid his sunglasses into his hair, his eyes narrowing as he inspected the writhing eel. "It could be plumper and thus sweeter. Perhaps if they'd allowed it to mature..."

"REEF, please. Put. The. Eel. Down."

"I have eaten these...." He contemplated the wiggling eel with new interest.

If he bit into it, it would bring a whole new meaning to sushi, one she didn't want to experience. "REEF, don't."

The owner ran out waving a sushi blade. "I call police!"

"Uncle Unagi, it's me, Evie Holloway. You know my kids. We get take-out here all the time. You know my sister too. Senator Jana Jasper? And my father, Congressman Jasper? Governor Jake Jasper was my grandfather." If she had to, she'd name drop everyone in her family.

"He play with eel!"

Evie blocked him from getting closer to REEF. "I'll take care of it. He didn't know. It's, um, a cultural thing. He's a tourist, visiting from...from far away!"

"Nevada," REEF supplied.

Evie rolled her eyes.

"Put eel back in water now," Uncle Unagi barked at REEF in his broken English. The rotund little sushi chef had no clue he was taking on a man who was once one of the galaxy's most feared killers, and Evie had no plan to enlighten him.

"As you wish." REEF let the eel slide from his hands into the tank.

"See?" Evie said as cheerily as she could with her heart pounding in her throat. "All better."

The owner stalked back to the restaurant to put the finishing touches on their order. From inside, the couple had watched the entire show through the glass. The woman turned to the man and whispered.

Evie turned on REEF. Her head felt ready to explode. "What were you doing? What were you thinking? You're supposed to be keeping a low profile."

REEF took off his glasses. His eyes were achingly blue and suddenly alive. His excitement made him look almost boyish, something she wouldn't have thought possible. It gave a glimpse of what he might have been like before he was made into a REEF. "I've caught creatures like this one and ate their meat...as a child."

It was hard to stay angry in the face of his wonder. To have his memories come back after so many years...she was afraid she'd cry if she witnessed it. She clutched Sadie closer. "Tell me more."

His expression tightened, his brows drawing together. "There was a sea, a vast inland sea, calm and pale green. I used to fish there with the man I believe was my father."

"And who still is your father. Not that many years have passed, relatively speaking. I'm sure he's alive."

The light drained from his eyes. "To me, he is dead."

He turned away, pacing a few steps, lost in his thoughts, before he stopped, his frown returning. "Nothing. I see nothing more. I was told that my memories will likely return all at once, like water breaking through a weakened dam. Yet, it's been months. I thought I'd remember more by now."

His confession about broke her heart. "You will. Soon. Even a small memory is a breakthrough." Even one of a man whose memory he'd rather forget.

"What if you and everyone else are wrong? What if I am condemned to live like this forever?"

"Then you start fresh," she ventured quietly. "You begin again. It's what we humans have to do sometimes."

He held her gaze. "It is all so complicated, being human. I think perhaps I need your Terran school more than you need my protection."

She was about to argue when a blue Ford four-door slowed as it cruised by. The windows were tinted, yet she felt the stares of people she couldn't see crawling over her skin. "REEF." She couldn't seem to draw in a full breath. "REEF. The car."

He stepped in front of her, placing his body in between her and possible danger. His hand lifted toward the holster hidden under his shirt.

"Don't shoot," she whispered. "It's a public place."

He made the smallest of exasperated sighs. "I let you do your job, yes? Let me do mine."

"Fine."

"I'm only guarding the weapon so that I'm prepared to use it if necessary."

She wanted to sob. A shootout at Uncle Unagi's. It wasn't so farfetched considering she'd narrowly missed getting blown to bits in the parking lot of a balloon-bouquet warehouse. What had her life become?

"Occupants—two," REEF rattled off. "Male, thirties—in Earth years."

"Earth years. Of course." She was trying very hard not to let her terror translate into sarcasm.

"Paint—new. It appears to cover lettering of some kind."

"What does it say? The Mob's Drive-by Shooting Service?"

He stiffened. "I...don't know."

"Well, I can't even see past the paint. I'll have to take your word for it. For someone who was supposedly 'dismantled' you have a lot of leftover powers."

The car accelerated and drove on. Evie closed her eyes and whispered her thanks. Sadie made a snoring sigh and went back to sleep in her arms.

"Don't be afraid," REEF said. "I will protect you."

"I'm not afraid for me. I'm afraid for my kids." And of losing them. "I can't afford to become a target." Evie realized she was trembling. REEF lifted his hands. For one held-in breath she though he was going to grab her shoulders to steady her, but he let his hands drop. She was relieved and disappointed at the same time. "Maybe we should call the police. No— Let's just get our food and go." She took another look up and down the street.

His fingers landed on the center of her back, and pushed gently. "I will keep watch. You don't need to."

"But—"

"You still have not learned how to be a damsel," he complained as he urged her along. His mouth had formed a frown again, but his touch was light, protective, nothing like the forceful shoves in Ka-bloom's parking lot.

"I haven't had much practice. You need a knight around to be a damsel." And now she had one...in the form of a down-on-his-luck interstellar hitman.

They moved closer to the door of the restaurant. Uncle Unagi was almost done with their order. The heat was blistering. It didn't seem to bother REEF much, but she was wilting. Her top clung to her damp skin. She tugged at the cotton to coax in some cool air, plucking and releasing until she noticed REEF's dark gaze. Her hand went still. His cheeks turned pink and he glanced away. Her own face felt hot, and her awareness of him spiked all over again.

"Number seventeen roll, no onion!" One of Uncle Unagi's servers offered them a foam takeout box.

A little breathless, Evie took it. It was too hot to eat outside at one of the plastic tables shaded by a Sapporo umbrella. They returned to the Hummer, leaving it in idle for air-conditioning. REEF adjusted the rearview mirror to keep watch on the stores behind them as well as the street they'd parked facing. No blue Fords lurked suspiciously.

Only then did REEF open the box. He ignored the chopsticks. With his finger, he dug out a sliver of *unagi* from beneath a layer of avocado and discarded everything else—the seaweed wrapper, the *tobiko,* the rice.

"Chopsticks?"

He frowned at the mangled roll as if he'd just now realized what he'd done.

She smiled. "Don't worry about it. Try it. See if it's what you remember."

"It looks as I remember..." He held the sliver of meat between his fingers, tilting it from side to side then sniffing it. "And smells as I remember."

Straight white teeth sank into the meat. And then he sighed. What followed was a prolonged, sensual reunion with a food he'd loved. His enjoyment was so blatant, his anticipation of each succeeding taste so sharp, that she found herself holding her breath between bites.

It wasn't hard to imagine that mouth on her...*everywhere*...as he kneeled over her naked body, tasting her from head to toe, just like that.

Her entire body clenched with arousal. She fumbled for the air conditioner vent and directed it at herself. What was wrong with her? *You're just out of practice, Evie.*

Way out of practice. She hadn't gone on more than a half-dozen boring, post-divorce dates before deciding she'd wait until the kids went to college before concentrating on a personal life. Her life was so happy and busy that she'd found the decision a surprisingly easy one. On the other hand, she hadn't been really, truly tempted into changing her mind, either.

Like REEF tempted her.

You can't date him, Evie.

Who said anything about dating? How about some memorable, no-strings sex?

He's an ex-interstellar cyborg assassin who's in the process of being relocated.

The reminder helped keep her attraction to him in perspective, if it didn't exactly cool the flames.

Closing her eyes, she tipped her head back to expose her neck to the chilled air. Her hair whipped around her face and shoulders. Everything felt better—more vivid, more sensual. It was as if she'd been doing a Rip van Winkle for years and had finally been shaken awake.

Then it hit her that it had grown very silent in the big car.

She popped open her eyelids to find REEF's heart-stopping blue gaze on her, burning with a hunger so intense it made her toes curl. Startled, they both forced their attention in opposite directions.

The atmosphere in the car had become strangely charged.

It was a damned good thing she was a responsible citizen and a mother of two, not to mention the daughter, grand-daughter and great-granddaughter of career politicians, making "good public image" her middle name, or by now she'd have been stripping off REEF's clothes in the backseat.

She willed the huskiness from her voice. "Save some room for dinner."

"I have plenty of room. I have been hungry since I landed on this blasted rock."

"Watch it. I like this planet."

"But there is never enough food," he lamented. "When I was hunting Caydinn, I ate little. Then I was ill for so long. The Gatekeeper and her mate were kind, but I think they've forgotten how much a man needs to eat."

"I feed people, REEF. It's what I do. It's what I love. Do you have a favorite food...that's not eel?"

He thought for a moment. "Italian."

"You're kidding me. How in the world did that happen? They don't have Italian where you're from."

"When I first arrived here, I ate to survive. Next to my inn, there was an establishment that allowed me to carry food back to my room."

When he was hunting Cavin. She tried not to dwell on that. "We'll have Italian tonight. Lasagna and garlic bread and Caesar salad. Layers of cheese and sauce and meat, baked until it's bubbling and delicious." He was hanging on her every word. She laughed. "You won't go hungry in my house. Trust me."

She wished she could summon as much confidence about allowing him into her life. In less than thirty minutes, she'd be introducing him to her kids. Maybe she should have been thinking about that instead of...his damn mouth. "We need to talk about you meeting John and Ellen, my son and daughter."

"I am ready." He looked as if he was about to receive an intelligence debriefing.

She might as well give him a little background information, then. "John and Ellen's father, my ex-husband, feels my family is a bad influence on them. He doesn't want them around aliens. I think he's being a bigot. Cavin's been nothing less than a hero to them, but you..." She sighed. "He—Pierce—threatened to remove them from the home if he thinks they're in any kind of danger."

"Yet you have invited me into your home."

"I told you, I owe you."

The fist he rested on his thigh tightened enough to squeeze the blood out of his knuckles. "No. There is too much risk for you in this arrangement. I hereby release you of your obligation."

For a split second she was tempted to agree. But she knew she couldn't, not now. "Don't argue or I'll drive you straight over to the FBI building and tell them to sell your spare parts for scrap."

"You would do that, Terran?"

"If you push me, *Cyborg*."

They glared at each other until her mouth twitched. She'd always had a terrible time keeping a straight face.

"You are teasing me," he said. He let out a breath and shook his head. "Tell me the rules for your home, and I will do my best to abide by them."

"First, you can't just go off and do things like pulling seafood out of tanks at restaurants. Second, don't pay for anything with paper money until I teach you about the denominations. And, third, quit frowning all the time. It makes you look...scary."

"No fishing. No buying. No frowning." The ghost of a smile softened the hard line of his mouth. "Is that all?"

"Oh, no. There's much more. But that's good for starters. As for the kids, they've been able to tell fact from fiction since they were in diapers. Whatever you say has got to be convincing. That means doing a better job of lying than you did when you told me you had another place to stay. Let John peek at your gun. That'll impress him. He's a mirror image of his great-grandfather Jake in looks and personality. He respects law enforcers, so he'll respect you. But Ellen, she's going to want to know the gory details. Blood, mayhem, the works."

He tipped his head. "Your *daughter* will?"

"She's my little enigma, always has been. She told me she wants to join the Space Force after graduation, or maybe the Marines. She loves video and computer games. Get her on the cyber battlefield, and she's as heartless as her brother, maybe even more so. But put her in front of the mirror the night of a school dance, and she can easily spend a half hour applying mascara lash by lash."

She smiled, thinking of Ellen putting up her hair,

exposing her long, graceful neck, courtesy of her ballerina grandmother's genes. Then she pictured Ellen eagerly interrogating an ex-assassin about what weapons he was carrying and how to use them, and winced.

REEF slid on his sunglasses. "I am Eric Sanders, secret service agent assigned to your family for additional security in light of the Jaspers' elevated role dealing with the Coalition."

"Perfect." With the sunglasses and his athletic, clean-cut appearance, he looked the part of a government agent, even without the ubiquitous dark suit and tie.

REEF lifted his T-shirt a few inches, exposing washboard abs and a holstered gun. "Sig Sauer, .357 caliber. Loaded. Not for play. It stays on my person at all times."

"That works." She relaxed a fraction. Maybe she was worrying needlessly. "They get out of swim in ten minutes. We'd better head over to the pool."

"As you wish." With feral grace he slid his seat belt around his waist. The move was confident, sleek, purposeful. Never mind about the .357, Evie thought; his body better fit the term "deadly weapon."

In all her life, she'd never seen, talked to, or met anyone like him, and now she was bringing him home.

Pathetic as it sounded, it was the most daring thing she'd ever done.

He was armed, he was dangerous. And for now, he was hers.

EIGHT

They arrived at the school. A short distance away, a group of boys and girls wrapped in towels waited to be met. At Evie's instruction, REEF parked the Hummer in one of the allotted spaces.

"They won't recognize the car. I'll get their attention." Evie transferred a sleepy Sadie to his lap and jumped out.

Appalled, REEF stared down at the slumbering creature. He didn't dare move and risk angering it. The dog circled once before settling down in a tiny ball of fur. With a lion-size sigh of contentment, Sadie closed her eyes.

REEF gaped at the tiny, fragile dog as it relaxed into a deep sleep. He could end its life with one quick snap of his hand, yet it lay on him in total trust. In his adult memory, he could not recall any creature, large or small, animal or human, tolerating his presence without fear. In awe, he touched two fingertips to the dog's little skull. Her ears twitched at the touch. He took a chance and stroked a silken ear. Incredible...

"Here," Evie called out. A boy and a girl walked over to her. The boy was blond and the girl's hair was darker like her mother's. They had Evie's eyes as well as a vague resemblance to Senator Jasper, their aunt.

"Mom, where's our car?" the girl asked.

"Listen and don't get upset. The car is in the shop. I was delivering berries today...and there was a shootout."

"No way!"

"Yes. The car was hit where it was parked."

Both children were clearly impressed. "Was anyone shot?" the boy asked.

"Several men."

"Were you close enough to see?"

"Pretty close."

And that's where he knew Evie would leave it. She'd already mentioned that she didn't want them to know how close they'd come to losing her.

"That said, I have someone I'd like you to meet."

Ellen appeared more suspicious than her brother as she peered through the tinted glass to the driver's seat, where REEF remained, pinned to the seat by a four-pound, seven-ounce Chihuahua.

Gingerly, he lifted the sleeping dog off his lap. It stirred once, uttering an odd snore-growl, but remained asleep as he set it ever so gently on the passenger seat. Over the course of his career, he'd moved explosives with less caution, he thought and stepped down from the vehicle.

He offered his hand in the standard Terran greeting as the Handyman had trained him to do. "Agent Eric Sanders. Secret Service. You are John and Ellen Jasper, yes?"

They extended their hands in turn, their introductions polite and automatic. Their backgrounds as the offspring of a political family showed in their composure and self-control even as he sensed their boiling curiosity.

"What model firearm is that?" John asked as Evie had predicted.

REEF lifted his shirt slightly. "Sig Sauer P229, .357 caliber. Loaded. Not for play. It stays on my person at all times," he added as he'd promised, feeling Evie's approving gaze on him.

"What else are you packing?" Ellen asked, also as predicted by her mother. She was as Evie had described, deceptively delicate but with fearless, miss-nothing eyes.

"These," he replied, showing her his hands and turning them over. "And my knowledge of seven different deadly forms of martial arts."

"Like what? Budo-kan, Aikido, Krav Maga, Kali...?"

"Okay!" Evie interrupted in a singsong voice. "Everyone get in the car. Agent Sanders has had a very long day. Isn't that right?"

"Quite," he said, his voice shifting to a slightly more intimate tone with her before he realized what he had done. Her cheeks colored as they always did, and she swept her gaze away. He didn't mean to throw her off balance, but he rather liked that he could.

Ellen and John threw their gear in the back. Barking, Sadie was up and recharged, excited by the children's return.

Another boy jogged over to the car. "Check this out," John told him, pointing at REEF. "We're being guarded by the Secret Service."

The newcomer's eyes opened wide under the rim of the hat he wore to shade his fair, freckled skin from the sun.

"Agent Sanders," Ellen informed him.

REEF nodded, extending his hand. The young man grabbed it heartily. "Andrew Strutz. Just call me A.O. Everyone does. It stands for Andrew Owen." He turned to Evie. "See you later, Mrs. Holloway."

"*Later?*" Evie didn't quite yell out the word, but it was clear she was unhappy about the prospect of a guest. REEF knew well the reason. Him.

"Mom, it's Friday night, remember?" John said. "Can't A.O. come over and hang out?"

"You betcha. I lost track of what day it was. Too many things going on today."

Like her business going up in a storm of bullets and an alien assassin showing up at her door.

"Can he stay the night, Mom?"

"Of course." Evie was full of false cheer that REEF noticed and the children didn't. Did anyone around her notice the part she played to perfection? Did anyone see the woman he saw? She was quick to say yes, to accommodate others. She took on everything with cheer and grace. But what did Evie Holloway want?

In his mind flashed a vivid image of her writhing beneath him as he made love to her. "Tell me what you want," he'd whisper in her ear. "Tell me...."

A bolt of heat hit him in the groin. Desire flooded his entire body. With a hiss of breath, he went still until he'd composed himself. He must stop thinking about her that way. It was pointless torture.

"See you later!" With a wave, A.O. jogged away, towel flapping.

Evie squeezed her eyes shut for a moment. REEF wasn't familiar with Terran religions, but he was fairly certain she'd just uttered a prayer.

REEF waited outside for everyone to climb into the vehicle before he boarded. He made a careful sweep of the parking lot before shutting the door. No cars followed. None waited, parked nearby. As he put the archaic Earth vehicle into Drive, the noise inside soared—voices chattering away, a cell phone ringing, Sadie's barking and music playing over the speakers. It was as loud and pulsating with energy as the squatter's ghetto in the bowels of the orbital space-city Keiron, but without the stench.

If Evie expected the noise and disorganization to frighten him off, she'd have to come up with something else, for the atmosphere of chaos didn't repulse him. Contrasted to the desolation of his life until now, it soothed like nano-salve on a laser burn.

Evie leaned closer. "Is it getting to you yet?"

He turned, recognizing the dare in her eyes. *He won't last,* she'd said. "Do you want it to get to me?" His question was serious, not meant to tease.

Astonishment filled her gemlike eyes. Then profound thanks. Didn't anyone ever ask her what she wanted? After a long, contemplative pause that left him feeling oddly turned inside out, she shook her head.

The urge to reach out for her, to touch her, to draw her close, surged all over again. He thanked the goddess for the children's presence. It kept him from risking something that would likely cause him to look foolish and Evie to be appalled.

Gripping the steering wheel, REEF maneuvered out of the parking lot. *"You're not sure how to give and receive affection. The ability is there, inside you, but locked away. Just as a picture, a taste, or even a random scent will open the floodgates of your past, someone you meet will provide the key to unlock your heart."*

And what would the Gatekeeper say if that woman did find her way into his heart...only to find him lacking in his ability to feel, to share, to commit: all the normal things a human being would desire from another? The solution was simple, really. The only way to keep Evie from unlocking his heart was to never give her the key.

The Goddess Keep, Sakka

The palace was abuzz with rumors that the high-maintenance queen had met her match in the Terran prince she'd been forced to marry. Rumor also had it that Queen Keira had fallen for the rogue-world royal. That they were inseparable.

Let the palace consume itself in frivolous gossip! It was just the distraction the Headmaster needed to keep the bored and curious diverted so that they wouldn't discover how deeply he'd plumbed the recesses of the Coalition's military intelligence files hunting for information that would lead him to his lost REEF.

He rubbed a hand over his bristly jaw. So consuming was his research that he often forgot his personal grooming. Forgot to eat. To sleep. However, that too went unnoticed.

His duties as headmaster did not require his day-to-day presence at the training academy. From the earliest days of the program, he'd supervised the recruitment, the initiation and the bioengineering of the youngsters, yes, but now others managed the years of intense training that followed.

Is one of your trainers to blame for your best REEF not returning to base? It wasn't the first time that the Headmaster sought to place blame for Oh-One's mysterious disappearance. But he could find nothing linking his training—or trainers—to what had happened.

"If that scowl were any deeper, it would be digging furrows into your desk" a voice boomed from the door to his office. "Are the boys and girls acting up and making their headmaster grumpy?"

"Atir!" The Headmaster rose to greet his old friend. Despite several decades, promotions, and a command of his own, Atir was still the bald and grinning second-officer the Headmaster remembered fondly from their days as young, cocky intelligence officers plying the Rim worlds. Atir always dropped in for a visit whenever he was in port.

"You look terrible, Kelmet," the major told him. "Are you not well?"

"It's still missing," he growled, pouring two glasses of royal ale.

"Oh-One," Atir murmured, taking the offered drink.

"Yes! I've dissected every kill order, torn apart every encrypted code. I've analyzed records of every craft in and out of this port, every ship overdue to return, and nothing. There is no record of him being sent out on a mission. No tracks. No hints. No one knows anything. Believe me, I've asked. The two ministers who could have provided me with information are both dead! Has my REEF simply vanished off the face of the galaxy? I refuse to accept that."

"I've been pondering this myself, and I have a theory."

The Headmaster tapped his foot impatiently.

"Earth," Atir said.

"Bah! The rogue-prince's homeworld? Why would Oh-One go to that backwater cesspool?"

"Especially since he came from one, eh?"

The men shared a nostalgic smile. Neither would ever forget the little wild thing Oh-One was before being crafted into a magnificent combatant. There hadn't been another one like him since. The closest was a young recruit brought in not too many years ago. The Headmaster had such high hopes for the feisty child, but alas it wasn't to be.

Such was the cost of freedom. It was never won and maintained without its casualties. "What is your theory, Atir?"

"Prime-Major Caydinn fled to Earth to avoid his royal obligations, yes? A REEF could very well have been dispatched to stop him."

"Hmm. The queen's runaway suitor." He rubbed his chin and pondered what he'd heard in the intelligence briefings he attended regularly. Round-the-clock analysis of Earth news harvested from space showed the Prime-Major was alive and well, living as a traitor to the goddess, even going as far as taking a Terran primitive as a lover. The Headmaster grimaced. "It still doesn't explain why the REEF didn't return."

"Caydinn got to him first."

"Caydinn..." The thought chilled him. "How could he possibly have defeated Oh-One?" Unless Oh-One was hobbled by a fatal flaw no one was aware of. It made the Headmaster even more desperate to find out what happened. If a defect did indeed cause the destruction of his best REEF, he'd see it removed and eradicated so all future generations of REEFs would be immune.

Atir shrugged and swilled his drink. "I've never been one to subscribe to palace intrigue, but I do feel it's worth a look."

"I do, as well." The Headmaster returned to his computer to enter parameters for the auto-search using file images of Oh-One and all the other data from Earth compiled thus far. "Done. If any Earth news or images of males resembling Oh-One surface, I'll find out."

"And if you find your prodigal REEF in the same condition as Caydinn—retired and growing fat with disuse in the company of a Terran lover? Then what?"

The Headmaster let out a belly laugh. "A REEF? They're monks! Every last one. They're engineered not to drink, not to gamble and not to fuck. I almost wish that were not the case. Else Oh-One might have left us a trail to follow, like Caydinn did."

"And if this new search does uncover a trail?"

The Headmaster's smile faltered. "We'll find out soon enough."

NINE

"Dad's here," Ellen announced when REEF pulled up to Evie's house a few minutes after departing the pool.

Evie tensed at the sight of a male leaning against a red sports car, his arms folded over his chest.

Protect. REEF narrowed his eyes at the man. He was almost REEF's height but fair-haired—not in top physical form, yet he'd not let himself fall victim to excess, either. *Evie's former lover.* Handsome, boyish, fair, he couldn't be more different from REEF in appearance or demeanor. Was this the sort of man Evie was attracted to?

A new emotion coursed through REEF, not quite jealousy, for he knew with one look that Pierce no longer held Evie's heart, but perhaps something closer to envy. This man had been given what REEF never would have—the chance to make Evie his mate. That Holloway had squandered the opportunity simply proved his stupidity.

Neutralize threat.

Three car doors opened. REEF held up his hand, stopping his passengers. "Freeze." It went instantly silent in the car. Good. His charges had complied. "You will not go anywhere until I state it is safe to do so."

"But REE—uh, Eric, it's just my ex-husband."

"As I said, Evie, when it is safe, you may exit the vehicle." REEF opened his door and swung his legs out.

"This is so cool," Ellen said from the back.

He centered Pierce in his vision and advanced. The man took off his sunglasses as REEF approached.

REEF kept his on. "Reese Pierce Holloway III?"

"Maybe. Who are you?"

"Agent Sanders, Secret Service." He took out his ID and let the man study it. "I have been assigned to protect your former wife and the children."

The man nodded, handing back the ID. REEF turned to the Hummer and gave them the all-clear signal.

Evie waited until he'd finished exchanging hugs with the children before demanding, "Pierce, what are you doing here?"

"I heard what happened."

She eyeballed him. "What are they saying?"

"'Congressman's daughter rounded up in major mob drug bust,'" he recited.

Evie pressed two fingers to her temple. "They make it sound as if I were involved."

"If you were there, you were involved."

"Pierce, I was making a candy delivery. How was I supposed to know the FBI was going to make a drug bust?"

"What if the children were with you?"

"They weren't!"

"But they could have been."

The undercurrent of fear he'd sensed in Evie all day had finally surfaced. She didn't show her fear, but REEF sensed it in her rapid breaths and quickening pulse, something his senses could still miraculously detect.

REEF took a step forward and deliberately invaded the man's personal space, causing Pierce to step backward and away from Evie. "No harm would have come to them had they been present, Mr. Holloway. Ms. Holloway is unharmed because I was there to protect her, as I will be for some time to come."

"Twenty-four-seven," Evie put in.

Pierce looked REEF up and down. "He's sleeping here?"

"How's he going to protect us if he doesn't, Dad?" Ellen pointed out.

"I will sleep only when it doesn't interfere with my duties," REEF explained. "Or anything else Ms. Holloway desires that I do."

Evie made a funny little sound, and he didn't know why. A sideways glance showed the color was back in her cheeks. She was most definitely reacting to something he'd said, but what?

"Evie, I knew this business of yours wasn't a good idea," Holloway said, dousing Evie's playful spark with amazing swiftness. He glared at REEF. "Can we have some privacy, Officer?"

"Agent," Ellen corrected. "He's in the Secret Service. He knows seven different deadly forms of mar—"

"Over here, Pierce," Evie interrupted.

Letting her walk off with Holloway was one of the more difficult things he'd had to do since arriving on Earth. The woman conjured many things in him, not the least of which was a fierce need to protect her.

Whether in her presence or not, her former mate seemed to hold an odd power over her—and the man knew it too. It was similar to the influence Evie's extended family had over her, except their control was steeped in well-meaning love and this was purely fear and intimidation.

Whether it was a verbal command or merely a sense of obligation, it was clear Evie allowed others to control her life. How could she be so passionate about the plight of others in slavery and not be able to break her own bonds? His mouth twisted with the irony.

"They've been moving us around like pawns in a chess game. I say we take our pieces off the board and make our own rules."

Her words, her desire, but how quickly she'd jumped back in the game. He'd like to help her fling away the board entirely, but it was like asking a surgeon to remove his brain implant: the risk of suffering permanent damage during removal was great. Independence would have to be her fully informed decision, not anyone else's suggestion. Unless Evie made freedom *her choice,* she'd wind up trading new bonds for the ones she had thrown off.

He knew all about surrendering free will. Now that he had it firmly back in his control, he had no intention of ever giving it up.

REEF took up a position standing guard outside the Hummer as the couple spoke in hushed voices.

"Evie, you don't need to work. I send that support check every month so you can stay home with the children."

"And eat bon-bons. Yeah, you've told me before."

"Not everyone is meant to be a high achiever. It's nothing to be ashamed of."

"Your argument's moot, Pierce. I've already made the decision to close Evie's Eden."

"You have?" the man asked.

She had? REEF was equally shocked. She'd been so enthusiastic over the venture. So passionate about her cause.

"I bit off more than I could chew. Today confirmed that. I'm no entrepreneur, okay? I get it. Is there anything else you wanted to discuss?"

"No. No, that's all." The man appeared to be satisfied.

Looking weary to the bone, Evie gathered her glorious hair up with one hand and fanned the back of her neck. Sadie seemed to be wilting where she clung, draped over Evie's shoulder. "I'm going swimming. Anyone joining me in the pool?" Her voice trailed off as a van sporting a large dish on top pulled up to the house.

"TV reporters, Mom," John warned.

"Just bury me right here. Deep," Evie murmured. Her dismay lasted only a moment. "Kids, go inside. Ellen, take Sadie out of the sun."

"I'm late for a meeting." Pierce hurried to his car and sped off before the journalist had a chance to exit the van.

It appeared the man couldn't flee fast enough, REEF thought, unable to fathom why he wouldn't want to assist in deflecting the nosy visitors from his family.

"Evie!" Two females hurried across the lawn.

"Cheryl and Sandy, my neighbors," Evie explained. "Happy face, happy face," she muttered under her breath, smoothing her shirt as she formed her mouth into a cheery smile. "Hey..."

"Evie, we heard," the female with long hair said. "Oh my God."

"What happened?" cried the other. "Are you okay?"

Evie sighed through her nose. "I was making a delivery, and I waltzed right into a drug raid. Except it's not as funny as it sounds. If not for my bodyguard I'd be in the morgue tonight."

In unison Sandy's and Cheryl's eyes swerved to REEF.

"Ladies." He nodded. "I'm afraid I must ask Ms. Holloway to step inside."

"Miss Holloway! I'd like to ask a few questions about what happened today," the reporter called from across the street.

"Let us know if there's anything we can do," the woman with long hair whispered, frowning at the reporter as she backed away. "You're one of us, Evie. You've got us, okay?"

"Thanks," Evie whispered, looking as if she were about to cry. There was much affection between her and her neighbors, which came as no surprise given her warm and generous nature. Generosity her family had taken advantage of—and him, as well, by being here.

Protect.

"Go inside, Evie," REEF urged as the reporter and a photographer crossed the street. "I'll get rid of them."

"Not literally, right?" she whispered. "You're in enough trouble as it is."

"No, not literally," he said dryly. The woman still did not trust him. "Go. I'll take care of this."

She stayed put. "But you've never handled the press before."

"My protection for your lessons—we have an agreement."

She remained planted where she was as if she were worried about him. Worried! For him? Bah. "I am doing my best to protect you, Evie Holloway." What happened to the woman who wanted to be a damsel to his knight? "Go," he commanded.

"But..."

He expressed his building frustration with a groan—an emotion, yes, and, thankfully, an appropriate one. Perhaps he was beginning to get the hang of being human—if not convincing Evie Holloway he could protect her. He took what she'd told him at Ka-blooms and turned it around. "If I were a damsel in distress, and my rescuer told me to seek shelter, I would do so without another word. Now go!"

The shifting tides of emotions in her eyes told him that did the trick. She made a zipping motion across her lips before she jogged after the children. Finally, he'd managed to persuade the woman to obey his wishes.

Not all your wishes.

Namely a few, very private wishes.

REEF put further futile thoughts from his mind and strode toward the journalists. A photographer was already capturing images. With any luck, his sunglasses and his cover story would be enough to douse suspicion in anyone who might view the photos later. He'd been sent to California to stay out of the news, not make it.

He wasn't two steps inside the house when the interrogation began. "What did they want to know? What did you tell them?"

"No comment." He shrugged. "No comment to all. I suggested they contact the FBI if they require more information, and sent them on their way."

For a heart-stopping moment, he thought she was going to hug him. Instead, she told him, "Let me show you where everything is."

After a whirlwind tour of the house, mentions of too many animals to count, the unceremonious tossing—by Evie —of his suitcase in the guest bedroom followed by yet another rapid-fire explanation of his bathroom and room's amenities, Evie left him in a room adjacent to and in full view of the kitchen. The "family room" she had called it.

"I'll get dinner going." She abandoned him for the kitchen. "Sit, relax," she told him.

He sat down on the couch to better accomplish the relaxation. He realized a moment later that he didn't know how. However, he'd make his best effort for Evie's sake.

More pets appeared out of nowhere. One, a large, fluffy, smoke-colored feline with a tattered ear, jumped up on the couch to stare at him, unblinking.

Oblivious to it all, Evie layered ingredients for the meal in a dish, checked the status of the oven temperature, directed Ellen to slice bread all while carrying on a cheerful conversation with the girl and boy, who stole unattended food, gulping it down in between carrying cutlery to the dining room table.

Rising above it all, Evie was confident and in charge. What he had seen as hesitation earlier wasn't apparent here. Evie Holloway was in her element.

And him? He couldn't be further from his. He remained sitting where Evie had left him, observing from afar. It was as if a planetary cyclone whirled around him and he was caught in the eye. He longed to step outside of that pocket of false calm and into the storm but didn't have the first clue how to do so, how to be part of the group.

He didn't know how to be an active participant in his own life.

"Take a chance." The suggestion came in the voice of his father; he was sure of it. The memory lingered long enough for REEF to remember that they'd been playing Sech one evening long, long ago, as the chaos of a household not unlike this one swirled around them.

And then the memory was gone.

A familiar frustration invaded, and the sensation of mourning for a past life he might never fully know. However, the glimpse had provided another small piece of his identity: even as a child he liked to hold back, studying situations from all angles before making his move. *"I fear I'll grow old waiting for you to make a decision."*

Not this time, Papa, REEF thought. He pushed off the couch. Soon he was striding toward the kitchen and the center of the hustle and bustle. He wasn't sure if he'd know what to do when he got there, but if life was anything like playing Sech, he wasn't ready to pull his pieces off the board. He'd set his sights on capturing the goddess.

TEN

Evie welcomed his appearance in the kitchen with two outstretched arms. In one hand was a green bottle; in the other was a black and silver contraption. It appeared to be some sort of primitive Earth utensil, but for what purpose? He took both items and awaited enlightenment.

"Terran lesson number three," she said out of earshot of the children. "Opening a bottle of excellent wine." She rattled off instructions. "Take the corkscrew, yes, that's it, and push it into the cork in the mouth of the bottle. Good. Now crank down on the lever."

He did as she said. Within a moment the cork was out.

"You have the support of your neighbors," he observed. A memory flashed and was gone. There were neighbors where he'd grown up too. What were they like? On what world did they live?

"They watch out for me. They won't talk to reporters, except to tell them to get the hell off the street. They know the toll my family's visibility takes on my private life. Here, I'm just another neighborhood mom. Until the invasion, it's how I thought of myself too."

Now she was anything but, he thought. He was a dark and frightening secret she was forced to keep.

"They'll help me keep a low profile until this blows over. And it will." She filled two glasses with the ruby-red liquid, handing him one. Then she tapped her glass against his. "Let's drink. God knows we deserve it."

She took a grateful swallow and waited for him to do the same. He sniffed at the beverage: fruit...with an underlying scent of fermentation. Alcohol. Hmm...

"It's okay. You're off duty."

Surely it would not hurt to give it a try. He'd seen many others imbibe alcoholic beverages over the years, seen its ill effects too. He simply had not tasted it for himself.

Warmth followed his first swallow. It was so pleasant, he took a second. He liked this Terran beverage. Wine. He took another taste. Yes, indeed, quite nice.

Curiosity about the conversation he'd overheard returned. "You told your former husband that you were quitting business. Why, when you're so passionate about helping the enslaved children?"

"What happened today wasn't obvious enough of a reason?"

"It is but one day."

"A pretty disastrous one day! It was a sign—a sign from God that I bit off more than I could chew, that I never set out to be a businesswoman, anyway. It happened by accident."

"I would like to hear the story."

Evie tried to gauge REEF's interest in the subject. It seemed genuine. "I was at a memorial service for my grandfather." She told him about her chance encounter with Leila Jones, the role of the International Labor Organization, and how the vast traffic in children was destabilizing so many areas of the globe. How her love of her own children made her want to do something concrete to help. "It's not only children that are enslaved. It's adults too of every race and on almost every continent. And yet we go about our daily lives as if it's not happening. I want to change that. If nothing else, I want more people to be aware. I might not have a college degree, but I can cook. And I'll keep on cooking as long as there's the chance it'll help a kid somewhere."

She glanced up from chopping carrots for a salad.

"Go on," he said.

He'd been listening to her, really listening, as if he thought her efforts were important. An unfamiliar feeling of confidence, of *accomplishment*, buoyed her. But she wasn't used to taking center stage. She didn't want to push her luck and bore him to death. "That's okay. You don't have to be polite."

"I don't know how to be polite."

She would have laughed if he didn't look so serious. "You don't know how to lie, either, if I remember correctly." She smoothed a hand over the front of her blouse. "I guess I'd better not ask if I look fat in this."

He made a small grunt of disbelief and his gaze swept over her with such raw appreciation that this time it was her turn to blush. "There is nothing not pleasing about your appearance. Not a thing."

She hoped to heaven the whimpering little sigh she heard in her head hadn't actually made it past her lips.

Twisting the pot holder in her hand, she pretended to check the lasagna bubbling in the oven. It wasn't the only thing at the boiling point. With one hot glance and a few words her composure had gone nuclear.

She'd been right about one thing: REEF was dangerous... but not in the way she'd expected.

***

As dinner became imminent, the noise level soared. Evie opened the oven and removed the dish she'd assembled earlier—lasagna. Drugged by the aroma—and the sips of wine —REEF breathed deep, shuddering with pleasure. It smelled as if the goddesses had crafted the aroma in heaven itself.

When he opened his eyes, Evie was watching him, amused. "You okay?"

"Yes. I am okay." He felt light, lighter than air. A soft laugh slipped out of him, to his surprise—and, apparently, Evie's. "Very okay," he assured her.

"It's the wine."

"I suppose that it is." He'd been sipping it for a while now. He lifted the glass to watch the play of light in its depths.

Evie appeared charmed by his reaction to the liquor. "You don't drink much."

"I don't drink at all. The desire to do so was programmed

out of me." He winced. Why had he said "programmed" when he wanted her to see him as human? *Bred* would be a better word. No, *trained*. Yes. "Rather, it was trained out of me," he corrected.

Hopefully she would not wonder what other desires had been programmed out of him, as well.

He'd like to assure her of at least one that hadn't been. Unfortunately, circumstances didn't favor stripping her naked, hoisting her up to the countertop and...*Focus elsewhere.* He gulped a deeper swallow on the wine. "I quite like this wine," he said gruffly.

"Pace yourself," she advised, smiling. She slipped on a pair of oven mitts and lifted the steaming tray of lasagna off the counter. "Kids," she called out as she carried the tray to the dining room. "Dinner!"

With laughter, chatter and the tinkle of cutlery and glasses all around him, he partook of his first experience dining with a Terran family. Despite the Gatekeeper's work with him on Terran manners, he took his behavioral cues from Evie—until he tried a bite of the lasagna. Goddess be. It was sheer heaven. He took another taste, and another, savoring each forkful. Before long he felt Evie's eyes on him and glanced up. "It is delicious," he told her.

"Thanks." Her cheeks were pink again and her voice was husky. She seemed to forcibly redirect her gaze to her plate.

Her reaction intrigued him. Was their attraction mutual? The awakening male inside him already knew the answer: yes, it was. Yet, he did not know why or how.

"Of course, you can take advantage of opportunity if the lady is available and willing," the Handyman had said.

And what if she were willing? Would he know what to do? Would he disappoint her? REEF reached for the wine to quench his suddenly parched mouth and in hopes of cooling the fever that raged in him all day in Evie's presence.

"Did you ever have to guard the president?" John asked as part of a steady stream of questions.

He welcomed the children's interest, although it appeared Evie did not. REEF shook his head. "My duties tend to more...ah, covert activities."

"So that's why you know all those forms of martial arts," Ellen observed. "I googled the Secret Service, and that's definitely not the norm for Secret Service agents."

Evie made a funny sound and grabbed for her glass of wine.

"They don't put everything on Google," John argued.

"No," REEF assured them. "They do not." Not even close.

"Thank the Lord," Evie murmured.

Ellen twirled her fork. "How many people have you actually killed, though?"

"Ellen..." Evie shook her head. "That's personal."

"No one likes to discuss that aspect of his job," REEF admitted. Evie gave him a grateful nod.

"But you've killed people," John persisted. "Right?"

"Kids. Please. Let the man eat."

"He has, I bet," Ellen murmured. "A bunch."

"I have an idea." Evie pushed away from the table. "How about we all cool off before dessert? To the pool, everyone!"

In another blur of motion, the table was cleared and the

entire family scattered, returning when they'd stripped down to "swimsuits."

A long white shirt covered Evie's arms and shoulders, but underneath she was almost naked in an iridescent black swimsuit that left no curve to his imagination.

She dropped a pair of short trousers into his hands. The garment was decorated with flowers and foliage in bright colors. "Jared's trunks should fit you. They're too big on him."

In a noisy herd, the family moved from indoors to out.

Trunks in hand, REEF followed them only as far as the deck overlooking the pool. Did Evie have to take so much back-arching, leg-flexing, hair-flipping pleasure in her floating lounger? He wanted to drag her off the damned thing and...

Focus elsewhere.

She waved at him from the water. "Come in, Agent Sanders! It's got to be over a hundred degrees out here."

And twice that in the water, REEF thought, trying not to contemplate the way her swimwear followed her every curve and hollow.

"Don't be shy. We're safe. I promise!"

Not as safe as you think, sweet Terran. Indeed. If she had any idea of the direction his thoughts had taken all blasted day, she'd see him to the door and tell him never to return.

Surveying the scene below, he shifted his weight from foot to foot. Dogs ran every which way on the grass, catching balls, splashing through a sprinkler. Her late grandfather's dogs, she'd explained, plus Sadie. Music blared from speakers. He'd missed this. On some fundamental level, he knew that this was where he belonged, here in the company of others, far from the endless solitude imposed on him. He wasn't meant to be alone. A true loner he'd never been and he hoped to the goddesses he never would be again. With emotions, with his emerging humanity, he would not survive it.

You've determined you want to reap the benefits of being part of the human race, but what have you to offer in return? The worry that he wasn't capable of giving what another human required or expected gnawed at him.

"Hey, you!" Evie swam up to the pool's edge, propping her chin on her folded arms. She was even prettier with her hair slicked away from her face. A smile broadcast her amusement at the towel and the trunks hanging from his hands, just as she'd left him fifteen minutes earlier. "Am I going to have to come up there and teach you how to relax? At least sit down and finish your wine."

That's when he noticed she'd placed his half-empty wineglass on the table with an arrangement of fruit, chips, and cookies. Evie had prepared the refreshments so quickly that they were on the table before he'd realized what she had done.

Dutifully, he sank into the chair and finished the last of the wine in a single mouthful. Propping one leg crosswise over his thigh, he folded his arms over his belly, sinking a little more into the cushions as he listened to the sounds of the family. He liked those sounds. Memories clamored from behind the wall in his mind, begging release. The home he'd grown up in was much like this one; of that he was certain.

REEF drifted on a cloud on contentment: not drowsy, but not fully alert, either, not in the way he was used to being. The length of the eventful day and his resulting fatigue combined with the heat, the wine and the enjoyment he took in Evie's hospitality gradually lulled him into a state of almost total relaxation, an experience as novel as it was pleasurable.

REEF lifted a lazy brow as Sadie and the other dogs converged on the back door in a frenzy of barking. *A.O. is here.* Using the memory of the sound and size of the footsteps from when he met the boy at the pool, he'd validated A.O.'s identity the moment the boy entered the house, beating even the dogs' sharp hearing. It was a mystery why his senses seemed to grow more powerful by the hour, but he welcomed their return.

The boy let himself outside. "Hey, Agent Sanders," he said.

"Hey," REEF greeted in a like manner.

A brimmed "Kings" cap was pulled low over the boy's face. He was shirtless, his fair skin covered by a towel draped over his shoulders. "Aren't you going in the pool?"

"I'm quite happy where I am." In fact, REEF was certain he'd never felt as tranquil in his life. It was almost as if he were about to lift off the chair and float into he sky. He chuckled at the thought.

"Well, I am," the boy said and tore off his cap, revealing a shock of bright orange hair.

Bright hair...light eyes.

Suffocating hatred pulled the breath from his lungs.

"I know of a school for special boys like you..."

Goddess help him. Squeezing the armrests, REEF fought to hide his reaction as long as he could so the boy would not sense anything wrong. Someone with hair that color that had done something to him in the past...something irrevocable and painful.

"Mama! Papa!"

"You might be the ideal age, size and temperament for the REEF program, little rimmer, but as for intelligence? The way you're hanging on to that hatch I'm having my doubts. Let go of the damned door!"

As he pretended to watch the family cavorting in the swimming pool, his mind opened to sweeping vistas of tall, green trees and rich, brown bark, the scents of moist earth and food cooking. As sweat trickled down his temples, he listened to distant thunder rumbling over misted hills, and a man's deep, affectionate laughter. A woman's arms came around him, warm and loving.... *My sweet boy,* she'd say. It was a life better than any other. One to which he was born, and was meant to live. A simple man on a simple world. Happy.

The bright-haired off-worlder captain took it all away from you.

REEF stifled the cry that tried to rip from his throat. Goddess. His hands convulsed over the armrests. *Maintain. Be calm. You do not want the boy to see.*

The ringing in his ears that he'd suffered ever since his command center was dismantled had turned to a sharp whine. He wanted to throw his hands over his ears to drown out the sound, but gripped the armrests instead as the past that had been a solid wall crumbled.

Dimly, he was aware of A.O. trotting down the stairs. As soon as he was gone, REEF lurched to his feet and escaped through the door.

Inside, it was cool, quiet, and still fragranced with the

spicy aromas of dinner. Laughter from outside told him that the children had not been alerted to anything unusual, thank the goddess, and A.O. had not glimpsed the reaction his hair color had caused.

He staggered into the house, ending up on the couch in the family room, hunched over, his elbows propped on his knees. At one time, he yearned for a glimpse of his memories. Now his entire past gushed forth with gut-wrenching force. He remembered summer evenings spent lying on his belly in the grass amongst his arrows and toys while he watched lantern bugs trace light patterns in the twilight.

He remembered how the thunderstorms boiled over the hills and rolled down into the valley. The memory of the acrid scent of the rain and the way it felt landing on his tongue was so sharp it was as if he were there, now, living it.

But on a wooded world, the most beautiful season was autumn, of course. He felt the weight of a little girl on his hip as he carried her to a stand of trees, struggling under her weight as her thin legs dangled, tangling with his. They gazed at all the gold and scarlet leaves. "It's like fire, Eriff!" she'd cried. He'd reached high and pulled down a leaf for her to hold. Love and admiration shone in her face. It had made him feel as if he'd given her the most precious jewel in the galaxy.

The enormity of what he'd lost came in a gut punch of anguish. He had two sisters. Sayree and Karah. *Would they recognize their brother if they saw you now?* He doubted it. They were too young when he left.

He'd thought he'd felt empty before, but not like this, now that he understood the extent of what had been taken from him. "Stolen," he cried hoarsely, seeing the off-worlder captain's lean face and bright red hair. *You took it all away. Damn you. Who gave you the right?*

As he gripped his head in shaking hands, memories bore him along in their rapids. He struggled to stay afloat, but there was no slowing it down. *Who gave you the right!*

"REEF!" Strong, cool hands gripped his shoulders and gave him a shake. "REEF!"

Gasping, he swung his blurred gaze to the woman standing in front of him. Her voice seemed to come from a long distance away. Evie gave him another shake. "Look at me," she said harshly under her breath.

"Evie," he whispered.

"Oh, thank God. I was calling you. You wouldn't answer." Breathless and soaking wet, she was angry and afraid, a roaring tide of emotions that somehow swept him closer to her. "What's wrong?" she demanded. "Do you feel sick? You look like you've seen a ghost."

He almost laughed. She wanted to know if he'd seen a ghost. A more appropriate choice of words she could not have picked. "I have," he rasped. "By the goddess, I have."

ELEVEN

"I know who I am," he said, shaking. "I have a past. I remember..."

Evie sank to her knees, water streaming from her hair. "You remember? Your name? Your home?"

"Everything." He had to pause for a moment to regain his composure. With emotion so new, it was difficult forging on when his feelings threatened to overwhelm him. "I was called Eriff... Eriff of Sandreem. It was my home, an isolated world far out on the rim of the galaxy."

Ah, Sandreem. He shut his eyes and let the images flow: the sharp change in seasons, the night sky and its bold brush-stroke of glitter that was the remains of a moon forming a ring around the entire planet. The sash of the goddess, Sandreemers called it. He saw the forests, leafy trees and conifers, as far as the eye could see.

In a torrent of words, he did it best to describe it all. Even before his mind was wiped clean, he wasn't much of a talker, he suspected. Now he couldn't hold back. What if he were to forget and lose his past again? It was imperative that he share as much as possible so that there was some record, some proof he'd once existed.

That he'd once mattered.

Evie seemed to sense his urgency, listening intently to every word as tears filled her eyes.

"Nothing compared to Sandreem,. I have visited more worlds than I care to count, and every one I found lacking. It wasn't anything I could pinpoint, just a sense, an impression. I kept it to myself. I wasn't supposed to feel anything but obedience. But Sandreem is my blood. It is my soul. Even the alterations done to me couldn't change that." Emotion welled up inside him. His sacrifice for the defense of the Coalition was greater than he'd realized. It was greater than any man should have to make.

You didn't make the sacrifice. Your hand was forced.

"My family didn't send me away," he said, his voice harsh. "He took me."

"Who took you?" Evie's eyes burned bright. *"Who?"*

"His crew called him Captain. He had orange hair. Like A.O.'s."

REEF described the arrival of the starship and how he couldn't resist running out to see it. "I used to play a board game called Sech. I loved it. The object was to move your pieces with the goal of capturing the goddess."

"Sech. Like our chess?"

He nodded. "I never made a move without considering

every possible predicted outcome. My father would sometimes fall asleep in his chair while I decided what to do. I
planned every move I made, analyzed all possible outcomes.
Yet, the day the spaceship came, I did not include capture as
an outcome when I went hunting that off-worlder. Why
would I? I knew every tree and every creature that lived up,
inside and below them. My capture was impossible. Yet, it
happened."

Changing his life forever.

"I tracked him through the woods. I stole his lunch.
Goddess, I even shot arrows at him. Was I insane?"

"You were a little boy! Those are the kinds of things little
boys do. I could tell you stories about John, like the air-soft
gun and our neighbor's cat. Then there was the time he was
grounded for half the summer—he melted a plastic army man
with a lighter he wasn't supposed to have and started a huge
grass fire at the ranch."

Two mischievous boys. Two very different sets of consequences. One lost some privileges. The other, his soul.

"I can't even touch what your mother must have felt
when she learned you were missing," Evie whispered. For
all the work she'd done on behalf of children forced into
labor, she of all people understood, REEF knew.
"Couldn't she and your father have lobbied for your
release? Couldn't they have complained to your
government?"

"*Complain* to the Coalition? Not if you don't want it to be
the last complaint of your mortal life. In wartime, forced
conscriptions are legal."

"It's always been wartime for you guys. How many

hundreds of years have you been battling the Drakken Empire? Too many to count."

"Children are not normally used as soldiers." He could ease her fears in that at least. As for the REEF Academy taking children against their will and their family's wishes, he had no reassurances. "The captain didn't come to Sandreem looking for recruits. My mistake was being noticed."

Goddess, what he wouldn't do to live that day over, to have a second chance. The lament was a familiar one. For weeks afterward he'd reviewed the details of that nightmarish day, analyzing everything he'd done, everything he could have done differently, or that he should have, from the moment he'd climbed high into the trees to the moment the ship's hatch slammed closed. When the first of the mind-wiping drugs was finally administered, he welcomed it. Anything to end the torture, anything to end the pain.

"Listen to me, Eriff of Sandreem." Evie's voice softened a fraction uttering his real name. "A child's mischief is no excuse for an adult to exploit their vulnerability. Nothing is an excuse to take advantage of a child—ever. You aren't to blame for what they did to you." Her eyes filled again. She lifted a trembling hand to dash away a tear.

He marveled at her ability to feel such powerful emotions for a virtual stranger. He could barely manage his own; his feelings ran either too strong or too weak. He'd yet to find a balance. His memories may have retuned, but not the confidence that he was fully human.

Not human. Not machine.

Because of one day. One man. One mistake. Regret and grief clawed at his chest, tightening his throat and making his eyes ache. The emotions were all at once appropriate and staggering.

Evie took one glance at his condition and pushed to her feet. Her wet hair whipped over one shoulder, splashing him, splashing the table. The thin, glistening fabric of her swimsuit covered her lush curves but barely, yet she didn't seem shy in the least; nor was she flaunting her body. She was confident and comfortable in her skin. Water still beaded on that skin, and dribbled down from her soaking hair, disappearing into her cleavage. He imagined following the rivulets with his tongue and...

"I know just what you need," she said.

REEF almost choked. So did he, but...

"Wait here." When she returned, her wet hair was slicked away from her face and she was clothed in another long white shirt that reached halfway down her suntanned thighs. She handed him a small glass. "This will help."

He smelled the alcohol from many feet away. "I've already had a glass of wine," he warned her.

Her mouth slanted up on one side. "Wow, a whole glass."

Was he not supposed to feel its effects? She gave that impression. He took the glass.

"It's tequila. Bite the lime." She held out a slice of citrus. "Now down the shot all in one swallow. Uncle José will make you feel better."

If it didn't render him unconscious first. The liquor burned its way down his throat, still on fire when it hit his gut. His eyes watered. The drink did help—to a degree. He wasn't numb exactly, but it had blunted the emotion. It explained why some drank to the point of sickness. They craved oblivion.

He, on the other hand, craved Evie.

She'd perched at the edge of the low table next to the couch, leaning toward him, her arms folded under her breasts, pushing them upward to form that cleavage he struggled not to stare at. She smelled of chlorine and faintly of the Earth substance he knew as vanilla. Underneath it all was her own scent. At some level, at all times in her company, he was aware of it. Why did it draw him so?

If only he had the confidence, the experience, to reach for her and pull her onto his lap. Now more than ever, he needed the physical contact. Desperately.

"You're not sure how to give and receive affection." His hands twitched with the thought of his fingers smoothing over the smooth skin of her thigh, sliding under the hem of her long shirt and higher. What would she feel like? Taste like? How would she respond to him? Would he know what to do if she ached for him as much as he did her?

"The ability is there, inside you..."

Lost to him because of one day, one mistake.

"You aren't to blame," she repeated. "No one made him steal you and abuse you. It was his choice."

He let out a bitter laugh. "His choice to rob me of the life I was supposed to lead. To destroy a family. In a flick of an eye, he *chose* to take everything, as if he were one of the goddesses. What gives one man the right to exert so much power over another, Evie?" His voice cracked to his dismay. He made a fist on his thigh, staring at his throbbing fingers. "What gives a man that right?"

"Nothing does. He had no right. You need to believe that, babe. You need to."

His head jerked up. She'd called him *"babe."* To his further shock, her hand came to rest on his cheek. The stroking of her thumb over his jaw was hypnotic, until she seemed to become aware of her actions and froze.

He went still, as well. He feared if he moved he'd frighten her away. To his relief, her warm hand remained on his cheek. Her bare knees butted up against his.

"He had no right," she whispered. Closing her eyes, she leaned forward and touched her lips to his cheek. Soft, warm...

He inhaled sharply through his nose, turning a fraction of an inch. The move brought his mouth brushing across hers.

Again, they both stopped, frozen, breathing hard, their lips almost touching. So close to a kiss.

How swiftly anger and grief heated into desire.

He ached for her. He wanted her so badly. "Evie," he said. "Evie." He curved his hand behind her head and touched his lips to one corner of her mouth.

With a sigh, she turned to offer him full contact, her soft lips parting.

"Mom, what's for dessert?" Ellen's voice came from the direction of the kitchen.

"Shit." Evie jerked away.

"Come here." He pulled her back to him.

What are you doing? her eyes screamed.

"There...I can see it." He touched his fingertips to her brow. "Don't move."

She shook her head.

"Hold still I said."

Her nostrils flared. Ignoring her anger, he pretended to take something from her eye. "A piece of lint. See? It's out now. Rinse your eye with water."

The tension went out of her. She realized the ruse he'd played. Goddess knew how he'd thought of it so quickly. As his memories returned, so had talents he never knew existed. "Downside of being a parent," she whispered. "No privacy."

A new memory filled his mind...of barging in on his mother sitting on his father's lap by the hearth fire. REEF didn't understand why her shirt had been pulled low on one shoulder, or why they were sitting in the darkness.

Now he knew.

Evie stumbled up and away from the couch. REEF stood, as well, but it wasn't easy reverting back to his habitual aloofness. Something had altered inside him during that kiss. In those few moments, he'd felt...human, the machine in him forgotten. His old REEF senses were sharpening by the minute, and he didn't know why, but for that brief period of time, he was a man kissing a woman.

Ellen observed the entire spectacle with a towel clutched around her slim shoulders. "Are you okay, Mom?"

Evie pressed a hand over her left eye. "I'm fine. Agent Sanders is as good at first aid as he is with—" she looked him over "—everything else."

He didn't need a translator to understand her meaning. So, she thought he was good at kissing? He could hardly feel smug. They'd barely touched lips. That he'd affected her in any way at all was a miracle—or beginner's luck, to use an expression of the Terrans. She'd been his first, his only. For that entire dizzying moment, he was winging it, going on instinct alone.

Animal instinct, he thought.

By now his head was swimming. From the alcohol, or from her? *By the Dark Reaches.* The pulsing ache where his jeans had pulled tight would not relent. *That* hadn't been caused by the drink. He was so aroused he could barely walk.

"I find mind over matter works best," the Handyman had advised. *"It's all you can do. Focus elsewhere. If all else fails, take a cold shower."*

All else *had* failed.

"Or, of course, you can take advantage of opportunity if the lady is available and willing."

His gaze swerved to Evie, who was overseeing the distribution of dessert amongst the children. Her willingness to be with him was no longer that farfetched of a thought. He hadn't scared her off; Ellen had. With equal parts dread and anticipation, REEF couldn't help but wonder what would happen the next time they were able to be alone.

"I will take advantage of your shower now." He stepped away but Evie's voice stopped him.

"A swim would be better," she said.

"Is the water cold?"

"It's perfect," her daughter, Ellen, chimed in. "Not too hot, not too—"

"Cold enough," Evie interrupted.

"Mom?" Ellen quirked a brow.

Evie busied herself with plates and utensils. "Why don't you go for a swim, Agent Sanders? I'll meet you when I'm done in the kitchen." Her glance was pointed and hot.

Hot.

Goddess help him.

If he'd been wondering what would happen the next time he and Evie were alone, he would not have to wait long to find out.

TWELVE

After the REEF went outside, Evie piled cookies, brownies and berries on a tray for Ellen to bring upstairs. She'd assumed her "perky mom" facade, the kind of mom who didn't come *this* close to making out with an alien cyborg in the living room, who didn't fantasize about shoving him into the guest bedroom later, stripping naked and throwing herself at the hot man sleeping in the bed.

"You like him."

Evie hesitated for a fraction of a second before adding the last berry. "What's not to like? Agent Sanders is a very nice man."

"Nice as in—" Ellen waggled her eyebrows "—*Nice, right?* Hot."

"He's our bodyguard. Keeping a totally professional relationship supersedes any attraction I might have for him."

"Whatever."

It didn't sound like Ellen believed a word she'd said. Only one problem with that—neither did Evie.

Ellen took the tray from her hands. "I thought you didn't like us eating by the computers."

"Let's just say that tonight I feel like letting a few rules slide." She kissed Ellen and gave her a little shove toward the stairs.

Evie grabbed a bottle of wine, two clean glasses and a platter of Evie's Eden berries. Shoving open the back door with her bare foot, she scampered down the stairs.

She wanted to finish that kiss, damn it!

All her life she'd sacrificed for others, especially her kids. She loved them to pieces, but there came a point where "Mom" had to draw the line. She needed that kiss, and she was going to get it too. Judging from the way REEF had looked at her when they were in the kitchen, she expected no arguments.

This is so not like you, Evie.

True. It was like the old her: the old self she'd wrapped up and put in storage after high school with the intent of throwing it away, but never quite having the heart to do it. It was as if a part of her always knew she'd want to take that old Evie out again, dust it off to look at and remember before putting it back on the shelf.

Her cover-up fluttered behind her as she walked across the lawn to the pool. The night was warm and dry. Frogs in the greenbelt behind the house belted out mating calls. The perfect background music, she thought, feeling predatory.

It was dark already, but there was enough light from the

underwater pool lights to see. Where was REEF? His towel was flung over a chair, as well as his t-shirt. She walked closer to the pool. There, under the surface, a long, dark form glided, silent and sleek, from one side of the pool to the other.

She arranged the wine and berries at the water's edge and slipped her cover-up off her shoulders, dropping it onto a lounge chair. Underwater, REEF touched the opposite wall and flipped, gliding back across the pool.

With his grace and physical perfection underwater, he reminded her of the rays he'd described from the seas of his planet, Sandreem. Even now as she watched him, he seemed otherworldly somehow, as if he were an exotic animal that had been caught and carted off to the zoo. He looked like someone who didn't belong here, on Earth, or anywhere except at home—his home. Sandreem. She was going to get him back there. She'd reunite him with his family. She just had to think of how.

Perched on the ledge, she hugged her knees to her chin as she waited for REEF's strong swimming to bring him back to her. When he reached the side of the pool, he surfaced explosively. "It's about time you came up for air."

He blinked up at her, his chest heaving. Water made spikes of his dark lashes, framing those amazing eyes. "Ms. Holloway." He nodded.

She nodded back. "Agent Sanders. Or should I say Eriff?" She chose a milk-chocolate strawberry coated with sprinkles and tossed it to him. He rose out of the water and caught it neatly in his teeth before biting into it with clear enjoyment. "Your news is so fantastic, I thought we should celebrate. A little wine. A little chocolate." She inhaled deeply and let it out. "A little night air."

A little naughtiness...

Swimming closer, he anchored himself to the ledge with folded arms. It raised his upper body out of the pool. Streams of water slid down his bare chest. Lovingly, she followed the rivulets as they flowed over every ridge, every valley. *It's not good manners to stare.* She didn't do much better with his eyes. They made her heart flip-flop and she broke into a sweat. Not to mention the other, more distracting sensations she was feeling in other, more private regions of her body....

He finished the berry. "I am not yet ready to be called Eriff. In my mind, I'm still REEF."

"You've got a lot of catching up to do. It won't happen overnight." The horror he'd been through, the indignity. She hugged her knees closer to her body. "You have one incredible story to tell. So much adversity, and you've overcome it all. It would tug at anyone's heartstrings."

"Bah!" He shoved away from the edge. "I do not want your pity or anyone else's."

"Oh, for God's sake. You have my sympathy, you grump. Not pity! Is that like your hot button or what?"

His perpetual frown evaporated into shock at her outburst. Then worried confusion. "Explain 'hot button.'"

"It means something that gets you upset easily. You're so worried about people feeling sorry for you. Get over it already. And another thing—when someone exhibits compassion, accept it gracefully."

REEF drifted backward. Water lapped over his upper body as he observed her. "Another Terran lesson?"

"Yes, damn it. Number four. Are you writing these down? There'll be a test."

There...that ghost of a smile again. "My humble apologies, dear teacher."

"Better." She sniffed. "The only one I pity is the monster that stole you and abused you. It's a horrible story. The public has to know."

"I think not."

"REEF, there's going to come a time when you're going to have to face the charges against you. What if they're not dismissed like Jana thinks they will be? What if she's wrong and you have to stand trial? In the media, you're the bad guy, the monster. You tried to kill Cavin. It makes it easy for everyone to hate you. You're everything we always believed about extraterrestrials. You're scary, you're hostile. You think you're superior."

"That last bit is accurate, at least." He chose another berry.

"That won't help you in the court of public opinion. They need to know who Eriff of Sandreem is, even if it generates that dreaded pity you hate so much. You're not the killer everyone thinks you are."

"I have indeed killed, Evie. Many times." His expression was unreadable, his eyes dark in the shadows. She sensed remorse and strength as well as ruthlessness. In that moment, he was no less capable of killing than he was before. The only thing stopping him now was his emerging humanity. A shiver of apprehension went through her. He was a stranger with a dangerous past. Thinking anything less was deluding herself.

"The circumstances of how I got to be an assassin don't change the fact that I was."

"I can't stomach the idea of them locking you up. I won't let it happen. Your life was hijacked. You lost your future. All over the world, the same thing is happening to other people—to children —of every race and on almost every continent." She thrust her hand at the stars. "And now you tell me it happens out there too!"

Embarrassed by her rising passion, she froze, hand in midair. *Carried away again.* Pierce's eyes would glaze over when she'd go on like this. "Calm down," he'd groan, wincing as if extremes of emotion, any emotion—joy, grief, anger— were almost painful for him. She'd tried hard to stay within the lines. After all, her entire family did. Why not her?

She snapped her hand back, instantly reverting back to her perky, politician's-daughter poise. "Sorry about that. I'm fairly passionate about the subject and sometimes I get going and, well..."

"Fairly? On the contrary, you are extremely passionate."

Blushing, she felt like skulking away.

"But I'm beginning to understand that the plight of the children deserves that passion, Evie. It is a gift. Do not underestimate the power of that gift. And do not ever feel as though you must apologize for it. Not to me."

Unexpected butterflies took flight in her stomach. He thought her opinions were important, not something to be dismissed. That her passion was appropriate, not freakish.

Suddenly, the need to prove her intelligence around him was gone; he assumed that she was smart. In his company, she could almost believe it.

With a whoosh of gushing water, REEF hoisted his body up and out of the pool, landing next to her. She could almost see the steam rising off his skin as pool water sloshed against her thighs. He chose a strawberry from the platter, turning it from side to side as he studied it. "Why then have you decided to cease operating Evie's Eden?"

"I'll still make berries. But I'll keep things small. Contained." *Safe.* "Going commercial isn't for me."

He focused those bluer-than-blue eyes on her. "Is that what you want, or is it a decision made to placate others?"

That stopped her in her tracks. No one had ever asked that question before. She had a loving family; she'd even had a good marriage—at first—and no one had ever challenged whether her decisions were made because she thought they were the right ones or because she thought they were what others wanted. "The reality is that it isn't just about me." If she strayed too far outside the lines of her life, she stood to lose so much. REEF had no idea.

Yet, something flickered in his eyes, as if he understood. How could he have even the remotest idea what she'd gone through during and after the breakup of her marriage, and what she was going through even now? To experience heartbreak you needed feelings. He'd been engineered to not feel anything at all.

Sure, he'd been "repaired," to be more human but to what extent? He wasn't easy to figure out. She wasn't sure she wanted to.

It would be all too easy to start to like him too much. Guys were safe until she fell in love with them. *Then* they became dangerous. Luckily, she didn't have to worry about that with the REEF. They were a total mismatch.

"I didn't want to quit, okay? I wanted to see where this would go." Feeling frustrated, frustrated with herself, she took the stray chocolate sprinkle she'd been twiddling between her fingers and flicked it away. "Evie Holloway, successful entrepreneur. I thought it had a better ring to it than Evie Holloway, Jasper black sheep."

"Black sheep..?"

"The member of the family who doesn't measure up to everyone else."

"As an objective outsider, I disagree with your observation. You more than measure up, Evie."

"You'd better not be buttering me up for letting you stay here," she said, half-afraid it was true.

"First I am being 'polite' *then* I am 'buttering you up'—a slang term I happen to know." He blew out an exasperated gust of air. "Do Terrans always say one thing and mean another?"

I promise to love, honor and protect until death do us part. Pierce's vows on their wedding day echoed hollowly in her mind. "Sometimes..."

"Then how does one determine what is true and what is not?" He sounded discouraged, at a loss.

Welcome to the club, she thought. *Club Human.* "You go with what your heart says. You trust. And hope the people you trust deserve your faith in them."

"And you, Evie? Do you say one thing and mean another?" Those intense eyes bored through her like twin ice-blue lasers, waiting for her answer.

She shook her head. "I've been known to say one thing and *wish* another, though."

"Like yes when you'd rather say no?"

He'd pegged her. "You figured that out pretty quick."

"It is not hard to see. And I would ask that you not do that with me." His gaze dipped to her mouth. Her face grew hot. Was this his way of asking permission for a kiss?

"I'll try," she whispered. *Promise. Promise.*

"Do or do not. There is no try."

She laughed, delighted, murmuring as she leaned closer, "That's Yoda's line from *Star Wars.*"

"The couple who cared for me during my recovery had me watch all the *Star Wars* movies. They thought they might spur memories..."

"Mmm. Princess Leia...Han Solo..."

Again his gaze lingered on her mouth. "You are so quick to say yes, to accommodate others. You take on everything with cheer and grace. But what does Evie Holloway want?"

"A kiss." Oh God! She'd actually said it. It probably wasn't what he'd expected to hear, but there it was. It was out. "We never finished it. I need closure."

She wanted that kiss, damn it. She'd thought he did, also. Now she wasn't so sure. They'd been out here a half hour now and all they'd done was talk. For once in her life she wasn't after conversation.

He smoothed his hand over her shoulder. "Evie..." The surprise in his voice, the pleasure...her name had never sounded sexier.

She was disappointed that he didn't pull her closer in the

darkness. "If you're worried about violating the teacher-student, damsel-protector relationship, don't be."

His fingers slid into her hair as he brought his lips to her forehead. She trembled. The chorus of lust-drunk frogs surged. Or was that the blood rushing to her head? He'd hardly touched her and she was shaking. It was crazy. Was she that starved for physical contact, or was he just that good?

He hovered there, the seconds crawling by as her blood heated to the boiling point. *That good,* she decided, stifling a sigh as the path his lips made along her hairline made her heart race. She looped her arms over his neck. His bare skin was so warm, so smooth; he smelled wonderful: like chocolate and spice and man.

He kissed the strands of hair lying on her cheek. Her eyes closed. She wasn't quite breathing anymore; it was more like panting, and nothing had happened yet. Part of her couldn't believe they were doing anything at all. "I'm saying yes," she coaxed in a whisper against his damp jaw. "And *meaning* yes. In case there's any confusion."

He pressed his lips to her throat, inhaling deeply as if he loved the way she smelled. "The children..."

"Inside," she assured him. "Busy."

His fingertips slid down the side of her throat to her shoulder and disappeared behind her, circling between her shoulder blades. Unconsciously, she arched her back. He was dragging out the anticipation so much that she wanted to die. "Is this how you used to play Sech? You said you used to take too long between moves. If you kiss anything like you play, I'm going to—"

He dipped his head and kissed her on the mouth.

—scream, she finished in her mind, melting.

His lips were firm and warm. And closed. He'd caught her midsentence, lips parted, yet he didn't use his tongue. Instead, he treated her to lingering, erotically charged little kisses from one end of her mouth to the other, savoring her, even nibbling her lower lip, everything but hauling her close and kissing the daylights out of her.

He moved back, brushing his wide palm over her hair. She stared at him in the darkness. Well, shit. Maybe he'd come to his senses. She surely hadn't. Or maybe he was just being a gentleman.

Lucky for REEF, she'd never been shy about making the first move. Or the second, in this case.

A girl had to do what a girl had to do.

She reached up, rolling her fists in his short hair to anchor him, and slipped her tongue inside his mouth.

REEF responded with a sound somewhere between a sigh and a low growl, his tongue searching out hers. A shudder coursed through his body, and he crushed her close, one big hand splayed on the back of her head. The kiss was so deep, so mind-wipingly *hot* that she felt the shockwave clear to her toes.

They lost their balance and fell sideways into the pool.

She never heard the splash. Her thighs were wrapped too tightly around his hips. His back muscles bunched, and he moaned in her mouth. Bubbles fizzed around them, heading upward as they sank. She locked her legs around his hips until she could feel every inch of him. Every ridge. Powerful and well-formed applied to more than the former assassin's muscles.

Bodies twined together, they hit bottom, her ears popping. He used his feet to shove upward with a powerful kick. They surfaced, gasping. He wasted no time in resealing his mouth over hers.

Oh, baby. Now *this* was a kiss. It had taken a while to get there, but it was worth it. And that mouth...that mouth; she'd dreamed about it all day, and now it was hers for the tasting.

It was a lush, sensual kiss that seemed to go on and on, their hands everywhere. Two thin bathing suits were all that separated them from a naked lovefest on the concrete ledge next to the pool. Well, that, three teenagers in close proximity, and the last vestiges of propriety.

Finally, they moved apart to gulp in air. He had her back pressed to the pool wall farthest from the house. She liked that he'd automatically hidden her from prying, teenage eyes. Her lips tingled. Every nerve ending in her body throbbed. "Wow. Now that's what I call a kiss."

Her face was so close to his that all she could see was his mouth as it curved, finally, into a brilliant smile. "So, experienced man-of-the-galaxy, how do Terran girls rate when it comes to kisses?"

His smile faltered. What was that about? Maybe he didn't like to kiss and tell. "No comparison," he said with conviction.

Suddenly, he tipped his head. "Someone is here."

"Where? Here? In the yard?" She blinked, confused. She didn't hear anything outside her heartbeat and the frogs.

He grabbed her upper arm. "Stay here."

She started to protest, but he squeezed her arm almost to the point of pain. "Do as I say."

Water sprayed as he dove away from her, sluicing off his

body as he climbed out of the pool and retrieved his gun she hadn't known he'd hidden under a lounge chair. He gripped the weapon in his hands, turning in a half circle, his face without expression.

"REEF!" Her heart beat in fear—for him, for her. For the kids inside the house.

His almost-scary focus fixed on the acres of oaks on the dark greenbelt behind the house. Not almost-scary, she amended. It was plain scary. He was a different man from the one she'd just kissed. This was a stranger. This man was the REEF.

"No shootouts allowed," she pleaded. "This is the suburbs." She squeaked as he vaulted over the six-foot iron fence and ran into the shadows, barefoot.

From inside the house, Sadie and Grandpa's dogs were fogging up the sliding door's glass. They hadn't started barking until REEF jumped the fence. Whatever REEF had detected was outside the range of even canine hearing.

She hurried out of the pool and swept a towel around her. The frogs had gone silent. All of a sudden the beautiful starry night seemed eerie—the stars themselves most of all. They twinkled almost malevolently. She shuddered with a premonition she couldn't explain.

She ran to the fence, holding on to the bars. The crunching of twigs and leaves out in the greenbelt carried back to her. Purposeful walking: REEF's. Then a louder crunch and the sound of more than one pair of running feet.

She almost swallowed her heart.

She gripped the bars on the fence, straining to see in the darkness until the sounds went out of hearing range.

An eternity seemed to pass. *REEF!* She wanted to scream out his name, but common sense told her it would put him in danger—more than he already was.

Come back. Come back.

From far off, the sound of footsteps returned. She couldn't tell whose.

Prying her hands from the bars, she backed away from the fence. The hammering of her pulse made it difficult to hear. Then a dark form emerged from the trees.

"REEF," she whispered. He was limping.

"REEF!"

He vaulted back over the fence. He slid his weapon into his holster. His eyes were back to normal, thank God. He had scratches all over his bare torso. His feet were a bloody mess.

"You're hurt. Let's get you inside and cleaned up." But even as she said the words, the wounds were closing. Healing. She swallowed, trying to reconcile this—this *being* with the man who'd kissed her just now.

He caught the look in her eyes. His expression of embarrassment about tore her heart out, and she cursed the fact that she'd let her shock show. "I'm just not used to seeing healing like that." But her reassurance didn't seem to make it any better. It was clear he didn't want reminders of what he once was.

"What was out there? Who was it? Tell me it was just some workaholic paparazzi. Please." She didn't want to consider the alternatives. Like Guido and his mob friends.

"Two men. Armed. Wearing black."

Wearing black. Not paparazzi. Something worse, but what? Who?

He paused to catch his breath. When his eyes came back to her, they were filled with self-censure. "I couldn't catch them."

"But you scared them off. Thank goodness for that. What do we do now? Call the police?"

He killed that idea with a shake his head. "Involving the police will do nothing but bring us attention we don't want. The intruders are gone."

"What if they come back?"

"I'll stay on watch tonight, but I doubt they will. They'll think twice about returning now that they know I can detect their presence."

She wrung the ends of the towel. "I'll set the house alarm so you don't have to stay up. I need you with all your wits tomorrow in case it's a repeat of today." *Please let it not be.* The queasy, quivering, back-of-neck prickling feeling she'd felt earlier at Ka-blooms had come back. She felt so helpless. It was like being trapped on a runaway train with no way to stop it before it crashed.

REEF took her by the shoulders. "Let me worry about that. I will protect you, Evie. I *am* going to keep you safe. I won't allow anything to happen to you or your children."

"Or Sadie." It seemed silly, but, somehow, if the little dog was okay, they'd all be okay. "Say it, REEF. *Or Sadie.*"

The certainty and pain dominating his fierce stare melted. "Or Sadie," he said.

Yet the awkwardness generated by her apprehension of his superhero powers remained. She wanted to fix that, but she didn't know what to say. Acting on instinct, she closed the distance between them in a couple of steps and slid her arms around his waist.

His body stiffened at the contact. She'd surprised him, she knew. His heart pounded away under her ear. And she said nothing. She simply stood there, hugging him until the frogs resumed their song and the tension went out of his body. When at last she felt his hand glide along her back to keep her close, she shivered with relief. Eriff was back.

THIRTEEN

Kill.

The order scrolled across his eyes, blocking out all other, extraneous visual inputs. The time and distance to his target decreased with each loping stride. He did not tire; his internal systems saw to that. That stamina sustained him on his run through the dark forest.

Target acquisition: 49.52 seconds.

Too long.

He accelerated his pace. *41.05 seconds.*

And closing.

A tell-tale red glow ahead signified heat, body heat. *Target acquired.*

The ground was boggy, slowing him down. *KILL.*

The trees closed in around him, further slowing him. *KILL.*

Urgency drove him not to fail. The trees were all around

him now, caging him in. The boggy ground sucked at his legs, sinking him to knee level. *Oh-One, do not fail me.*

The voice, easy and familiar, and always there, drove him relentlessly. He had to obey at all cost. The red glow danced, closer now. He kicked at the greedy mud that entrapped him. *KILL.* The trees formed a solid wall. The red glow teased.

Do not fail, Oh-One.

Blind desire drove him to succeed. No other choice. He would prevail. One last kick and he was free of the sucking mud. Stealthy in the shadows was his normal mode of operation, but this was no normal night. The wall of trees would not stop him. No, indeed. With bioengineered might, he thrust his fist between the tightly packed trunks to grab his target's throat.

An explosion of pain in his arm jolted him out of the dark forest. The pain was knifelike, shooting up his right arm. Gasping, blinking, he peered into the confines of a comfortable room, Evie's guest room, and at the wall he'd just punched.

All hells. He hadn't punched a hole in the wall but he'd blasted sure tried. Clutching his throbbing hand to his stomach, he sat heavily on the bed. The sheets were tangled and half pulled off the mattress. The mud from the dream, he realized. In reality he'd struggled to get out of bed.

He shut his eyes as the echo of the kill order still thrummed in his skull. It reminded him of the machine he once was, the tool of others. Acting with no free will was something he'd hoped to the goddesses above he'd never repeat.

You will fight this. You will not go back to what you were before. You will prove with your deeds and your desire that you are part of the human race, not an assembly of hardware.

He unfurled his fist and assessed the damage. He'd broken two fingers. The torn, bloodied skin on his knuckles was already healing, but the bones needed to be set—and fast —or they'd heal crookedly.

He needed something with which to wrap them. He grabbed the sheet, and stopped. He'd already plowed through Evie's wall; no need to worsen the deed and ruin her sinfully soft bedding. He reached for an extra T-shirt instead, shredding it. In short order the middle fingers were secured in a decent battlefield dressing.

It was, in fact, as if he were at war. With himself.

When his past came rushing back to meet him yesterday, he fully expected it would distance him from his other past as an assassin. But last night's dream-hunt through the woods did not let him forget so easily. Was he fated to live as a human by day and as a REEF at night? Dread clutched at this throat, yet another new addition to his ever-expanding repertoire of emotions.

You will fight this.

His senses were stronger than any human's. He healed faster than he ever had. What if his bio-implants were regenerating somehow, microscopic threads forging new connections between his numerous implants, reactivating them one by one? Would he once more be under the control of a machine? Would he once more *be* a machine?

You will not go back to what you were.

To his knowledge no REEF had ever suffered the

complete removal of the master implant. Who knew what his makers had bioengineered into his body in that unlikely event? The answers, if any, were back at the REEF Academy.

And that's where the answers would stay. One or more persons in the Coalition had wanted to see him dead. Not likely he'd be giving them a second chance. A few months ago, he'd wanted to die. No longer was that the case. He had his memories now.

The sounds of footsteps from upstairs warned of a waking family. The bedside clock read 5:47. Upstairs the family was already stirring. Evie's children had a sporting event to which he'd drive them at seven. He'd looked forward to a day in the company of her and her family as a man reunited with his past. He'd looked forward to feeling *normal*.

And he would. He would not let the nightmares stop him. If it turned out that his REEF abilities regenerated while he slept, he would not sleep. It was as simple as that. He'd gone without sleep before while on missions; it was not difficult for him to do. No sleep, no nightmares, no bio-cyber-regeneration. Within the week he'd know if it was working.

He unraveled the bandage, wiping away the blood before tossing it aside. His hand would be all right as long as he didn't move it too much. Dressed in jeans and a fresh T-shirt, his holstered gun hidden beneath it, he entered the hallway, following the aroma of the Earth stimulant coffee. Caydinn detested the beverage, had warned against it, but REEF had taken to the drink from his first sip at the farmhouse. Now he knew why. On Sandreem, the nuts of the papatat tree were dried, baked and ground into powder and brewed much like coffee.

Sandreem. Home. Family. He smiled. His. He savored the images, drew them close. The sensation of knowing who he was and where he'd come from was so deeply satisfying, so much a part of him on an elemental level that he found it difficult to imagine what it had been like *before*.

Evie's late grandfather's dogs were clustered around the rear glass door when he entered the empty kitchen. He poured a cup of coffee from the pot Evie had told him would be ready when they woke and sipped, walking over to greet the canines.

They whined and backed away, tails tucked.

A low-pitched growling came from behind him. REEF turned, finding Sadie glaring at him with her upper lip curled back, exposing tiny fangs. Trembling, she radiated menace. "Come now, Sadie. We were friends." He extended a hand in peace. The maddening little dog foamed at the mouth, snarling and snapping.

He sat on a kitchen chair and patted his thigh. "You liked this lap yesterday. Care to try again?"

The dog would not be consoled. He gentled his voice, reaching for her. "Do not fear me."

Sadie backed away, shivering and barking.

"What's gotten into her?" Evie sailed into the kitchen, bringing the scents of vanilla, flowers...and her own warm skin. His gloom dissolved in an explosion of color, joy, and warmth. Her form-fitting short pants curved around her swaying hips and bottom. An equally snug, colorful shirt pushed her breasts high. A necklace with a single pearl dangled in the valley between them. Silently, he groaned. It would make his job protecting her far easier if she wore shapeless sacks.

Sadie barked then whined.

Evie bent down and picked up Sadie. "What's wrong, baby? Scary kitty outside?" Evie turned, hugging the little dog and finally turning in his direction. Her gaze softened at the sight of him. "Hi..."

The heat from last night's kiss simmered.

If there was any doubt she'd wake today repulsed by what they'd done at the pool, it was erased in that moment. He nodded. "Good morning, Evie."

"We've got a problem," she said as she busied herself preparing breakfast, one-handed as she clutched Sadie. "My family called—Jana and my father—about a half hour ago."

"And it is not good, I presume."

"Apparently your face is plastered all over the news, social media, everywhere. It's because I'm involved. Evie, the black sheep Jasper. The press hasn't had any good shots at me in, oh, about fifteen years." She took a long drink of coffee. "They say I was involved in major drug bust. Give me a break. As if there's any doubt why I was there." She put down the coffee cup, hard. Tension tightened her mouth.

"You family will intervene on your behalf," he assured her. "Don't underestimate their power, particularly in the wake of the Coalition's attempt to invade. As well, you've already been debriefed by the law enforcement officials. They're certain you weren't there to do ill deeds."

"I'm not the issue here. It's you. REEF, they got your photo. Someone's going to recognize you." She grabbed a loaf of bread and cut slices. "What were we thinking? We should have taken that camera away."

He started to reach for her, intending to give her arm a reassuring squeeze—with children nearby he dared risk no more—but Sadie snarled.

"Stop it, Sadie."

"I'm dead," he reminded her. "I was killed in Nevada."

"You're staying home. I'll take the Hummer and bring the kids to swim. I'll be fine—"

"No."

"You're being stubborn."

"And you are not, Evie?"

Her eyes flashed with fire, no doubt equaling his own anger. Remembering they weren't alone in the house, they lowered their voices. "I do not know who the intruders are who I chased off last night. Without that knowledge, I will not under any circumstances let you go off without my protection. Like it or not, we are together today, all day. And all night, if we have to."

Her hand flexed around the knife. The pink was back in her cheeks. "That's not fighting fair. Sweet-talking me."

The slang baffled him. "Sweet-talking you?"

"It's like buttering up, but with sex."

He almost spilled his coffee.

She glanced sideways. "If anyone tries to arrest you, I swear, I'll fight them. It won't be pretty, because I am totally uncoordinated. But kicking, slapping, that I can do."

"Evie, I'm a government agent with an uncanny resemblance to the dead REEF. It's a solid cover story. That's no reason for arrest."

"They don't need a reason. That's the thing. They don't need a reason any more than that captain who kidnapped you needed a reason. But it doesn't matter, because I have a plan in case this all goes to hell." She moved closer, lowering her voice even more. "You're going home."

"Evie... Sandreem is very remote. And there is so much left to do here on Earth before—"

"You need to go home, to your family. You won't be whole again until you reconnect with who you were."

"And how am I to get there? The Coalition gave Earth a fleet of spaceships as part of Queen Keira's dowry, but they're at your Terran military base under lock and key and the tightest security in the history of your planet."

"The ships on my family's ranch aren't."

He couldn't help laughing. "My fighter? Caydinn's? They're wrecks."

"Cavin's is. Yours is dinged up and dented, but when Jared went inside, the day he met Queen Keira, he was able to power it up. That was last spring. I don't know what kind of shape it's in now. But I know no one's touched it since. With everything else going on, everyone's forgotten about those ships, including my family." She caught his hand, her eyes dancing with excitement and hope that was contagious. "It just might be your ticket home."

"You would help me escape," he said, incredulous. "That's your plan..."

She nodded. "If it comes to that, yes."

The dog snarled louder.

"Stop that, Sadie." Evie groaned. "I don't know what's gotten into her."

"She and the other dogs can detect changes in me that humans cannot."

"What do you mean? What kind of changes?"

"I've been having nightmares, Evie. In them I was a REEF on the hunt. Last night I punched my fist into your wall."

"Omigod."

"There was no damage to speak of. A smear of blood—"

"Who cares about the wall? Give your hand."

She set Sadie down and tugged his hand from behind his back. "Your fingers are swollen. You need to ice them." Her green eyes were filed with concern as she pulled ice from the freezer and wrapped it in a damp towel. "Here. Look at those fingers." She shook her head. "You could have broken them."

He cleared his throat.

She gasped. "You did. Oh, REEF."

"I've had two such dreams in as many nights." He remembered waking gripping the Gatekeeper's fragile wrist, the fleeting terror in her eyes. Shame at what he was capable of seeped into his gut. Determination to never let Evie see that side of him ran hard on the heels of that shame. It meant he had to give her some warning. Better to have some inkling of the danger than none at all and be caught unawares. He'd die before he hurt her.

"I believe the bio-hardware in my body is regenerating while I sleep. I've seen the signs already—my heightened eyesight and hearing. My rapid healing. Animals are sensitive to such activity."

"REEF, please, she's a dog. She's in a bad mood. She's Sadie, for God's sake. It has nothing to do with your nightmares, which I'm sorry you had, but you are not, I repeat, not in danger of changing back to a REEF. If you were, you would have broken the wall. Instead the wall broke you."

She'd taken away his main argument. Without superhuman strength, he was, in fact, merely a human. He looked down at the ice he held on his fingers. *The wall broke you.* For once in his life he was glad for defeat.

REEF surveyed the swim meet from behind sunglasses. The noise was deafening. Besides splashing, cheering and intermittent applause, music blared from speakers attached to tall light posts and to a small building known as Krusty Krab Snack Bar, where Evie was doing her volunteer shift for the next two hours. The area nearby was thick with the odors of frying food and the particularly cloying smell of "hotdogs." Chlorine formed the foundation to the less powerful scents of sweat and hot concrete.

Evie considered her home the "epicenter of chaos." He now knew she was incorrect. The swim meet was far worse than anything he'd experienced at her home since he'd arrived.

He loved it, every minute.

He breathed deep, as if he could take in the morning sunshine on his arms, the noise of children and laughter. Even the hotdogs smelled good. If he had to guess, he'd say this was what freedom tasted like.

Here, he could blend into the crowd. Here, he could feel...almost human.

The area surrounding the swimming pool had been transformed into a city of tents. Families milled in and out of the makeshift shelters, spilling into the crowd seemingly without order or purpose yet somehow appearing at the required races at the appointed time. Butterfly, freestyle, backstroke, breaststroke: all the ways he swam as a boy were now defined and broken down into races of various distances called "heats." The thought of Sandreem's High Sun Day festivities being handled in such a way made him chuckle. With a pang of longing, he recalled the festival that celebrated the first day of summer that the sun didn't set.

Hands clasped behind his back, he moved into position to watch John participate in his race. Something plowed into him from behind—a herd of small boys on their way to the pool. Then a group of girls Ellen's age squeezed past. It was impossible to remain in a position to keep watch on Evie or any other Holloway without being jostled by children of all sizes.

The horn sounded. John appeared to fly through the air before slicing into the water. A memory of diving from the high branches of an ebbe tree into a crystal-clear lake followed, and REEF remembered. It had indeed been like flying....

"Which one's yours?" A slender woman with a bouncy blond-streaked ponytail stood next to him. "Mine's in six."

"Lane eleven," he replied, his focus on John as he took an early lead.

The woman jumped up and down, whooping as the boys reached the wall and flipped. "Go, Kyle!"

"That's it, John!" he encouraged. It felt somewhat strange

shouting to the children, but Evie said they loved it. After a life of being silent and stealthy it was invigorating to release his hold on his emotions, his demeanor, his voice.

On the final stretch, John fought for victory against two other boys, nearly head-to-head. REEF made fists, mentally urging him faster. In the end John lost energy and the heat by a fraction of a second.

"Blast it," he muttered. Ah, but the boy had fought hard. Ellen's race was coming up next.

But first...Over a sea of heads, he located Evie—a flash of glossy hair and her floral shirt. The area around the snack bar was clear of danger. Satisfied that she remained safe, he turned to go.

"Oh, darn," the blond woman said. "I can't tell if Kyle came in fifth or sixth."

"Sixth," REEF informed her, mentally replaying the order in which the other boys had reached the finish.

"You noticed!" She seemed to take it as a personal favor when it was simply the way he was, a fact best kept private. *Just tell people you have a photographic memory,*" Evie had advised in case he raised suspicion.

"And yours? How'd he do?" she asked.

"Third."

"It was a strong heat." She scrutinized his face. "By the way, do I know you?"

REEF tugged his NorCal ball cap lower over his eyes. "*It's okay to be my bodyguard,*" Evie had said. "*We just don't want you looking like one.*"

The cap was another acquisition from Jared Jasper's

stockpile of abandoned clothes. "No, we have not met," he told the woman. "Now, if you'll excuse me, I must go."

"I just love your accent!" She flipped her ponytail and fluttered her lashes. "And you *do* look familiar. I'd never forget a face like yours." An appreciative glance from his face to his legs broadcast her opinion that she wouldn't have forgotten his body, either.

By the goddess, she was flirting with him. His gaze veered to the snack bar to see if Evie had noticed. Animatedly, she took an order from two little girls who weren't tall enough to reach the counter. She seemed to come alive around children. He wondered why she never had more than two. Perhaps it was not her choice, he realized, thinking of Pierce.

"What country are you from?" the woman was saying.

"Nevada."

"And I'm from China." She laughed. "Excuse me for noticing, but you're not wearing a ring. Me, neither." She showed him her left hand. "Wow, a cute single dad who's here instead of off playing golf. Let's go view the time sheets. Come on. I'll even buy you a Coke."

Movement caught his eye. On the far side of the pool, near the entry, a couple of police officers stood peering into the crowd. Adrenaline exploded throughout his body. Were they looking for Evie, or for him?

"Hello." The woman waved her hand in front of his eyes. "I lost you there again."

Protect. He grabbed her wrist to move her hand out of the way. She gasped as he held on tight. That gasp of fear reached down to the human part of him, calling him back. As the red rage subsided, he processed the look in her wide blue eyes. It was the same terror he'd seen in the Gatekeeper's eyes when he'd woken from his nightmare, gripping her arm. *Monster.* In horror, he released the woman.

Almost immediately, Ellen was at his side. A green swim cap framed her small, heart-shaped face. "He's really sorry."

The girl pulled him away from the dumbfounded woman. "He was in the military—a sniper. A *Marine sniper.* Ever since he got back from Iraq he's been suffering post traumatic stress disorder. If you ever try to block his vision, look out."

The woman's fear melted into sympathy. "Iraq?" she asked.

"I—" REEF started to protest but Ellen interrupted.

"He doesn't like to talk about it." Her strong, lean arm linked through his as she propelled him away.

Stunned and repulsed by his behavior, he glowered straight ahead. The REEF in him was possibly regenerating at night. Was he to fight its return by day, as well? Apparently so. The necessity to clear away all obstacles between him and his goal had overwhelmed all other thought. All *human* thought. Yes, his goal this time was to protect and not to kill, but what would he have done had the woman persisted in thwarting his efforts to guard Evie? Had the human part of him not intervened? Had Ellen not interrupted and pulled him away?

A shudder of revulsion ran through him. *I will fight this. I will not go back to what I was before.*

"That's Kayla's mom." Ellen didn't seem the least bit concerned by what had happened. "I can't believe she was hitting on you."

"She did not hit me. It was I who made first contact."

"Hit *on* you," Ellen enunciated. "Not hit."

Slang, he realized.

"She needs to get a clue. You were so not interested. You pushed her hand out of the way because you saw the police officers, right?"

He blinked at the sudden change in subject. "That is correct."

"I thought so. That was Michael Spencer's dad and his partner. He stopped by to see him swim the two-hundred-meter free. I'd let you know if I saw anyone here we really needed to worry about."

He smiled. "I appreciate the help, Ellen."

"I appreciate your helping my mom."

REEF glanced over at the snack bar and caught Evie's eye. She tipped her head at him, smiling her mischievous, flirtatious smile, one that he sensed she used only with him.

Wishful thinking? Perhaps. After a lifetime without wishes, he deserved a few, he decided.

Perhaps a few had already come true. He fought the urge to pull Evie from the snack bar and draw her into an embrace. He needed that contact, needed it to remind himself that he was human, that what had just happened and happened last night was not him. Not Eriff. Only in Evie's arms was he sure of it. She didn't think he was a monster, and neither did her daughter, apparently. His violent reaction to the blond woman didn't frighten young Ellen at all. Then again the girl didn't appear to be frightened by much.

She stayed by his side as they wound their way closer to

the snack bar and Evie, looking as if she wanted to continue their conversation. "Can I ask you a question?"

"Certainly."

"You're not really from Nevada, are you?"

At his hesitation, she said, "I knew it." A small, smug smile curved her mouth. "You're the REEF."

FOURTEEN

REEF's shock appeared to delight Ellen even more. He had the oddest sensation of being in the hands of a master interrogator—and someone about twenty years older than her chronological age.

He narrowed his eyes at her. "How long have you known?"

"Since you picked us up at the pool after practice. I tried to get you to confess at dinner, but you wouldn't. Secret Service." She made a derisive snort.

Evie had been adamant about the children not finding out. She feared the reaction of her ex-husband. Would this mean he'd have to leave? He knew that would ultimately come to pass, yet he couldn't help thinking that this brief time of happiness had been too fleeting.

"Don't worry, I'm not going to say anything," Ellen whispered. "Not even to John. In return you're going to tell me all about what it's like to travel in space. You're going to tell me about other planets too. And how you used to kill people."

"Yes to the first two. No to the last."

She shrugged. "Okay for now. Fifty-meter butterfly—in five. Are you coming to watch?" She turned and scampered off.

REEF watched her go, his arms hanging useless at his sides. To use a Terran expression, he felt as if he'd just made a deal with the devil.

The smell of French fries and cheeseburgers filled the car along with laughter and the sounds of fast food being unwrapped. They were almost home after a detour through In & Out Burger. The expression on REEF's face when he experienced ordering food from a drive-through was priceless. They hadn't taught him much in Nevada, not at all, Evie thought. And they definitely hadn't fed him enough, according to his earlier complaints. Not so at her house. Not only was she planning to keep stuffing him full of delicious home-cooked meals and snacks, she had no problem contributing to his nutritional corruption by introducing him to cheeseburgers, fries and chocolate milk shakes. He'd have no more room to complain. Or in his stomach.

REEF's gaze went to the rearview mirror as they turned into Evie's neighborhood. "We have company."

Evie pulled off her sunglasses and turned around. A California Highway Patrol coasted behind the Hummer. In one breath, her pulse jumped from a slow, contented thump to hard kicks.

Goose the gas, she wanted to cry out. They'd speed down the street and to the airport, where she'd purchase four tickets, cash, to a third-world country and hide in safety. Of course, her custody agreement didn't have a fugitive clause. So much for that plan.

Evie tried to keep calm for the sake of the children. Problem was, keeping calm wasn't her forte. Modulating her voice, she spoke slowly to give the appearance of composure. At least to the kids. REEF would know better. "What do you think they want?"

"They might not be intending to follow us," REEF pointed out.

True, but it sure looked like they were. Sandy's husband was outside working on the sprinklers. He stood to watch them drive past, trailed by the police car. Across the street, Cheryl and her husband paused to stare in the midst of unloading groceries from their car. Evie waved cheerily as if there was nothing strange about a police escort home.

REEF pulled into the driveway, then the garage. The police car stopped in front of the house, ending the question of being followed. REEF killed the engine.

Ellen gnawed on a fry. "Maybe they want to bring us in for questioning." To Evie's horror, her daughter seemed delighted by the prospect. *Nothing exciting ever happens to me,* Ellen always complained. Evie would have thought the threat of alien invasion would have qualified as "something," but now that Jared was married to the queen and the threat of immediate danger had passed, it had probably lost its allure.

"We're not going anywhere with anyone," Evie said.

"If they arrest us we'll have to go."

"We haven't done anything to get arrested for."

REEF unbuckled his seat belt. "I will go see what they want. Stay in the car." Opening the door, he appeared calm, in control, but the muscles in his jaw were tight. He was uneasy. Her heart squeezed. He had so damn much to lose.

"Good afternoon," one officer said. He was muscular, bald with barely there eyebrows and eyelashes. His skin was pasty white, but his lips were plump and pink. He reminded her of a department-store mannequin. The other cop was older, nice-looking with a salt-and-pepper crew cut. He looked familiar. She'd seen him before, but where? He seemed to spend an inordinate amount of time studying REEF's face. "We'd like to bring you down to the station for questioning, Agent Sanders," the bald cop said.

Not on her life. Evie was out of the car in a heartbeat, marching over to stand at his side. REEF touched her shoulder before she could say anything. She bit her lip, boiling to tell the cops to go to hell.

"What is the nature and reason of this inquiry?" REEF asked.

Evie winced at his affected speech. She'd gotten so used to it that she didn't give it much thought, but now it was painfully obvious. Anyone familiar with Cavin would recognize it.

Salt-and-pepper's eyes sharpened, but Bald answered. "Your presence at Ka-blooms," he said.

"I already gave a statement to the FBI," Evie said. REEF tried to glare her into silence. She glared back. Those ice-blue eyes of his didn't intimidate her. The less he talked the less chance there was of the men figuring out who—and what —he was.

"We need a statement from Agent Sanders, as well, ma'am. Someone will give you a ride home when you're done, sir. It won't take long." The men backed away as if expecting REEF to go with them. Evie's arm was spring-loaded to grab REEF's belt if he so much as moved an inch.

"Got a warrant?" Ellen asked. She'd popped out of the car, pink-cheeked from the sun, the fast food bag dangling from her hand.

Evie gasped. "Ellen!"

"Well, do they? They can't question him without a warrant."

The kid was right. Hands on her hips, she turned to the police. "Well?"

"Look, ma'am, all we need is a statement to assist with the ongoing investigation. A small amount of administrative paperwork and we're done. Agent Sanders, you're in the force. You know the drill."

"We won't let you take him!" her daughter cried.

Evie took her daughter into her arms. "Damn right," she muttered.

Silent but self-assured, John walked up to the women in his family, laying a hand on each of their shoulders. Her son had that cautious, naturally protective streak characteristic of Jasper men. Ellen, on the other hand, seemed to have no such self-preservation skills, much like her mom when it came to protecting her own. A category into which REEF now belonged, she realized.

He saved you. You'll save him.

Something softened in REEF's expression as he took in the sight of Evie, Ellen and John forming a phalanx of protection around him. His surprise and pleasure made her want to weep. Hadn't anyone stuck up for him before in his adult life?

"As much as I'd like to accommodate you," REEF told the officers, "I cannot. I'm tasked with providing protection to this family. Therefore, I cannot comply with any request that interferes with my duties. Good day, gentlemen."

"Cooperation is in your best interest, Sanders," the familiar cop said. He uttered the name with distaste as if he found it personally offensive. "I sincerely ask you to rethink your decision."

"I stand by it."

The officers turned on their heels and returned to their car. A small gathering of neighbors moved back to let them pass.

"Yes." Evie gave her fist a little pump. "Victory."

"Omigod, that was so cool," Ellen said. John grabbed her by the arm and tugged her inside.

"Everything okay, Evie?" Cheryl called out.

"No. They won't leave me alone about what happened at Ka-blooms. I already gave a statement. They wanted to drag us down to the station for more. On a Saturday afternoon!"

The neighbors made noises of sympathy and support as they returned to their homes.

Evie sighed. "Thanks for handling that so well," she told REEF.

He scoffed at her gratitude. "It was not hard. You require search warrants, and arrest warrants. Had it been the

Ministry of Coalition Intelligence that wished my coopera-tion, they'd have extracted it whether I was in agreement or not."

Evie's heart skipped a beat, her gaze snapping up to the white-washed sky. His words were a stark reminder that the real threat to REEF wasn't her people, but his.

The Planet Sakka

The palace was in chaos. The Headmaster plowed through a sea of palace officials of every rank streaming into the Halls of Parliament. He needed to reach his superiors before the queen's address began.

"The Goddess walks amongst us..." Murmurs of awe whispered through the grand hall. Not once since assuming the throne as a child had the queen addressed parliament. Speculation had centered on rumors of dissent within the Holy Keep's walls, and how the queen would address them.

Nevertheless, an air of excitement filled the palace. It magnified the Headmaster's own good cheer. He'd found Oh-One. He'd found his precious REEF! *Just a little longer and you will be safely home,* he thought. *Patience, my boy.* The Headmaster chuckled at that. Of all the good qualities of his best assassin, patience was at the top. Obedience was a close second. His REEF would return to him. He had no doubt about that.

People had come from all over the Keep to glimpse the

queen, from lowly maintenance workers to Prime Minister Rissallen to the queen's consort, the Terran prince, Jared Jasper.

Terran, the Headmaster sneered. Oh-One had been held on the barbarian prince's homeworld all this time. If not for Atir's breakthrough advice to check Earth news, he'd be there still. Physically, the REEF had appeared unharmed in the photo he'd intercepted that morning. He wore a frown; his eyes were cold. It gave the Headmaster hope that Oh-One would be back to his duties within a short time.

"Praise the Goddess!"

As Queen Keira moved through the crowd, some touched her, some simply stared; still others dropped down on a knee, hands clasped under their chins.

"Rise and go with the goddess," the queen told them. More bowed, paying homage, their hands circling over their chests. The walls displayed images of simultaneous gatherings on Coalition worlds. A wave of her royal hand in greeting sent thousands of worshippers down to their knees all through the galaxy.

The Headmaster wondered what the godless Drakken thought of this. He was grateful for the Drakken, regardless. If not for the Coalition's age-old enemy, there would have been no need for the REEF program.

Must reach Minister Vemekk. Only Vemekk could authorize communication with Earth. The procession slowed, and he couldn't get around it. He boiled with impatience as the queen and her consort were enveloped by the pale blue robes of her attendants who formed a protective barrier between her and her subjects. Still, hands slipped through the bodies to touch Keira's sleeves or some other part of her. Serene, she smiled.

Odd that she'd remained in seclusion all of her life. Was it to keep her from learning how much power she possessed? Her subjects loved her. They'd do anything for her.

Much like his REEFs would do anything for him. His precious children.

Oh-One, I will have you back soon. Then we will fix what happened to make you disappear.

Everyone had finally entered the halls of parliament.

The Headmaster found Minister Vemekk. He despised the woman, but she was his direct superior. "Madam Minister," he said, bringing his fist crossways across his chest. His rows of war medals glittered.

But Vemekk brought her finger to her lips. She was eavesdropping on the queen's conversation with her prince.

"Give them hell, Sunbeam," he heard the Terran prince tell his queen, giving her hands a squeeze.

Sunbeam? The spoiled, tantrum-prone goddess?

"I love you," the queen said.

"I love you too," the prince replied.

Together, the Headmaster and Vemekk vented their disgust in a groan. So they did in fact agree on something. She glanced at the Headmaster, one silver brow going up. "What do you need?" Her dislike of him was less apparent today. Her focus was on the queen's address.

"I've found my REEF. Oh-One-Alpha is on Earth."

"Earth." Her eyes narrowed, shifting to the prince. "Whatever is your lost REEF doing there?"

"Apparently he is being used by the Terrans in the capacity of a guard for their royal family."

"Royals." She made a sound of disdain. "Jared Jasper, his family, they are commoners, all."

Shocked to the core, the Headmaster turned his attention to the prince. "Prince Jared is not of royal blood?"

"The queen is not aware." She lifted her finger to her lips, telling him the prince wasn't aware his secret was out.

"How long have we known this?"

Vemekk waved a hand. "Long enough to know Earth is no threat to the Coalition."

Granted, he'd buried himself away running the academy which served a double purpose of keeping him safe from the annoying intricacies of palace intrigue, but this revelation was huge. The queen's marriage was a sham!

The prince's life was now worth nothing. How long before he was dead? The rumors were correct—something was very wrong within the Coalition government. Whose side had Vemekk taken?

It didn't matter as long as she took his side.

Vemekk stepped away to take her designated seat in the front row along with the other leaders of the Coalition. He followed. "I must contact the Terrans and see about the return of my REEF."

She looked as if she were about to say no, but her gaze drifted back to the prince and narrowed malevolently. "Permission granted. Follow the contact protocol."

"Senator Jasper, you mean. The prince's sister."

"Yes."

She started to walk away. "Feel free to act as outraged as

you wish. Make it an intergalactic incident for all I care. Earth has fared too well for too long."

The Headmaster stood frozen in place as the intelligence minister left to take her place next to the prime minister. Her hand touched the man's arm. He leaned sideways. His gaze sharpened for only a moment before he turned away to view Queen Keira ascending the stairs leading to the podium and the throne that had gone empty for her entire reign.

Treachery was afoot.

The crowd hushed as the goddess lifted an arm in a signal she was about to speak. "Greetings," she began, innocent of the fact that betrayers might be in the audience. The Headmaster scanned the faces of those officials in view.

Should he sound the warning of what he'd just witnessed?

And start the rebellion early? A hearty no to that! He was going to reclaim his REEF first. Then for all he cared, the Coalition could go to hell.

But as he reached the exit, ignoring the curious glances of those in the audience, the queen's clear, regal voice carried to him: "I order an investigation into the series of assassinations and attempted assassinations that have been dismissed as tragic accidents."

Vemekk's predecessors, the Headmaster realized. Both intelligence minsters had died "tragically". Suddenly, he saw the intelligence minister in a new light. She was indeed a crafty bitch. If she rose to power from this, he'd be in a world of hurt—she hated him. Today she'd granted his request to seek repatriation of the REEF only because it was another way to destabilize relations with Earth.

He wouldn't give her that. He refused to be her puppet.

After a short pause to allow uneasy mumbling and hearty applause, Keira declared, "I will find out those responsible and, by the goddesses, I will rid the queendom of the collaborators!"

The Headmaster didn't walk to his offices; he ran. There was no time to waste. It was imperative that Oh-One be back in his possession before the Coalition government came crashing down.

———

A night without shut-eye loomed in front of REEF. He leaned against the closed door of his bedroom, arms folded over his chest, waiting until all sounds ceased upstairs and the family was finally asleep before he returned to the main part of the house. The hours ahead, he knew, would be interminable.

When it was silent, he proceeded to the kitchen to make a cup of the Earth beverage coffee that he'd come to enjoy. Tonight more than its taste would keep him drinking it. He'd come to rely on the stimulant to stay awake. If there was one thing he missed from his REEF days, it was the ability to go long periods without sleep, doing so without flagging energy, without mental cloudiness or confusion.

Perhaps, this night, it would be easier.

Even if it wasn't, he would not sleep. He would not give the REEF in him the chance to regenerate. There had been no more incidents like what had happened at the pool, but he didn't dare risk it by giving in to sleep and possible regeneration.

Staying awake would be a true test of his discipline. He wandered the darkened, quiet house, pacing to keep watch as much to stay awake.

His pacing brought him on a circuit of the rooms downstairs. He avoided the upstairs, not wanting to invade Evie's privacy—or tempt himself into invading it. Thoughts of her sleeping, soft and warm under her sheets, conjured a familiar ache between his legs. He willed away the images of slipping into bed with her, sliding his hands over her bare skin to find her breasts and hold them, to taste them, heavy and full. To roll her onto her back and love her...

To be inside her.

The ache sharpened and he swore, pausing by the window to peer outside into the night. A breeze blew in through the screen, cooling his skin if not his fever for Evie. He thought of her day and night, but most intimately at night.

Instinct, he thought. *Human instinct.* It was the time of day when a man should be holding his woman...deep in the night, the person with whom you were closest cradled in your arms. While he'd never experienced even the most tenuous emotional connection with a woman all these years, he knew that was what was missing in his life. He knew it without a doubt.

You are a man. Not a machine. If he said it enough, perhaps then he could win the battle waging inside him.

"I present to you the greatest game in the galaxy." REEF unfolded a cardboard square, placing it on the kitchen table. "Sech," he said proudly.

Evie smiled, carrying plates of scrambled eggs, bacon, toast, mixed fruits and home-fried potatoes to the table. John and Ellen were sleeping in. The house was quiet except for Sadie snorting in her sleep as she dozed in her doggie bed on the family room floor. "That's our Monopoly board!"

"*Was.* It is better served in this capacity. Not to fear, my alterations are not permanent." Shaking his head, he muttered, "Monopoly. Pointless Terran game, acquiring money and property—to what end?"

"To get rich," Evie said, biting into a potato.

"Bah. One's wealth is home and family. That is all that matters. Material possessions are but a temporary salve."

His voice took on a certain thickness that made her heart catch. *You're going to get him home, somehow.*

"Show me how to play Sech," she said softly.

He opened the board, smoothing both hands over the surface. "There wasn't as much to do in the evenings on Sandreem as there is here," he explained.

"No TV? No computer? No video games?"

"No."

She sipped some coffee. "Sounds like heaven. Although, I'd miss the Food Network."

"We probably could have used some better communications equipment but upgrading would have been complicated, I believe, and would have involved off-world travel. I'm sure that's why they never did. There were always more important things to do—like fishing or swimming."

Evie laughed. "My kind of planet."

"To my knowledge, only three individuals ever left Sandreem. My father, who enlisted as a teenager, and my great-uncle Magnus, who left to become a scientist and never returned. And me."

"What happened to Uncle Magnus? Was he killed?"

"I believe he was prevented from returning. We never received word of his death."

"You don't think he met an amazing off-world woman and had ten kids with her and just lost track of time?"

"No. He would have come home. No one leaves Sandreem and doesn't return." REEF's face took on that serious look when he was trying to hide emotion. Emotion was still new enough for him that at times he seemed self-conscious about it.

Soon, he'd go home too, Evie thought. He'd return to his faraway planet and she'd never see him again. She should be happy about it. Ecstatic. Yet, she'd learned the hard way that there was an awful poignancy in helping someone find their way and losing something when you let them go.

"My father did, however, bring home one treasure from his travels—Sech. It was a family treasure. As soon as I could hold a game piece in my hand, he taught me how to play."

He emptied a bag of plastic chess pieces that he'd altered. She picked up what used to be a pawn. It was etched to resemble an archer complete with a belted tunic. "How did you do that?"

"I heated a sewing needle with a lighter and used it to carve the lines."

"That must have taken you all night."

He shrugged.

"Didn't you sleep?"

"My rest was sufficient." He was focused on arranging the pieces on crisscrossing stripes made with electrical tape. Fatigue made small lines to either side of his mouth and shadows under his eyes. He'd drained his cup of coffee but hadn't touched the plate of scrambled eggs, potatoes and toast.

"Your eggs are getting cold," she pointed out, spreading homemade strawberry preserves on her toast as she pondered him.

He shrugged again. "My appetite is absent this morning."

That was a first. "Instead of playing, you should take a nap."

He gave her a long look.

"We had a crazy weekend, and you've been extra-vigilant making sure no one's stalking us." He'd scoured the area around the house after dark, making sure no one lay in wait, watching them, like the night before. "You were still up when I went to bed, and you were already awake this morning when I got up."

He answered with a dismissive grunt, taking the first of the Sech pieces between his strong fingers and setting it in line with the others like it. "You begin with your archers spaced so," he growled.

"Oh, no. I'm not letting you go grumpy on me again. You've been in a good mood for, what, almost twenty-four hours now. A new world record!"

His crystal-blue eyes stared at her in disbelief as she got up to add more cream to her coffee.

"Do you know what I think? I think the chaos here is finally getting to you. I tried to warn you, but, no, you wanted to come anyway. I figured you'd last a week, because you're tough, maybe ten days on the outside, but it's only day four and you're wiped out. I knew you wouldn't last—"

A chair scraped back. His hand landed on her shoulder, spinning her around. She almost dropped her cup of coffee, somehow having the presence of mind to hold on to it as he pulled her into a kiss, muffling her squeak of surprise with his mouth. She sagged back against the counter. He steadied her, holding her face between his hands, ever-so sweetly, as he deepened the kiss, exploring her mouth with confidence until she was clinging to him, her breasts aching to be touched, her crotch throbbing, as she made plaintive little sighs.

He moved away, but she caught him and tugged him back.

His chuckle was rich and deep. The sheer maleness of it made her tremble. His hot kiss turned the shivers into fire. If he could turn her on this much with his lips, she couldn't wrap her mind around what it would be like doing more. Her knees went weak at the very thought of taking him upstairs to her bed.

But REEF, ever the gentleman, the consummate professional, tenderly but firmly ended the kiss. Inches away, that amazing mouth filled her vision. It had formed a smug curve. "Just to prove a point," he said.

"Point?" she asked, breathless.

"That I'm not as tired as you think." He gave her one more quick, hard little kiss before he snatched the coffee mug from her hand's precarious hold and left her swaying on her feet.

He set the mug on the table, sitting down in front of the Sech board. Exhaustion was a condition that he obviously wouldn't admit to, not that she minded the method he'd chosen to prove his point. Mental note: inquire after his fatigue more often—*Are you tired, REEF? Oh, poor baby. You must rest! A nap will do you good.*—and especially when the children were otherwise occupied.

She grinned evilly.

His brow went up. "Coming? I do not wish to play alone."

"Keep kissing me like that and you won't have to...*play alone.*"

To her delight, one of his famous man-blushes colored his cheeks with a hint of red. Evie, the old Evie, the sassy, original-edition, dusted-off, almost-mint-condition Evie, sashayed back to the table and slid into the seat, more determined than ever to discover the truth behind the former assassin's illogical sense of innocence.

FIFTEEN

"I'll be right back." Fresh from a whirlwind cooking session wherein she'd created several dozen extravagant chocolate-covered berries for a neighbor's party, Evie left the kitchen with a basket full of confections.

REEF noticed she'd attached a card to the handle that said Evie's Eden: a Garden of Berries. Excellent. It meant her dream was still alive. She smiled as he opened the front door, letting her out. "You ought to take a nap. We don't have to drive anywhere until noon."

"My rest is sufficient."

Since when had he become such an adept liar? Or perhaps not so adept. Evie didn't look as if she believed him. He was fine, though, perfectly fine. As long as he was on his feet, that was. Sitting was dangerous. Reclining was out of the question. "I should accompany you."

"No," she said almost harshly, as if she feared for him. "I

mean, no," she amended in a softer tone. "It's just three houses down."

He lifted a brow. "Too dangerous of a venture for me?"

They exchanged challenging stares. "No. The less visible you are, the better," she reminded him.

He let an unhappy grumble reveal his opinion on the matter. However, if it made Evie feel more comfortable, so be it; he'd comply. Only because she was going to be three houses away, as she said.

"Agent Sanders?" Closing the door, he turned. Ellen stood in the center of the foyer, her hands hidden behind her back. A suspiciously hopeful expression lit up her face.

"So. In your mother's absence, you've come to collect on my debt, eh?"

"Not all of it. The first part." From behind her back she pulled a large book. PHOTOS. He recognized the word from his sessions with the Gatekeeper.

She brought it over to the dining room table and opened it. As he watched over her shoulder, she leafed through the album. He caught glimpses of the years gone by: Ellen as a baby with her brother and parents—Pierce with his arm around a younger, more innocent-looking Evie (who was far more beautiful now, he decided)—sitting smiling on a blanket at the beach, Ellen snowboarding with her Uncle Jared, Ellen in a blue dress with her grandparents and great-grandfather in the front of the White House, Ellen with an assortment of pets of every description. A happy, normal childhood. He'd experienced enough years of his to know how very fortunate she was.

She stopped turning the pages when she reached a spread

of older, black-and-white photos. He immediately recognized the Coalition scout ship the Terrans called the "Roswell saucer."

"Cavin gave me these. They were taken in Nevada, you know, the same place you stayed when you were sick. It's also where the saucer is hidden. It's so cool! Did you get to see it too? Did you go inside?"

REEF smiled at the girl's bold curiosity. Her eyes were alight with wonder as if expecting to discover the secrets to the universe in his face. "I have seen photos only, like you."

"But you know all about spaceships, right?"

"I have my share of knowledge, yes."

"I'd like to know what some of the parts do"—she pointed to the faster-than-light stabilizer vanes and the over-pressure relief conduit on the underbelly of the star drive—"and what to call them." She lowered her voice. "These pictures are secret so please don't tell people outside my family that you saw them. Or that I have them. I promised Cavin."

"You have my word. However, your mother should know we had this conversation. My duty is to protect her, not keep secrets from her."

Ellen looked a bit guilty. "I should probably tell her I know."

"She told me it wouldn't be long before you figured it out, but, yes, the sooner you tell her the better." He gazed down at the small, vintage Coalition scout vessel. "The ship's name is *Shakree*. That's an unusual name for a spacecraft but fitting due to its tiny size. A shakree is a type of seed pod found on many worlds. When opened, it releases tiny seeds attached to silken sails that can be carried off by the winds."

Ellen sighed, smiling. The girl was a space explorer at heart, he realized. An Earthbound girl with dreams of the stars. If he had the power, he'd bring peace to the galaxy so that she could achieve what was obviously her dream.

He returned his attention to the ship. A marking to the right of the name gave him pause. A familiar marking, one he didn't recall seeing—or recognizing—during the photo album sessions with the Gatekeeper. *Then, you did not have your past unlocked. Now you do.*

He blinked as his pulse picked up. Surely his tired eyes were playing tricks on him. A closer look proved the image was no trick. The little scout ship was emblazoned with the Sandreem symbol for High Sun Day. "Always be with the sun," he murmured.

Sandreemer... His hand shook as emotion welled up inside him. A Sandreemer flew this ship. A Sandreemer like him! He swallowed, his throat aching with unshed tears.

"Is that part of the name?"

He shook his head. "It is a symbol from my homeworld. It represents High Sun Day. It's a festival that celebrates the first time every summer that the sun stays above the horizon all night. 'Always be with the sun.' It's good luck to have it painted on your boat—or ship."

They pondered the dented and scratched little scout vessel.

"It didn't work," Ellen said after a quiet moment.

"No, it did not." Dying on a remote world was not unusual for an exobiologist, but an exobiologist painting his ship with the High Sun good luck symbol was—a ship that met a bad end on Earth so many years ago. It was like meeting a long-lost brother across time.

Or great-uncle...

Goddess be. Great-Uncle Magnus. Could the *Shakree* have been Slipstream's vessel? Had Earth's infamous Roswell saucer, the spearhead of Coalition contact, been piloted by REEF's relative?

"Are you okay, Agent Sanders?" Ellen watched him curiously.

"Yes. Yes, I am." REEF shoved fingers through his hair and smiled at the girl. "In your quest for knowledge, you have given me an unexpected gift."

"The High Sun Day symbol?"

"Indeed. And I believe I know who piloted the saucer. He may even be a relation."

"Really?" The wonder was back in her eyes.

With Ellen's rapt attention on him, he described the various parts of the ship. "We have improved over this technology many times," he explained. "It is a very old ship."

Footsteps skipped up the front porch steps. The door flew open and Evie breezed in. It always amazed him how much cheer and energy she could bring to a room. "So, Ellen's holding you captive with her pictures, I see." REEF exchanged a meaningful glance with the girl, who nodded.

Evie closed the door, her thick hair swinging from her ponytail. She turned back to them and paused, her smile faltering. "Okay, what?"

"Mom," Ellen began, poking her thumb in REEF's direction. "You don't have to worry about keeping it secret anymore. I know who Agent Sanders is."

Evie's shocked attention swerved to REEF. "You told her?"

"She told me."

Evie sat down at the table. She saw the album opened to the photos of the saucer and pinched the bridge of her nose. "Dare I ask how you figured it out, Ellen?"

"I remembered him from the police picture. And I just knew we'd help if Jana asked. That first day I tried to get him to confess at dinner, but he wouldn't."

REEF folded his hands over his chest. "A confession she finally won while at the swim meet."

"Yeah. Kayla's mom was hitting on him, and—"

"Kayla's mom was?" Evie's cheeks took on a pink tint. Her green eyes blazed as she glanced from REEF back to her daughter.

"REEF was trying to blow her off and—"

"You were?" Evie asked him, softening.

"—then Michael's dad showed up in uniform, and REEF thought it was trouble. Kayla's mom got in the way and—"

"My combatant instincts took over," REEF finished. "I shoved her hand out of the way perhaps a little too forcefully. I frightened her."

John had wandered into the conversation. "I would have done anything to see that."

Evie threw up her hands. "And where was I when all this happened?"

"In the snack bar," Ellen said.

Evie sighed, tucking a lock of hair behind her ear. REEF's fingers twitched. He'd do that for her, if he could.

"Why didn't you tell us, Mom?" Ellen asked.

John sat down too. "You never keep secrets from us."

"I was afraid your father might not understand if he learned we were providing help to the REEF, who as you know isn't a REEF anymore. He's human now, and we're trying to get him home." With her characteristic compassion, she related his history, his capture and his desire to return home to Sandreem.

"I suppose now the right thing to do is to tell your father the truth," Evie finished.

"No," both teens chorused.

"A lie of omission is still a lie," she said.

"But if he makes us live with him..."

"I'd hope that's not what the courts would decide, but if they do, that is your father's legal right."

Bullshit, REEF wanted to say. Pierce claimed he cared about Ellen and John's welfare, but it seemed his intention was to use them as leverage—to hurt Evie.

"Does that mean Agent Sanders wouldn't be our body-guard anymore?" Ellen asked.

"My loyalties lie with you," REEF told her. "And your mother and brother. I will protect you, all of you, until I cannot do it anymore."

"Well, we're not going to say or do anything that's going to make you leave us," Ellen put in defiantly. The girl snatched her photo album. Hugging it to her chest, she stormed away from the table. John's departure wasn't quite as dramatic but no less unhappy.

REEF spoke up when they were gone. "Would you stand by idly if I were to give up my freedom as easily?"

"It's not the same thing." Evie studied her hands.

"Isn't it?"

"There are courts and judges and family law attorneys. We have laws..."

"Just because something may be legal, it doesn't necessarily make it right. You have spent your life standing up for others. At some point you have to stand up for Evie Jasper Holloway."

The pearl dangling on a chain between her breasts trembled. With his heightened senses, he could almost sense the flutter of her rapid pulse. "I think you're right."

He took her hand. The soft, warm strength flowed from her to him. He brushed his fingers over her knuckles in wonder. How casual his ability to seek out human contact had become, he realized with a start. Only last week he'd found it difficult giving and receiving hugs from the older couple who had nursed him back to health. Or perhaps it was easier now because the object of that touching was Evie.

His vision blurred. Blinking gave the sensation of sand in his eyes. Too many nights awake, he thought. Coffee no longer helped. He had to fight off mental confusion at every turn. It took every last bit of clarity and focus he had.

He feared he was close to hitting empty. He didn't know what would happen when that occurred. He hoped to the goddess that when it did, Evie and the children were nowhere nearby.

He arched his back, stretching stiff muscles. Too many pushups. Too little rest.

"I'm really getting worried about you," Evie murmured. "What's going on?"

"Leave me to fight my demons," he growled, and prayed

Evie respected his wishes. If she did not, the compassion she gave so freely to others could very well see her killed.

Hours into another consecutive night without sleep, REEF wandered back to his bedroom. He glanced at the soft bed. He'd slept in it but once during his stay, the first night here. If he continued to be successful in his efforts to go without sleep, he would not lie in it again.

Ah, how he longed to lower his body to the plush mattress, to let his head sink into the pillows, to inhale the fresh scent Evie had misted on the bedding as he drifted away into slumber...

He blinked awake, staggering. Goddess help him, he'd almost fallen asleep standing up. He dropped to the floor and pumped off several dozen pushups.

On his feet again, he once more faced the luxurious bed. Sleep sounded so appealing on a basic, elemental level. It lured him closer to the bed.

No. He pushed away from the door and shut it behind him. *I will fight this. I will not go back to what I was before.*

Only a few more days, he thought, dropping to do more pushups followed by a punishing floor exercise routine; all he needed to do was stay awake until the end of the week. Then his bio-mechanics could have him for all he cared. Once he was no longer in Evie's company, it did not matter. If she were out of arm's reach too far away to kiss, he wouldn't be able to hurt her.

The next morning, Evie walked through the house looking for REEF. She found him in the garage, using John's weights to work out. It looked like he'd been there for hours, sweating, his tank top clinging to his damp, golden skin as he pumped iron.

She leaned against the door frame, savoring the view. An empty coffee cup sat on the floor nearby. He'd been drinking a lot of it lately, bypassing alcohol completely. It was almost as if he was compelled to keep moving. He refused to relax, jumping to his feet before it could happen. With each passing day, his lean features looked gaunter. He claimed nothing was wrong, that he wasn't feeling sick or tired, but the hollow look around his eyes scared her.

Obviously, he took his job of protecting them too seriously. Yet he'd kept them safe all these days. He'd chased off the press, and the police he sent away hadn't returned. Never in her life had a man taken the job of looking after her so seriously, or done it so well. The deal they'd struck had gone beyond simple obligation. With each other all day long, they'd begun to care about each other in a way that neither felt comfortable addressing.

Sadie snarled and snapped in her arms. "Hush. I wish you two would get along again. I like him." But the little dog's upper lip slid higher, revealing tiny fangs.

Her phone rang, startling them both.

"Go outside with Grandpa's girls, baby." Evie pushed an indignant Sadie out the doggie door to join the pack of adopted dogs clustering around the glass door.

The phone kept ringing. Evie hummed as she cooked breakfast, taking a peek at the caller ID. It displayed Cavin's cell number. He and Jana checked in daily. Yesterday had been a double-contact day with REEF asking Cavin to pass along word to the Gatekeeper on his discovery of the symbol on the Roswell saucer.

Turning, she poured a cup of coffee.

"Aren't you going to answer?" Fresh from a shower, REEF appeared in the doorway, a towel slung over his shoulders.

"Yes. But waiting before I do gives me a sense of power and control."

He snorted softly and walked into the kitchen, carrying his empty cup to the coffeemaker to refill it. The dogs behind the glass door immediately backed away, tails between their legs. All except Sadie, who stood her ground, growling from behind a cloud of steamed-up glass.

"Good morning, little canine," he called out, to her obvious outrage.

The cats observed him from their perches in the living room, no expression in their drowsy eyes.

In the midst of all the noise, Evie finally relented and answered the phone. "It's a great day in Roseville. Evie Holloway speaking. May I help you?"

"Evie," her sister's fiancé said.

"Cavin," she replied, imitating his accented, serious tone.

"We have news."

Instead of feeling excited, a wave of apprehension washed over her. "What kind of news?"

"A breakthrough. For REEF. Very good news."

She took the phone from her ear a moment. REEF stood in front of a window in the family room that looked out at the oak trees in the backyard. He stood there, framed in leafy sunshine, *Earth* sunshine, his hands curved around a Starbucks mug. It was as if the moment were captured in freeze-frame, a turning point, from where every moment past and every moment from that point forward would diverge. *He's leaving.*

She knew it without a doubt.

And you have to let him go. More, you have to encourage him to go. It's the right thing to do.

He didn't belong here. He was a fish out of water, a caged exotic animal.

He needs to go home.

Last week she'd have jumped for joy at the prospect. Now she felt nothing but desolation. REEF had brought something back to her that she'd thought was lost: the old Evie.

"REEF?" She cleared her throat to get rid of the nerves she heard in her voice. "Cavin says he has news for you. It's good."

He took one look at her face and said, "Put the call on the speaker."

"I think he wants to talk to you in private."

"No." He appeared adamant. "What I hear, you hear."

She tapped the speaker icon, sending Cavin's voice into the room. "REEF?" he said.

"I am here, Caydinn." REEF walked closer.

"Jana and I have spent all night in conference with the president of the United States and the few leaders who know of your existence and predicament. We have been in conference since yesterday when we were contacted by the Coalition's Ministry of Intelligence. They want to repatriate you, REEF."

Evie sat down. It was more like her knees gave out; there just happened to be a chair under her butt to catch her.

REEF wore no expression. She hadn't seen his face so completely devoid of feeling since he'd first arrived.

"The Headmaster of the REEF Academy contacted us personally. He wants to bring you home."

Sharp hatred appeared in REEF's eyes along with a flash of fear. "Home? Or back to the Academy—and the lab—where they can *repair* me?"

Evie heard Cavin consulting with Jana and other unknown voices in the background. Then arguing. It sounded as if Jana and Cavin didn't agree with what was now being proposed.

"REEF, this is Laurel Ramos."

"The president," Evie whispered, her eyes growing wide.

"The Coalition is very concerned. You are, to them, a valuable weapon that they do not want to lose."

"Tell them I'm broken. That I'm no longer of use to them." REEF stalked across the room to the phone. "Tell them I was dismantled by one of their own."

"If we refuse to hand you over, it might be seen as an act of war."

"We're already at war," Evie cried out. "Ms. President," she added, wincing, as an afterthought.

The voices rose on the other end of the phone. More arguing. "He can't refuse," someone said. "This will cause untold problems...." "He's not really human." "Yes, he is!" "What defines a human, tell me? How do we know he is in fact one of us?" "What rights do we allow him if we don't know what he is?"

REEF walked to the coffeepot to pour a cup. His hand shook once, spilling some coffee on the counter. Evie walked up behind him and slid her arms around his waist. He stiffened at first then relaxed in her hold. His free hand came around to cover hers.

"The Coalition wants him back," President Ramos said. "Quite frankly, their reasons make sense. The REEF is a powerful weapon."

Evie slipped her fingers between REEF's warm ones, silently assuring him of his humanity. "You're no damn piece of equipment," she whispered fiercely, tears spilling from her eyes. "You're a man I admire very much."

His breath shuddered, his hand convulsing over her fingers. She felt the brush of his wrist scar over her knuckles. "You're free," Evie whispered to REEF. "No one can make you go anywhere, or do anything you don't agree to."

"If he refuses," the president was saying, "we're looking at a grave threat to what admittedly is a very shaky peace treaty with the Coalition. Our prince is married to their queen. That's all we have. And he's not even a prince!"

"But they think he is," Evie argued, turning to the phone. "Jana, can't we squeeze out a little Jasper family influence and get the queen to help smooth things over? She's a goddess. All she has to do is say the word and REEF's off the hook."

Jana's voice sounded strange. "We've lost contact with Jared."

Evie couldn't wrap her mind around anything happening to her big brother. She pressed her hand to her stomach as a wave of terror and nausea swept over her. "But he's okay, right?"

"Don't know. Communication's been sporadic for a while now. We thought the worst, maybe a coup or a Drakken attack. Finally, yesterday, the intelligence ministry assured us that the absence of communication is due to Jared and Queen Keira being caught up in their royal responsibilities."

"That doesn't sound like Jared."

"I know," Jana said almost too softly to hear over the debating going on in the background. Her sister was scared to death. It was contagious. They were both extremely close to Jared. It took all Evie had to push her fears for her brother aside in order to focus on the problem at hand.

"If REEF doesn't want to go back, why does he have to? What if he defects? Can't Earth grant him political asylum?"

"Evie," Jana said in amazement. "That's brilliant."

Evie managed a brief but smug grin. *Brilliant* was a word often used by or about members of her family—but not her. Never her.

REEF appeared shocked. "Defection would mean renouncing my allegiance to the Coalition."

"Your allegiance for your freedom. Say it," Evie urged. "Say you want to defect and you'll be free."

A spark of hope lit up his sky-blue eyes. In those eyes she saw the flicker of his memories, all the years he'd lost. She saw how he'd suffered at the hands of others, the powerlessness

he'd felt having no free will. The hard line of his mouth softened as he turned his gaze to her. He wanted his freedom.
One look in those eyes, and she knew.

"Quiet!" Jana's voice broke through the chaos in the Oval
Office. Cute, blond, small, her sister was a force to be reck-
oned with in the political arena, as she was now, facing down
an anxious president and her top brass. "REEF—political
asylum, if granted, means giving up your Coalition citizen-
ship to be a citizen of Earth. Is that what you want?"

"I am a Sandreemer, not an off-worlder. Not a Terran."
His voice carried clear and firm. "The choice I make is based
not on loyalty but on freedom."

He took Evie's hand, as if such a big, strong warrior
needed her support. Yet the way he gripped her, almost to the
point of pain, she knew somehow that he did. "I, Eriff of
Sandreem, guest of California, formerly REEF-01A, hereby
request political asylum. I wish to defect—to Earth."

SIXTEEN

Reef paced across the deck in front of where Evie sat in the big cloth hammock under the oak tree. The day was warm but under the enormous tree it was cool and still. For once the house and yard were quiet, with John and Ellen spending the day with friends. The dogs were in hiding—from both the sun and REEF—under the deck.

Evie had brought two iced teas outside to the table after they'd hung up the phone but REEF refused to stop pacing long enough to drink. "Just watching you exhaust yourself is exhausting."

REEF's intense, bloodshot gaze swerved to her. His jaw was rock hard, stubborn. "I will not be the cause of tension between our worlds. I will not be responsible for us going to war."

"This is not your war! It's been going on for centuries. We just got dragged into it."

"Know this, Evie. If it comes down to my freedom or the

threat of Earth's annihilation, I will not choose freedom. I would choose repatriation if it keeps the peace."

Evie wanted to scream "no!" but it would mean stripping him of his inborn sense of honor. He'd been stripped of nearly everything a man could lose. She wouldn't take the last of what he had as much as it broke her heart to keep silent.

Besides, she still had her backup plan. The crashed spaceship. If they lost all their other options, they'd still have escape as a last resort. *If* it were flyable.

He continued to pace. Turning, he almost staggered. The stumble was almost undetectable and corrected quickly, but in a man whose every move was blessed with the beauty of agile grace, it demanded attention.

"Sit down. Rest. REEF, this time I'm not taking no for an answer."

He exhaled. "My rest is—"

"Sufficient," she finished for him, rolling her eyes. "That's what you keep telling me. I see something different. I see a man who's gone beyond exhaustion to the point where he can hardly stand up."

He was tuning her out. She changed tactics. "How can you protect me in this condition?"

Angry, he spun around. "I am in this condition so I *can* protect you." His throat moved. He ran his arm across his forehead. He seemed strung out to the limit, tense beyond belief—and so very tired.

"When was the last time you slept?" she asked. "When, REEF?"

"Not since the first night I was here."

"What?"

He refused to meet her eyes. It was almost as if he knew she'd be pissed—and she was! "You can't be serious." She was sitting forward in the hammock as it rocked precariously. "You haven't slept since *last Friday?* You've been up for five nights? REEF, tell me I'm wrong."

His eyes gave her the answer she didn't want to know.

Shit! She thought back to their conversation where he'd revealed his fear of turning back into a REEF. "This was what you meant when you told me you had to fight your demons."

His jaw moved. His fists opened and closed. "Yes."

"Sit down." She patted the hammock next to her. "Just sit with me."

"Evie..."

"You need to get off your feet before you go catatonic."

He lifted a skeptical brow. "Catatonic? I think not."

"I think so. And then where will I be? I'll be facing the mob alone. And the FBI. What am I going to do when the press comes to the door? Or those annoying policemen? How am I going to get rid of them if you're facedown on the floor?"

He heaved a great, put-upon sigh and joined her. Deep and doublewide, the hammock creaked under the added weight. They sat crosswise, rocking gently, legs dangling.

He wore his heavy shoes. Her feet were bare. His hands were clasped in his lap. Hers clutched a plastic solo cup of iced tea. "Just kick back and look at the leaves, REEF. I do that when I need to relax. I look at the pretty leaves." She tipped her head back to admire the ancient tree's green-blue canopy. "Ah..."

He sat stiffly, or as stiffly as someone could sit in a hammock. She elbowed him. "Look at them, I said."

He let his head rest on the hammock. "Evie," he tried again.

"What is the main issue here? That you'll have a REEF dream and try to hurt me?"

"Yes."

"A quick nap. I'll watch you. If you don't get some sleep soon, we're going to be bringing you to the hospital next. Then they'll make you sleep—with drugs."

He made a grunt of disapproval.

"I didn't think so," she said, smirking. "So, nap time with Evie, or an Earth hospital pumping you full of tranquilizers? Your choice."

He reached across their thighs and found her hand, clasping it in his strong fingers. "A nap would be nice," he admitted. "A short one."

"Short," she agreed.

Holding hands, they rocked back and forth, listening to the soft noises of the leaves rustling above. After a few minutes, his eyelids drooped, opened, and fell again. Finally, he let them stay closed. "So tired, Evie..."

"I know," she whispered. "Just a short nap."

"Short..." His breathing deepened.

She lifted her head and took a peek. He was asleep. It happened that fast, proving he must have been exhausted beyond belief.

Evie smiled. The way she saw it, this was her chance to cuddle without repercussions. She let her head fall to his shoulder as her hand flattened on his stomach. His breathing remained slow and steady. She cuddled closer and sighed. He smelled like the spicy soap she'd bought for his shower. He smelled like REEF.

It had been so long since she'd been with a man like this, snuggling close, inhaling his scent, drawing strength from his warm body. Far longer, she was sure, than it had been for REEF being with a woman.

What kind of lovers had he chosen over the course of his life? Had any of them ever affected him? Pierced his REEF armor and touched his heart? A pang of jealousy met the thought.

She smoothed her hand possessively over his abs, aching to explore him, all over. She wanted to lose herself in him. To see him lose himself *in her*.

Her body came alive with desire, and she muffled a groan. He was *asleep* and he was turning her on! It was crazy!

He needs to rest. And you need to behave.

She popped off the hammock, leaving it swaying. REEF shifted position, his hand searching for her in his sleep. "Trust me, my hot spaceman, I want to be there too. But you need to sleep undisturbed."

Making him more comfortable, she lifted his heavy legs, dropping them on the hammock proper. Now he was stretched out all alone and comfy. She settled onto a lounger to sip iced tea and watch out for him as she'd promised. When she'd been next to him, he'd slept, still and calm. With her gone from his side, he was increasingly restless, his muscles tensing.

"Okay, you miss me. I like that." She walked back to him, trying to figure out where to fit her body on the hammock. His arms flung wide as he shifted position. His facial muscles tensed, his eyes moving side to side under closed lids. He was dreaming. Probably, she should wake him up. No. He was exhausted.

Luckily, he settled down. A subtle tremor ran through his body, his nostrils flaring. Then he fell unnaturally still.

Her heart skipped a beat. Was he breathing? Yes, but barely. Too shallow. "Hey, you. Time to wake up."

His head rolled sharply in her direction. He'd reacted to her voice. She froze. Instinct stopped her from going any closer. "REEF—?"

His hand shot out and grabbed her throat. It happened so fast she had no time to scream.

The world spun, and she was slammed up against a vertical deck post. Wind chimes over her head jangled. Sparkles exploded like confetti behind her eyes, fiery pain lancing across her throat. She clawed at his hand, but she didn't stand a chance in hell of budging it.

REEF! His chokehold wouldn't let even a whisper of sound leave her throat.

His eyes were wide-open, locked on her. Flat, frigid, it was the scariest gaze she'd ever seen.

He will watch you die and feel nothing.

This was why REEFs weren't seen as human. *This* was why he considered himself a monster.

But inside, he was REEF—*her* REEF!

Dimly, she was aware of Sadie, snarling as she tugged on REEF's pant leg. His grip was immobile, an iron vise. The pain where his fingers squeezed her neck, the pounding in her head, the indescribable hunger for air, the cold terror— she was drowning in sensation, all of it bad.

You're going to die, here in your backyard. And when REEF finds out what he did, he's going to kill himself. The thought ranked right up there with the idea of leaving her kids to be raised by Pierce and Angela.

She wasn't sure what possessed her to do it, but she stopped fighting. She threw her arms over REEF's shoulders, her knee sliding up his thigh as she molded her body to his, a lover's embrace. *REEF, see me. Feel me. You know who I am.*

Something sparked in those cold eyes. Shock. Torment. Self-awareness.

Humanity.

His hand released some of its pressure, allowing her to sob in a breath of air.

She didn't run; she embraced him tighter and pressed her lips to his sweating jaw. *Come back. Come back, baby.* "Eriff," she gasped. "You are Eriff of Sandreem. REEF, not *a* REEF. Hold me, babe. Hug me back."

He made a horrible sound of pain that seemed to come from the depths of his soul. The machine was battling the human inside him for control. It played out in his unblinking gaze, and in his body. Still curved around her windpipe, his fingers convulsed but didn't clamp down. REEF would not allow the REEF to choke her.

"Goddess," he said harshly, looking down at her. The ice in his eyes had thawed, leaving behind raw, human emotion. He whipped his hand away, staring at it as if it were a smoking gun. Then his horrified gaze shifted to her. "Your neck...I hurt you."

"I'm fine." She fought to catch her breath. "You let go the minute you knew it was me."

He wasn't hearing any of it. "I can see the outline of my fingers on your flesh. The bruises. I could have killed you."

She grabbed his wrist. "But you didn't. You realized what you were doing. You stopped yourself—"

"I can't be trusted to protect you anymore. I'm too dangerous."

"I didn't stop you, REEF. *You did.*"

"What if I was armed? What then, Evie? What if I had my gun in my holster?"

"You fought the machine and won. I watched you. REEF, this is huge. You can beat this. You can beat it. You have the power to override the kill order."

"I'm too dangerous."

"You have the power."

His expression told her that inside, he knew she was right, that he'd controlled the hardware inside him. He wanted to believe he now ruled the REEF inside him, that he called the shots. With all his heart, he did. "If I hurt you again..."

"You won't. You can't."

His voice cracked. "How do you know?"

"I trust you." Tears streamed down her face. "Let me show you, baby. Let me show you how much." She took his hand and gave him a fierce tug.

She led REEF through the family room and the kitchen, and up the stairs. Once upstairs, she headed straight for her bedroom. Amazing that he let her get that far without protesting or asking questions. He was probably too dazed to argue. He was taking it hard, what happened outside. How could he not? It was what he'd warned her about, what he feared most. Now it had happened.

The incident had been intense but over in seconds. The ache in her throat had already faded. REEF, however, would no doubt beat himself up over it. He'd glower, he'd grump. He'd probably keep threatening to leave. She was going to redirect that emotion. She knew exactly how she was going to do it too. Call it Terran Academy, graduate level.

"Evie," he said finally, crossing the threshold of her bedroom. "What are you doing?"

"Taking you to bed."

The former assassin peered at the frilly, feminine richness of her room, a fluffy comforter, ruffle-edged pillows, plush carpeting in cappuccino, surrounded by cream-colored walls. How many times had she imagined his hard body stretched out on those sheets?

He followed her gaze to the bed and frowned. "I do not think sleeping is a good idea."

"Who said anything about sleeping?" She shut the door with her foot.

He stood there, dumbfounded, as she unbuttoned her blouse and slid it off her shoulders. She felt a little shy doing a striptease—she hadn't tried to seduce anyone since Jason Behar, the captain of their high school water polo team, drove her home in his brand-new pickup—but she couldn't stop now. She was a woman on a mission.

Unsnapped, her denim shorts fell to the carpet. Dressed only in her bra and panties, she walked to REEF. Letting her hair spill forward, she gave him a come-hither look she hoped was hot enough to melt his defenses.

"Evie," he tried again.

"Hush." She dragged a finger through the valley between

his pecs, following the line down to the waistband of his jeans, stopping just short of the bulge below. His breath hitched. Good. The more he thought of himself as a cyborg, the more determined she was to remind him that he was a man.

"There's only one way we're going resolve this trust issue, and that's by making love. It probably sounds like an ulterior motive on my part, and maybe some of it is, but I don't know how else to prove my complete and unconditional trust than by being in bed with you, naked."

She reached around behind her back and un-hooked her bra. "Skin to skin." Her breasts fell free. She was standing in front of a fully dressed man in nothing but her panties and those weren't much more than a few strips of cotton and lace.

His eyes had turned a deeper blue, radiating a different kind of intensity. For a second or two, self-consciousness threatened her plan. She hadn't been with a man in three years, and the sex with Pierce had hardly counted. Then she heard a harsh breath, and REEF saying gruffly, "You look like a goddess."

Smug, she smiled. As long as he thought that, she had a chance at the rest. "And you're wearing too many clothes." Dressed, he could still run off. Naked, he'd have to think twice. She tugged on the top button of his jeans.

"Evie..." His tone held a note of warning.

She sighed. "Evie, what? Evie, I'm dangerous? Evie, I'm changing into a cyborg? Please." She popped the button. "If you don't want to be with me, you're going to have to come up with a different excuse."

"Evie," he said. "I'm a virgin."

SEVENTEEN

"You, a virgin?" She laughed. "You still don't know how to lie." She grabbed the hem of his T-shirt and helped him pull it over his head.

He wadded up the fabric and threw it aside. She smoothed her hands over his ripped abs. His stomach muscles clenched, reacting to her touch. His skin was so hot, so smooth. Falling slowly to her knees, she dragged her mouth down to his belly button, kissing him there. His next breath was a hiss. One yank opened the remainder of the buttons. He sprang free, his huge erection straining the thin cotton of his black boxers

She heard the thud of the back of his head hitting the wall. "Evie," he warned, his hands covering her hair. "You are about to cross the point of no return."

"Oh, thank God." She closed her fingers around him, moving from tip to base in one firm stroke. He jerked in a spasm of pleasure. She smiled. Playing fair was not part of the plan.

He swung her off her feet. The room spun and she landed with a *whoosh* on her back in bed. The weight of his body pressed her deep into the plush bedding. His kiss was hungry and thorough. Ah, that mouth...that incredible mouth.

He was better than chocolate. He was the best thing she'd ever tasted.

She wanted more.

A deep sound rumbled in his chest in reaction to her greediness. He hadn't uttered a single protest since they'd hit the bed, she noticed. Good. The point of no return had been passed.

Virgin—ha! Her hands slid over his back as they kissed. Down, down, down went her fingers until she'd wedged her thumbs in the loosened waistband of his jeans and pushed them over the tight rise of his butt. Together they rid him of his jeans and boxers, and then her panties.

His mouth was on her breasts, plucking, licking, and suckling the aching tips. Sensation arced from that point of contact, settling between her thighs.

His hands smoothed down her torso, then the insides of her thighs as he kissed his way lower. "May I, Evie?"

"What? Yes, yes," she gasped. He felt he had to ask permission?

When his lips found their target, the spasm of pleasure was so intense that her body gave an involuntary jerk. If that's what his mouth could do, then she could only imagine—

His tongue answered her prayers, and her eyes rolled

back in her head. She thought she might have shouted, "oh fuck," but she wasn't sure. All coherent thought seemed to have evaporated.

His eagerness drove her wild. It made her wanton, wild. Her thighs fell open, and her hands closed in his hair. "I want to give you pleasure, Evie." His fingers slid through her folds then dipped inside her. "Do you like this?"

His question translated to fireworks. He was asking her what *she* liked? How did that happen? she wondered, dazed. This was supposed to be about him, not her. He'd changed the rules.

"Or, *this?*"

"All of it," she gasped as he brought her to the brink. The pleasure pooled, throbbing hot. The quivering built to an ache that swelled until it was almost unbearable.

She grabbed the bedsheets in her fists, panting, trying for some kind of control, but she lost it, too fast, way too fast, her body clamping hard around his fingers, climaxing after only a few more intimate caresses.

REEF popped his head up, his weight on his elbows, observing her from between her thighs with a mix of wonder and smug satisfaction. "You found your pleasure," he said in that adorable accent.

Nodding, she tried to form words. "*You* found it, baby. I want you to find it again." She reached for him. "Come here. Let's make this good for you too."

He rose up over her. His handsome face was darkly intense as she guided him into position, hugging him with her legs.

"I only hope I do not disappoint you, sweet Evie." The

feel of his blunt tip nudging her opening made her shiver as he breathed, "My goddess..."

"Disappoint? Are you crazy?"

"Only a realist." He pushed a little deeper, and she could feel him tremble. "The fact remains that I've never been with a woman. I have never even kissed one. Until you."

Her eyes widened. "You really are serious." She realized he hadn't been exaggerating about being a virgin. Finally, the aura of innocence about him made sense. "Oh, REEF," she whispered. "I'm honored to be your first."

Something softened in his eyes that made her heart twist. He maintained that eye contact as he penetrated her with one thick glide. He groaned, and she twined her arms around his neck, her pulse spooling up with anticipation.

His eyes scrunched half-closed, his expression shifting from wonder to astonishment to tenderness, and finally hunger as he withdrew slightly then pushed deeper, sending delicious spasms into her belly.

His slow, forceful strokes reflected the level of control he had over his body. REEF might be a virgin but he was no teenage boy.

You are his first. She'd never been anyone's first anything. The realization made her giddy. It made her laugh with joy. And it made her cry. She smiled and sniffled, raining kisses anywhere she could reach, his jaw, his heaving shoulders, his throat. "You feel amazing," she told him, taking him deep inside her body. "Incredible."

Perspiration beaded on his forehead. His expression tightened with her praise and the pleasure he must feel. She guessed he would not last long, it being his first time, but she was wrong. He seemed to draw on that discipline he so often talked about, his rhythmic motions gaining force and confidence, stoking her desire.

Her moans of delight urged him on, until he at last rose up on his arms, his face contorted in pleasure. Then a groan burst from him, his body clenching. "Ah, Evie!" His peak seemed to last forever before he pulled out, collapsing in an exhausted heap next to her.

Reaching blindly, he hauled her close. His entire body shook in the aftermath of the orgasm.

She cuddled with him, inhaling the scents of his skin—soap, sweat and sex.

A few beats of silence went by, then he let out a quiet chuckle. "Wow."

She grinned, smug as she trailed her fingertips over his chest. Mission complete.

Their first time, Evie had practically torn off his clothes. The second started and ended with an in-depth exploration of her body. Now, REEF lay on his back, holding her close while she recovered. Her thigh was flung over his leg; his hand rested on the curve of her buttocks. Life, as the Terrans liked to say, was good.

Evie's fingers moved in a lazy circle over his chest. "Was going without sex a personal decision or just a matter of following the rule of abstinence?"

"It was neither." The issue of his virginity fascinated her no end. To his amazement—and relief—the idea aroused her rather than repulsed or disappointed her. "Physical desire interferes with a REEF's ability to carry out missions. The same command device that ordered me to kill regulated my sexual drive."

"You were medicated." She came up on an elbow, her expression furious. "The control they had over you was sadistic. And the Headmaster thinks you'd come back voluntarily?"

"He doesn't know my master implant was removed. He thinks I'm merely damaged and able to be repaired."

"Tell him to go to hell. You're not a piece of equipment."

"I wouldn't know who the Headmaster was if I met him face-to-face." His yawn was huge and jaw-cracking. The lovemaking had made him forget his sleep deprivation. They'd been so focused on discovering each other to worry about anything else. Now, once more he was reminded of his battle with fatigue. "I don't ever recall meeting him," he said. "Caydinn told me the Coalition military lives in fear of him assembling his own personal army of bioengineered combatants. Thus contact between REEFs and the Headmaster is forbidden."

"I'd like to see all you REEFs turn on him. Now that would be sweet justice." She rolled onto her belly, her breasts swinging free, her hair spilling forward. Her lips were plump and kiss-swollen. The musk of their lovemaking lingered along with a faint echo of vanilla. Goddess, he loved the way she tasted, and the cries she made when he did so.

A note of mischief crept into her voice. "It would also be sweet justice if you didn't let *that* go to waste."

He followed her sly gaze. He was fully erect. He'd

expected it would be necessary to wait for the passage of some sort of recovery period. Not so, apparently.

He smiled. "Sweet justice, indeed." His fatigue forgotten, he rolled her onto her back.

Evie hummed as she made a circuit around the bedroom, closing the curtains, lighting scented candles, putting on soft music. Chamomile and lavender; he recognized the scents that she had taught him.

REEF lay on his back in bed, watching her. "What are you doing?"

"In cooking terms, preparing the ingredients."

A ceiling fan stirred the cooled air. The room was already a haven. She'd taken all that was peaceful about it and amplified it. "There," she said, rubbing her hands together. "Now you're going to nap."

"Evie..."

"No arguing." She returned to him, slipping between the sheets. "Resistance, as we Earthlings say, is futile."

"Actually, that rather sounds like a Drakken expression," he said, coming up on an elbow. Smoothing back her hair, he gazed down at her. Sunlight filtered through a crack in the curtains, casting light on her shoulder and the faint, pink bruises mottling her neck. A gut punch of shame accompanied the sight.

She saw the direction of his gaze—and his thoughts. "I'll hold you while you sleep. You won't have the nightmare. You know I'm right."

Human contact was the tether connecting him to the world. When she'd embraced him outside on the deck, he was able to escape the REEF impulses. He'd overpowered the KILL order. If not for that, he wouldn't dare contemplate closing his eyes now. "Hold me," he said harshly. "Do not let go."

"I won't."

He held her tight to his body—Evie...his saving grace, his anchor to humanity. The sharp edges of exhaustion softened, blurring. His eyes grew heavy. Finally, he let them close—a conscious decision.

If he could not trust his ability to be human, who else would?

———

In the time it took to blink an eye, it seemed, Evie was kissing him awake. Her fingers trailed over his chest. "Wake up, sleepy-head. It's been almost three hours."

"Three hours!"

"Yes." She appeared proud and excited.

"With no incident?"

"None." She circled her fingers over his stomach. "You slept straight through. And you don't snore!"

He laughed, grabbing her close for a kiss. Holding Evie had staved off the REEF. He had a vague memory of hunting while he slept, but no KILL orders got through. He'd maintained power over the monster inside him. He couldn't explain the phenomenon any more than he could explain how his bio-threads could regenerate in the absence of a master implant, but surely it was reason to celebrate!

"We've been lying abed for some time now, my goddess. It's time for some refreshment." Scooping her into his arms, he carried her, laughing, from the bed to the bathroom and into the spacious shower. He turned on the water with a shove of his hand, kissing her as they bumped up against the wall.

Water gushed down, shocking cold then blissfully warm, sluicing over their bodies. He chased streams of water over her breasts with his mouth, suckling the pink tips to the sound of her sighs of delight. As she clung to his neck, he returned to her mouth, kissing and nibbling her soft lips before angling her head to kiss her with a surge of hunger. She kissed him back even harder, making her desire known.

She was as hungry for him as he was her. Intoxicating, that. His lack of actual experience no longer fazed him. Animal instinct had long since taken over, guiding him, potent and insatiable.

The wet heat of her body, her snug passage squeezing him, nearly undid him as he thrust into her.

"Baby, give me *more*..." Her voice was throaty, demanding. He thought he might hurt her with his force, but the harder he took her, the more she cried out in pleasure. He'd made it his goal to indulge her desires, and he did so now. It was about time Evie Holloway was on life's receiving end. After all the taking he'd done in his past—taking lives—giving was something he relished.

He pleasured her until he felt the throbbing that he'd learned signaled her orgasm. She cried out. Her back arched as her thighs squeezed him. "Omigod," she panted. "You are so amazing."

Her exuberance made him smile. She held nothing back, his Evie. Her passion was evident in every aspect of her life, but never more so than now, making love with him. In life, she walked carefully inside the lines; with him, she was utterly uninhibited.

It was how one should live always—no holding back, each day savored. It was what he vowed to do with his own life now that he'd won it back.

When he finally let go, he lowered his head and kissed her with an intensity and depth of emotion he never knew he possessed. As recently as last month, he *hadn't* possessed it.

Evie Holloway had awakened more than his humanity. She'd awakened the man.

———

With a picnic of foods spread over the kitchen table between them, they shared a snack, pausing every few bites to caress and kiss. So, *this* is what you feel like after having the best sex of your life, Evie thought. Muscles unused for years ached. She was tender in places she hadn't remembered were there. Yet, with a few kisses for encouragement, she was ready to jump back into bed with him. Maybe it was because no one had ever made her feel the way he did.

Or maybe it was because nobody ever made him feel the way *she* did.

She loved the way he'd been acting since they'd made love and since he'd napped—carefree, almost boyish. Happy.

The bitter, remote assassin was gone. He'd completed his transformation before her eyes.

From the other end of the house, the front door slammed open. Evie jumped apart from REEF, startled.

"Mom!" It was John. *"Mom!"*

Something was wrong. Her son never yelled; the kid was as cool as they came.

She scraped her chair back and ran to him. John crashed into her. *Alone.* Horrifying visions of Ellen crushed under the tires of a car flooded her mind. "Where's your sister?"

"With the protesters. Come on!"

Evie's heart lurched—again. "What protesters?"

"Come on!" John repeated and ran. She stumbled outside after him, and stopped short. Her neighbors were gathered in the front yard gawking at a small group waving signs that said ET GO HOME!

"Who are these people?" Evie demanded.

Cheryl folded her arms over her chest, wary as she glanced at REEF then looking hard at Evie. "They think your bodyguard is the REEF."

"They never did find the body," Sandy put in, equally suspicious. Her husband thrust a flyer into Evie's hands.

COINCIDENCE OR COVERUP? On one side was REEF's photo from the front page of the newspaper; on the other, a police sketch of his likeness. She remembered that sketch. It had been based on details given by the security guard, an off-duty patrolman, the night REEF and Cavin had their shootout showdown. The rendering brought back memories of when she hated the REEF as much as everyone else. The sketch and all the others made from eyewitness accounts of REEF's hunt for Cavin were supposed to have been destroyed.

Evie crushed the flyer into a ball. "There goes our cover story."

It was as if she'd pulled the ring on a hand grenade; her neighbors stepped back that fast. "But he underwent surgery," Evie assured them as REEF stood stoically by her side. Weariness shadowed his gaunt, pale face. She wanted desperately to hold him and soothe him, but it would be too much too soon. He wasn't supposed to be an alien let alone her lover. "He's just like us now."

The neighbors' attention shifted to REEF. Standing there, cold, remote, silent—no doubt in an attempt to hide his real feelings—he looked anything but like them.

Cheryl pulled her aside. "You brought him into our neighborhood? He's been walking amongst our children? Oh, Evie."

Your family is dangerous. She dreaded Pierce's reaction once this went viral.

"It was by order of the President of the United States and my family. I couldn't say anything. I was sworn to secrecy. It was a witness protection program. I was asked to hide him."

Except, hiding REEF wasn't what she'd done. She'd brought him into her life, her world, treated him like part of the family. *Got naked with him.* She remembered his tender kisses afterward, and swallowed hard.

"Good God, Evie. You're in love with him."

Heat exploded in her face. *In love?* Too soon, way too soon. Yet the thrill of possibility drowned in the fierce denial that followed. "That's crazy, Cheryl!"

"ET, go home...ET, go home..." the people in the street began to chant, seeing REEF.

One shouted, "It's time he paid for his crimes against innocent people!"

"He's a *monster!*" cried another.

REEF, stoic until now, seemed to flinch at that. Her heart twisted. The hours they'd spent in bed should have convinced him he was no monster even if nothing else had the entire week they'd been together. Yet, underneath it all, she knew he harbored secret doubts about his humanity. This would only make it worse.

"ET, go home...ET, go home..."

"You're the ones who don't belong here!" Ellen's voice rang out. Her daughter stood in the middle of the street in a face-off with a man Evie didn't recognize. Her daughter didn't reach higher than his barrel chest, but she was advancing on him, giving him hell. "You go home!"

"Ellen!" Evie cried, horrified.

She ran to her daughter, John and REEF following. REEF would not hesitate to protect Ellen if he thought she was in danger. It was the last thing Evie wanted him to do. It would feed into exactly what the protesters thought he was: a hostile monster.

"Where are your loyalties?" the protesters shouted at Evie. "With the aliens or with us, your own people?"

"It's time he paid for his crimes!"

"He saved my mom's life!" Ellen shrieked.

"No, Ellen." REEF took her by the arm, pulling her away from the protester. "Go inside."

"But he called you a monster," Ellen argued tearfully, trying to wrench free.

"Don't hurt her, space invader!" The man took a swing at REEF with his sign. It whooshed toward Ellen's head. REEF used his arm as a shield and tore the sign from the man's hands. His piercing blue eyes didn't do anything to help his cause. Murderous glares weren't conducive to public sympathy.

Evie took a weeping Ellen into her arms just as a highway patrol car rolled up the street, lights flashing. Her heart hit bottom. Her mouth went dry.

The Highway Patrol car pulled over to the curb and stopped. Inside, a bald officer was on the radio. The other officer observed REEF with narrowed eyes. Heaven help them. It was the same two cops as before.

"What seems to be the problem here?" Bald Cop called out pleasantly. As he and his partner approached, REEF moved closer to Evie and the children. His natural instinct was to protect, not to kill, but these people didn't understand that.

"REEF, let's go." To her own ears, Evie's voice was fierce, guttural.

"ET, go home! ET, go home!"

The protesters were chanting louder now. Evie glowered at them. She couldn't help thinking of Disney's *Beauty and the Beast* when the villagers came to rid their town of the perceived monster. All that was missing was the burning torches.

"Are they going to arrest him, Mom?" Ellen asked.

"I don't know."

"It was only a matter of time, Evie," REEF murmured to her. She hated the inevitability in his tone. "The officer on the left is Greg Rowe. He was the guard I encountered during the incident at the motel."

Incident, hell. It was a shootout. Evie's stomach knotted out of fear for REEF. Greg Rowe. Of course! Now she knew why the officer with the salt-and-pepper hair was familiar. Soon after the invasion was averted, she'd watched an interview from Rowe's hospital bed. REEF had melted his gun, burning his hand, before he floated him twenty feet in the air. He'd called REEF a cold son of a bitch. When it became known that REEF was dead, he'd expressed disappointment that REEF would never be held accountable for his crimes.

REEF could have killed Rowe that day. His mercy had created an enemy.

"We received a call about a disturbance," Bald Cop said, glancing around. "And that's what we have. Sanders, I'm afraid you'll have to come with us."

"Not without a warrant." Evie would call her father, or Jana. Surely Jasper political clout would diffuse this incident. It would definitely send a "hands-off" signal to the police.

Rowe produced the warrant for REEF's arrest. She was sure she saw a flash of triumph in his face before it was gone. All he needed to legally arrest REEF was probable cause, and they had more than an adequate reason to believe REEF had committed a crime. Namely an eyewitness—Rowe himself.

"I'll call Jana." Evie patted her pockets and swore. "My cell's inside."

Rowe opened the back door to the patrol car. "Sanders?"

"Wait!" Evie cried. "Senator Jasper won't allow this. He's part of a witness protection program."

"She can come down to the station and fill out paperwork."

"And President Ramos? I'll have you know his presence here has the blessing of the United States government!"

Rowe said. "Please, ma'am. It's only for some questioning."

"That's all," REEF assured her.

"How do you know *that's all?*"

"Because this has been accomplished through proper legal procedure. Your system has safeguards."

How could he be so calm? As soon as he was out of her hands, something bad was going to happen to him; she knew it.

"ET, go home! ET, go home!"

Blinking back sudden tears, she pleaded with him silently not to go. *I have to,* his eyes said. He squared his shoulders and stepped toward the car. Rowe patted him down, found his holstered gun and confiscated it. Then REEF slid into the darkened backseat, behind the cage separating him from the front seat.

Captive, all over again.

EIGHTEEN

Evie ran after the departing police car for a few stumbling steps. Feeling helpless, she stopped, arms hanging limp at her sides, watching the car until it disappeared down the street.

Sickened, she turned back to the strangers in the street and her shocked neighbors. Cheryl stepped forward as if urged by the others. "Evie." The woman sounded quiet but her eyes radiated the kind of protective determination seen in the eyes of mothers who lifted two-thousand-pound cars off their kids. "We don't want him living here."

"It's for the best," Sandy agreed, nodding.

Evie looked at each of her neighbor's faces in turn. They'd been through years of raising kids from preschool to now, block parties, borrowing of cups of flour and lawn mowers, and countless barbecues both before and after the end of Evie's marriage. Sandy and the other neighbors were her main social support outside her family. They'd helped out in tough times, celebrated the good times. She'd been one

of them. No more. "You're kicking me out of the neighborhood."

"We're sorry, Evie."

She almost grabbed her "perky Evie" face and slapped it
on. *You're right, it's for the best,* her automatic response would
have been, staying true to her image as an upstanding,
suburban mom and helpful neighbor.

REEF's words echoed: *"You are so quick to say yes, to
accommodate others. You take on everything with cheer and
grace. But what does Evie Holloway want?"*

She thought of REEF and the long chain of events and
people that had brought him to this point, alone and lost on a
faraway world, separated from his family, grappling with a
stolen life, a *ruined* life. Would she be yet another link,
someone who turned her back on him, who treated him as if
his rights didn't matter, that he was inferior to everyone else
here? Would she abandon him when with his resiliency and
capacity for affection against all odds was head and shoulders
above them all?

What does Evie Holloway want?

She wanted justice, damn it.

Evie stood tall. "If he goes, I go."

Her neighbors appeared shocked by her resolve. She was
sure she heard someone gasp. Sweet Evie standing up for
herself? Yes. Damn it, yes.

The desire to do what was right heated her passion. "Let
me tell you about your 'monster,'" she said, emotion straining
her voice. "Your 'monster' was abducted from his family as a
little boy and turned into a weapon against his will. His mind
was wiped clean of all his memories. *All* of them—of a mother

who loved him and now thinks he's dead, of a father who lost his only son. He had sisters, a village. A future. Until the recruiters came and forced him to be a REEF. Your *monster* was a child, surgically invaded by hardware designed to take away every last bit of his humanity. When he came to Earth to assassinate Major Caydinn, it was on orders he couldn't ignore because they came from inside his head. He was programmed to kill a man he'd never met, whether he wanted to or not."

She could have heard a pin drop on the street that sunny afternoon. Even the protesters had gone silent.

"The heroes responsible for saving Earth found him, broken and almost dead in the desert. Instead of killing him, or imprisoning him, they took out the machinery that controlled him. We on Earth gave him back his life. We gave him back his *humanity*. And now you want to take it away. I won't let you. I won't."

Warm fingers slipped inside her left hand. Ellen's. Another hand covered her shoulder. John's. Standing flanked by her children, she managed to catch her breath but was unable to stop the tears tracking down her cheeks. "He saved my life, you know. He protected me from a gangster's bullet by putting his body in the way. He would have died for me. He'd die for you too, if he thought it was the right thing to do. When it comes to honor and courage, he equals the men in my family, and maybe even surpasses them because of what he's survived in his life. Yes, your *monster*," she added with contempt. "He has a name. Eriff of Sandreem. I won't turn my back on him."

"Me, either," Ellen said.

"Or me," John said.

Evie drew them close. Her voice carried louder now. "What happened to Eriff is happening to other people of every race and on almost every continent all over the world. Kids, over a million a year, some as young as five, are being forced into sexual exploitation, begging, plantation work, even the military—just like Eriff was. Parents give their children away for a new goat or a few coins, thinking they're doing them a favor. Or slave brokers pluck them right off the streets in broad daylight. You're fooling yourself if you think the police care. A missing kid in a Brazilian slum generates about as much interest as a dead fly. Yes, the odds against defeating slavery seem overwhelming, but we must not let that—or apathy—silence us. The consequences are too terrible to imagine."

Trembling with emotion, she met her children's eyes. They didn't appear embarrassed by her outburst. On the contrary, they seemed proud, enormously proud of their mother. She choked back a sob of relief, of joy, and, yes, even pride in herself.

This is your moment of truth. The idea lurking unspoken in her subconscious burst to the surface. *This was what you were born to do.* Not selling berries—that was just a path to this point—but taking her passion for human rights and instilling it in others. The silent crowd gave her no confidence that she'd had any effect on them at all, but tingles swept over her all the same.

"One by one by one," she finished. "One by one, we can beat this. Until the day comes where no more people own other people."

She dashed a hand across her nose and sniffled. "Come on, kids, we're out of here. Get the dogs, load them in the car. We're going to the ranch." It had been the headquarters for every Jasper crisis. Then she'd get REEF out of jail, even if it meant storming the precinct herself.

The Earth warden's station was crowded and noisy. Officers came out of every nook to stare at REEF as he was ushered past. After running the gauntlet of uniforms, he reached the front desk. A heavyset officer wearing glasses halfway down her wide nose shoved some paperwork at him. "Fill this out."

REEF tried to make sense of the small print. His barely mitigated fatigue did not make the job any easier.

"Name, address, date of birth and Social Security number," the woman snapped, tapping her pen on the jumble of symbols.

"I cannot read this language," REEF said stiffly.

From behind him, Rowe snickered. "What language *can* you read? Martian?"

"Speaking of reading, have you read him his rights yet?" The woman with the wide nose sounded annoyed with both REEF and the other officers. She shook her head and sighed when there was only silence in response. "You have the right to remain silent," she told REEF. "Anything you say can and will be used against you in court. You have the right to legal counsel now and during any future questioning. If you cannot afford an attorney, one will be appointed to you free of charge if you wish. Do you want to call someone?"

I have no need of advice on how to deal with moronic Terran bureaucrats, he wanted to say but he bit his tongue for Evie's sake. He would not put more strain on her reputation than he already had. Today he would make her proud. "My own counsel will be sufficient."

More muted laughter. REEF's fists twitched. He could take them out, all of them, easily, breaking necks, snapping bones. For Evie he'd behave. He'd come here to answer to his crimes and, he hoped, atone for them, helping bring closure to a part of his life he'd rather forget. Only then would he be free to start his new life. If enduring a short time of annoying Terran procedure was necessary to further that goal, so be it. A few questions, some administrative details, and he'd be done.

After producing ID and enduring the halting, rather humiliating process of having to recite his answers for the booking paperwork, he was led to the room for his questioning. It was small, approximately twelve Earth feet square. There were two chairs and a small, bare table. A storage cabinet lined one wall. A phone and a device for putting out fires were the only decoration on three white walls. A window dominated the fourth wall.

"Inside, please." He entered the room. Rowe and his partner came with him. Before shutting the door, they signaled silently for two others to stand guard, one on each side of the hallway, keeping the area in front of the window clear of onlookers. It was REEF's first indication that something was amiss. The second was the crackling tension coming from the two men in the room.

They had something to hide. What? REEF tried to

summon his sharp senses but weariness dulled the ability. Three hours of sleep in nearly a week. He could barely keep his eyes open and focused.

"Sit, please." Rowe waved at a wooden chair.

REEF did as he asked, folding his hands in an unthreatening way on his lap. The men's blood pumped with adrenaline. Bald walked behind him. REEF focused on the man's actions, his every muscle braced. Perhaps it was why he never saw the back of Rowe's hand before it flashed in his vision.

The blow was powerful too painful to have come from bare knuckles. His ears rang; his left cheek was on fire. Blood streamed from his nose. His hands hadn't moved from his lap. He hadn't cried out. He would not. It was a test of sorts, a trial by fire. Accepting the punishment the Terrans dealt out would prove once and for all that he'd won the right to be called human.

REEF lifted his head as blood ran from his nose and a cut on his cheek as Rowe was walking back and forth in front of him, ranting, "You thought you were so fucking tough that night, the big bad alien assassin, invincible robot. *Terminator*," he spat. "Well, this ain't no goddamn Schwarzenegger movie."

Silent, Bald continued to stand guard behind REEF.

Rowe ground brass knuckles against his open palm. "It's payback time. Here's a little vigilante justice, Terran style." He hauled back his arm and punched REEF in the gut.

REEF's breath exited in an agonized "oomph."

"How do you feel now, *alien*? Not so easy to be tough now, is it?"

This coward had the gall to question his fortitude? REEF

peered at the officer through a red haze of anger. In an instant he could have the man's throat in his hand. His windpipe would be crushed before Bald could do anything about it. *And what would you be then? A monster. A REEF.*

You will fight this. You will not go back to what you were before. You will prove with your deeds and your desire that you are part of the human race, not a conglomeration of hardware.

"That night you ran the poor senator down I should have killed you," Rowe said. "You fired your fancy Martian gun and melted my goddamn weapon. The burn was so bad, I almost lost my chance to stay on the force. That wasn't good, alien. It's time we evened the score."

KILL. Sensing a threat to his survival, his REEF impulses commanded neutralization. *You will prove with your deeds and your desire that you are part of the human race, not a conglomeration of hardware...* REEF chanted the words in his head like a prayer even as his mind urged him to do what he was designed to do—Kill.

Locked in battle with his other self, REEF focused on the floor and the splatters of blood by his shoes. Although the pain had lessened, his exhaustion was almost too much to fight. He swayed in the chair, his eyes unfocused.

"Look at my partner!" Bald kicked the back of his chair, jerking REEF to alertness. Rowe's hand floated in front of his eyes. The skin on the palm was unnaturally shiny and rippled with weblike scars. *You did that to him.*

It was only a fraction of what he'd done to others over the years. Visions of the kills he'd accomplished flickered once more through his mind. The vast majority of the hits had been quick, yes, but a few hadn't gone as planned. For the rest of his life he'd carry the images of those stares of terror before he administered the final blow, the futile pleas for mercy. Remorse filled him as never before. *You are human now, that's why.* Those same emotions he used to dread now gave him hope. They gave him power over the REEF inside him.

Love, he thought with sudden, overwhelming realization. Yes, love, the most complex of human emotions. Through Evie, he'd regained the capacity to love. It gave him the tools he needed to defeat the REEF. Now all he had to do was use them.

"Look at my hand," Rowe bellowed. "What do you have to say about that?"

"I spared you," he replied honestly, quietly.

"What did he say?" Rowe demanded.

"I said I spared you."

Rowe's fist came out of nowhere, hitting him in the face, the same spot as before, with a fresh explosion of pain.

KILL.

The urge to comply was strong. *No!* He battled the REEF, fighting the impulses his regenerating hardware launched as he despaired of the creature within him. It was growing stronger all the time. *What makes you think you had a chance at being human again? Is that enough to call yourself a human? Because you saved a life? Because you made love to a woman?*

No. Because he'd more than made love to Evie; he was falling *in love* with her. If anything gave him the chance to be fully human again, it was loving Evie.

You will prove with your deeds and your desire that you are part of the human race, not a conglomeration of hardware.

His head hanging low, he waged a silent battle with the REEF inside him.

Oblivious to his inner war, the men conferred, walked around him. He detected a new scent in the air. Something was burning. It smelled like hot metal. He heard the clank of something metallic on the counter behind him, and the hiss of a flame.

"Still good out there, Rowe?" Bald asked.

Rowe threw a tense glance out the window. "Yeah, still good." He now hefted a metal rod as he returned to REEF. The tip glowed, the light reflecting in his dark eyes. "Your secret's out," Rowe said, a strange expression on his face. "No one on Earth's going to want you hanging around now. But before you go home, ET, I've got a little souvenir for you." He brought the rod closer. "Call it a little Earth hospitality. Okay —hold him."

At Rowe's command, Bald caught REEF in a choke hold. He grabbed and held his wrist, turning his hand palm up. Rowe aimed the red-hot poker at his flesh. He was going to burn his hand the way REEF burned his.

Instead of anger or fear, calmness came over him. He knew the kind of men these two were. They were of the same vein as the red-haired captain and his sidekick, Major Atir. They were like the bands of Drakken skullers who raided planetary outposts, killing after raping and pillaging. The more horror the better. They thought of themselves as part of the human race, and yet the cruel acts they perpetuated told the truth.

They were the monsters.

You are better than them. Yes, no matter what the sins of

his past, no matter how imperfect he was now, he possessed something they did not. Decency—human decency.

"Just do it already," Bald snapped.

The rod hovered above REEF's open hand. The calm had turned into serenity. He sensed Rowe's increasing frustration in not being able to provoke or frighten him. If only the man knew how close to death he'd skated, multiple times.

"Lift his head. I want to see the son of a bitch's eyes when I stick him."

REEF's hair was grabbed, his head yanked back.

Rowe jabbed the rod down. "Holy fuck." He stopped inches from REEF's hand, close enough to feel the heat of the metal.

"He healed himself already!" Rowe sounded horrified. "Look at his face. Jesus. The skin's sewn together."

Shouting echoed from outside the room. The door crashed open to reveal what seemed to be half a squadron of soldiers. Armed to the teeth, they aimed their weapons at the two rogue policemen.

Evie, REEF thought with a weary, relieved smile. She'd gone to the highest levels to win his freedom. For once he was glad she was not very good at being a damsel in distress.

NINETEEN

When REEF walked into view, bruised and flanked by national guardsmen, Evie's heart sang out.

You're falling in love with him. The realization was clear and pure. She took her discovery and tucked it close, wanting to protect it and relish it before revealing it to anyone. It was like placing the most delicious piece of chocolate on your tongue. If you consumed it too fast, you lost the magic before you had the chance to appreciate it.

REEF walked stiffly as if he were trying hard to disguise an injury. What had they done to him? Blood stained his shirt. His face sported fading bruises. The cops had abused him. His bio-assisted healing hid the true extent of that treatment. Well, by the time the day was done, she'd make sure everyone knew.

REEF had suffered enough.

His eyes, ice-blue and wary, searched the crowded room. For her, she knew. She wanted to go to him, but was acutely conscious of the officials surrounding her: some members of her father's congressional staff, police, military, and two men in black suits and sunglasses—sunglasses *indoors*—who'd flashed CIA identification and looked suspiciously like Men in Black. And a colonel named Tom Connick, representing Jana and Cavin. They'd notice if she ran to REEF and greeted him in the way she wanted to greet him. They'd see her feelings for him. What would they say then?

She ached to run to him, hating that she couldn't. All her adult life the perceived expectations of others had held her back, dragging on her like a lead ball chained to her ankle. She acted on an overwhelming desire to please, not what she really wanted. She'd always come last, where she'd chosen to be. No wonder others treated her the same way. She allowed it.

Not REEF. From the first moment they met, he'd put her first. More, no one had ever challenged her the way he had: "What do *you* want, Evie?" he'd asked.

She knew what she wanted. She wanted REEF.

Driven by urgency, she squeezed out from between Connick and a guardsman. *Baby,* she thought. *I'm here.* REEF's gaze found her and went soft. Everything she could ever wish for she saw in those eyes.

She pushed past the people surrounding her and ran to REEF, flying into his arms. He caught her with a pained "oomph."

"Oh—I'm sorry! They hurt you, the bastards." He might be healed on the outside, but internal injuries took longer to mend. True anger blazed inside her. "I'll kill them myself. Where's your gun?"

He didn't let her escape. One handed, he crushed her close enough to feel the tremble that coursed though his body, to feel the gentle press of his lips on her hair. "No more killing," he said quietly. "No more."

No more pain, she thought. Only loving.

I love you, Eriff. She thought it hard, hoping the secret words somehow sank into his skin and made their way to his heart, to grow and flourish. The short time she'd known him allowed her neither second thoughts nor the courage to say the words aloud.

She'd tell him when they were *both* ready.

But for now, she'd love the way this big, strong soldier acted almost bashful when he caught sight of her. She loved that she'd been his first, and that he called her his "goddess". She loved how he made love to her as if he meant it. She loved that her discerning daughter idolized him, and that her son approved. She loved that he devoured her cooking bite by savored bite. And she loved his quiet strength, how it made her feel in his arms: safe, happy, *loved*.

Without saying a word, he conveyed with a long, grateful hug that he felt the same way she did. And so they stood there in the police station, embracing, their feelings for each other no longer a secret.

REEF was ordered to serve house arrest at the ranch. For his own safety everyone but him agreed. Official custody was out of the question—no one knew how many more police were bent on vengeance, or who would try to hurt him out of morbid curiosity, which they couldn't do to Cavin because of his protected status as a global treasure. REEF on the other hand was viewed as a global threat.

Ellen was the first to detect the shift in public opinion from hostility to sympathy. Someone had recorded REEF's arrest and Evie's impromptu, teary antislavery speech on their cell phone. The hits on social media were already in the low millions, headed fast for higher. The United Nations reacted within hours, calling a televised press conference. Promising to look into REEF's situation, the General Secretary said Evie had brought the issue to the American table.

It was surreal, seeing her little rant being used by the United Nations as a springboard to finally, seriously gather world support to end human servitude. Not just talk this time, or promises that were never fulfilled, but real, get-something-done support. It was everything she'd dreamed of, but she was too numb from nearly losing REEF to absorb it all.

By evening, Jaspers began gathering at the ranch. First to arrive was Evie's mother and father, tired, concerned, and fresh from a private jet ride from Washington. They sat with her and REEF in the kitchen at the same table where Evie had eaten most of her meals growing up. From intruder-invader to honored guest, he'd come full circle.

News from Jana and Cavin had put a damper on the celebration. Her father held an iced coffee as Evie's mother sipped strong Russian tea. "We've been unable to dissuade the Coalition from wanting you back. They've threatened to send a ship to pick you up—presumably for emergency medical treatment. They act as if the fate of the galaxy depends on it," her father said.

REEF reacted with a weary but contemptuous snort.

"All this has been discussed, or is being discussed at levels far higher than mine. Meanwhile, what it means for us as a family is this. Your ability to remain anonymous has been compromised, REEF. You will no longer be able to provide protection to my daughter in the way you would like and, I have to say, have done quite well. I understand you saved her life. For that you have the eternal loyalty of this family." Her father struggled for composure.

Equally moved, her mother added in her husky, Russian-accented voice, "Yes, you do, REEF."

"If I lose my career over it, by God I'll see you free," her father promised REEF.

REEF's eyes had turned very blue. For a moment Evie thought he might join everyone in tears, but he seemed to grab control of his emotions in time. "Thank you, sir," he said. He blinked, rubbing his face, looking as if he were going to pass out from exhaustion.

"I also understand that you have not slept in some time."

"Six days," Evie tattled.

"Five," REEF corrected. "Nights."

"Thanks to Evie, I've spoken with Cavin regarding your problem. There may be an experimental surgery to try, micro-surgery using lasers, to sever the regenerating bio-threads."

"I have had my fill of surgeries in my lifetime, but this is something I will try." *For you, Evie, I will,* his solemn expression said.

REEF emptied his cup of coffee. His yawn was huge and eye-watering.

Evie rose. "We'll talk more about it when Jana and Cavin

get here, and after REEF's gotten some sleep." She crooked a finger at him. "It's bedtime. Remember, resistance is..."

"...futile," he finished with a wry smile. Pushing to his feet, he followed her out of the room.

Smiling, Larisa Jasper turned to her husband. "I think we can safely expect to add one more extraterrestrial to the family, yes?"

"Agreed. But safely?" The congressman paused, sighing. "Barring a perfectly timed galactic miracle, no."

PEACE AT LAST!

Nearly bloodless revolution topples Drakken Empire. Earth to be holy shrine.

Reuters—one hour ago

WASHINGTON, D.C. (Reuters)—The Coalition has accepted the unconditional surrender of the Drakken Empire, President Laurel Ramos announced today at a press conference, ending days of speculation over the welfare of Queen Keira and her Earthborn consort, Prince Jared Jasper. For the first time in nearly a thousand years, the galaxy is at peace.

Planet Sakka, the Goddess Keep

After generations of mistrust, hatred and killing, once more the realm of the goddesses would exist under one flag, within one border and in peace.

The Headmaster felt like he was going to be sick.

How dare there be a revolution in the midst of rescuing Oh-One? It was as if the goddesses themselves were conspiring against him!

He strode through the palace, absorbing the celebrations, the tears, the scenes displayed on the wall screens of billions of secretly religious Drakken proclaiming loyalty to the goddess-queen. It was shocking. Some called it miraculous. From what he'd gathered from the streams of news, before their warlord's body was even cold, Drakken believers had started pouring out of the cracks. After millennia, they still worshipped the goddess. The war was over.

Over...

What happened when wars were over? No longer needed for defense, military forces shrank. Programs were cut. Nothing was too holy to fall under the ax of budget cuts, including the REEF Academy. *Including you.* The niggling dread he'd carried around all morning swelled until it choked him.

The wall screens now displayed Queen Keira's address to the entire galaxy. At her side was her barbarian bedmate and fake prince. Embarrassment simmered in the Headmaster's gut at the sight. The Coalition was better than this. Where was their pride?

"I declare planet Earth as a holy sanctuary of the goddess in honor of its being the birthplace of my beloved husband and hero of the realm, Jared Jasper," the queen began.

"Oh, please." The Headmaster groaned. Onlookers threw

him funny looks. "Cretins, all of you," he snapped. "This means peace. Peace! Do you not understand the consequences?"

Apparently not, judging by their blank stares.

"This holy ground is never to be defiled," the queen continued. "Earth will be defended for all time, but will never have to defend itself. Earth will forever remain under its own independent rule. Earth's leaders, you have stipulated 'no visitation' and we will respect your wishes."

No visitation? That further complicated his rescue efforts. The Headmaster hunched his shoulders, clutching his fists behind his back as he stormed toward the offices of the Ministry of Intelligence. The doors were locked and sealed. "Where is the minister?" he demanded of a palace guard.

"Why, in custody with the rest of the traitors." The soldier gaped at him as if he were a dolt for not knowing.

Vemekk, gone. There went his in-house support in retrieving his poor abducted REEF just as events on Earth had taken a turn for the worse. The Headmaster had been poring over Earth news. Obsessively Atir said.

Necessarily, the Headmaster argued. And now, Vemekk had the nerve to get herself arrested. And likely executed next, being that she was implicated in trying to overthrow the government! She'd abandoned him when he needed her the most.

He, however, would not abandon his precious Oh-One. *Do not despair, boy. I do not need Vemekk's permission to continue harassing Earth into giving you up.*

Time was of the essence. News revealed the horrifying fact that they were planning to operate on Oh-One, destroying him even further than they already had. Worse, the Terrans pitied him, calling him a victim. A victim! The Headmaster had never heard anything so outrageous in all his life.

Oh-One-Alpha was a thing of beauty, the pinnacle and perfect example of technology married to biology to create something far better. It nearly brought the Headmaster to tears thinking of his REEF mutilated. Thankfully, the basic inner structure of his bioengineering was still intact; it could not be removed without killing the human body. With a new master device installed, and with a little patience and therapy, he could be returned to normal operations, perhaps even better than before once the Headmaster uncovered and eradicated the flaw that made him go missing in the first place.

The Headmaster would work with the REEF himself. He'd bring Oh-One back to life with his own hands, just as he brought him to life all those years ago.

With that, an image of a small boy with black hair and pale eyes danced before his vision. Something inside the Headmaster went soft. Ah, yes. The child had been like a piece of raw clay begging to be molded into a masterpiece—a masterpiece to serve the Holy Queendom, his beloved Coalition. The Headmaster had achieved all that and more.

And now the meddling Terrans sought to shatter that work of art. They would not! As long as he had breath left in his body he would not give up on Oh-One, even if it meant putting his greatest, and now flawed, creation out of its misery.

TWENTY

The impact of "holy shrine" status was felt almost immediately. Earth was showered with gifts from all over the galaxy. If only those gifts could be distributed evenly throughout the planet.

To Evie's disgust, there were still people on Earth empowered by the enslavement, physical and economic, of others. The fight to end slavery was not yet over here, or elsewhere in the galaxy. While her involvement was closer to home, thanks to REEF's story Jared and his royal wife had promised to launch a full investigation into allegations of child servitude in the Coalition military, starting with recruitment practices by the REEF Academy.

With the war over and Earth breathing a sigh of relief, life for the Jaspers was slowly returning to normal. After saving the world, Jana could begin her long-delayed life with Cavin, and after helping save the galaxy, Jared was free to strengthen the love he'd forged with his wife, Keira. As for Evie, her immediate goal wasn't to save trillions. Just one man, and making him whole again. Step by step, she was helping him get there.

Everything was set for his trip home. To Sandreem. The spaceship was repaired and supplied for the journey—only a couple of day's distance from Earth due to their home planets sharing the same remote corner of the galaxy. They'd practically be neighbors, she thought, trying to ignore the ache of knowing he'd soon be gone. Oh, they'd keep in touch, she was sure, but it wouldn't be the same.

She decided to listen to the old Evie who said it was best to live in the moment. Problem was, present-day Evie wasn't so sure anymore that the old Evie was right.

REEF's upcoming trip to Sandreem was a source of fascination around the world. It seemed everyone loved the story of a long-lost son returning home, no matter what planet he came from. But first, surgery.

In a bedroom at the ranch converted into an operating room, a hospital mask covering her face, Evie stood by REEF's side as he prepared to go under the knife.

Everyone hoped the operation would stop the REEF part of him from issuing commands until he could be seen by a trusted Coalition medical team with the technology to repair him permanently.

The Headmaster of the REEF Academy had even offered to help, multiple times, but REEF wanted no part of the academy or its staff. Before anything was settled, the Headmaster had disappeared, surprising no one. Post-revolution, a lot of Coalition cronies were diving into cracks like roaches escaping from the light, disappearing into the Borderlands, the lawless buffer zone between the two former enemies. For now, "primitive" Earth surgery would have to do.

A surgical team specializing in micro-surgery had arrived by helicopter along with Jana, Cavin and Colonel Connick. Evie wasn't clear on who the colonel was, exactly, but apparently he'd been involved in the invasion crisis since it began and trusted by Jana and Cavin to deliver REEF to California.

"I'm leaving." Jana clutched Evie's arm. "Come get me when it's over, Evie." Her sister's pale face revealed her utter squeamishness when it came to blood—or the thought of blood. As brilliant and brave as she was, Jana fainted at the sight of a paper cut.

Evie smiled. "I will."

The only people left in the room were the surgeons, Evie's father, Connick and REEF, reclining, prepped and ready, in a special chair. His forearms had been swabbed with surgical antiseptic and strapped down. His biceps bulged as he unconsciously resisted the restraints. An IV ran into a vein, delivering valium and painkillers. "Need to stay awake, Evie," he slurred drowsily. He feared an ill-timed kill order could jeopardize the surgery. Against everyone's wishes, he'd demanded and won the right to be conscious during the surgery.

She crouched next to him, stroking his hair. It only made him sleepier. Then inspiration hit. Smiling, she leaned close and whispered in his ear, telling him in detail all the things she was going to do for him and to him while he lay helpless in her attentive, post-operative care. By the time the first cut was made, he was smiling too.

REEF woke to the sound of Sadie's barking. That infernal creature!

He winced, opening an eye. He couldn't see the little beast, but by the sound of clattering claws on hardwood, it was circling the bed. There was a soft thumping noise against the side of the mattress, as well. That he couldn't figure out. Perhaps the dog had armed herself, prepared in Evie's brief absence to do him in once and for all.

With his REEF functions once more disabled, his senses, his strength, everything had come back down to normal human levels. It was the best sign yet that the surgery had been a success. Unfortunately, it also meant that his self-healing had slowed considerably. He'd even relented to taking some Terran painkiller pills called Advil to dull the aches after the surgery.

Claws skidded, scraping the edge of the comforter, and he heard a snorting sound. So, this was how it would all end, he thought, a wry smile curving his mouth—the once-deadly assassin, a super soldier cyborg, feared throughout the galaxy, hunter of Imperial spies and Coalition traitors, would now meet a most-dreaded end.

Death by Chihuahua. Needled to death centimeter by centimeter, there would be no mercy shown by Sadie.

Then, something landed on the bed. Perhaps he *should* be worried.

Sadie poked her head over the mounds of bedding, her big brown eyes wide and moist. He could smell her bad breath as she struggled toward him, wading through a sea of blankets. She bounded onto his chest and crouched down playfully, her tail whipping. The thumping noise, he realized. Then the attack began, although not in quite in the way he'd expected.

Squirming, Sadie joyfully licked him on the face.

Proof that his internal hardware had been silenced.

REEF laughed. He circled her tiny rib cage with his hands and lifted her, grinning.

Sadie barked, trying to lick him.

"Oh, so that's how it is." Evie burst into the bedroom carrying a platter of something that smelled like heaven. "I leave you for a minute and you waste no time taking a new woman to bed. Humph, Sadie. I saved you from Sacramento County Chihuahua rescue. I thought that meant something. I guess not." She set down the tray. The dog seemed to grin from where she was curled up on REEF's chest. "Fine. You can have him." She turned to go.

REEF snatched her hand and pulled her onto the bed. She squealed, giggling as he kissed her.

"So, it's a threesome then?" Evie murmured as he slid his hand under her shirt to cup a lace-covered breast.

"Not unless you consider a threesome me, you and—" he gave her breast a gentle squeeze "—these."

"That's four," she said, laughing as he returned for another kiss.

There hadn't been much privacy at the ranch. He missed being with her. "Come home with me," he said in her ear.

She pulled back. "REEF, you know I can't."

"But you want to make the journey. I see it."

"I know, but, REEF..."

"Your parents said they'd watch John and Ellen. We wouldn't be gone very long."

"Two weeks!"

He tucked her hair behind her ear. "The children think you should go. Ellen, especially."

"Hell, *she* wants to go. It's all she talks about. 'Mom, I want to see another planet. Haven't you always wanted to see Earth from space? REEF says there's a ring about Sandreem. I bet it's amazing to see at night. Come on, Mom. Please?'" Evie heaved a big sigh. "It's been day and night."

"Then let's take her."

Her laugh was quick, harsh. "Pierce would have me back in court so fast my head would spin. I'm surprised he hasn't done it already. I keep waiting for that certified letter to show up."

Her back muscles were like steel under his hands. It amazed him how much tension came into her body when she thought of her former husband. The man still held such power over her.

It was a blasted shame, he thought. The woman who had done so much to shatter the bonds of millions of people around the world was unable to break her own.

He slid the tray of food toward him and inhaled deeply. "Ah, Evie. Italian food?"

"Baked penne. Jana asked for it, so I made us all a batch."

He brought a forkful to his mouth, closing his eyes in

deep pleasure as he chewed. "From the heavens," he murmured.

Evie glowed.

"I'm going to miss your cooking."

"It sounds like there's plenty of food there." She waggled her brows. "Fresh eel."

"But not like your cooking, Evie. I'll probably lose weight."

"You have to eat, REEF. The doctors warned you."

"I'll try."

"I can pack you some meals to bring on the ship."

"It won't be the same."

He made a show of savoring another bite. He tried not to smile at the way she stared at his mouth. He'd spent his fair share of time gazing at her kissable lips. He supposed it was only fair. "I've missed you these past few days," he admitted in a huskier tone. "I miss making love to you."

Her eyes darkened, her cheeks turning a pinker hue. "Me too..."

"No privacy here. Lots on the ship, though." He chewed slowly, deliberately, as he let his gaze roam over her body. The hunger he felt wasn't an exaggeration.

"Is there a bed?"

"Not as wide as this one; we'd have to snuggle. I wonder," he continued, feeling the heat building between them, "what it would be like making love in zero G."

She made a soft noise, maybe a swearword.

"But—" he shrugged "—you're staying behind, so I guess I'll never know. Two weeks..." He exhaled. "Alone, hungry, starved for companionship. And back on Sandreem with a family undoubtedly hell-bent on marrying me off after all these years."

"You're trying to get me to come with you," she accused.

He tried for a look of innocence.

"I was daring once, you know. I was wild. I wasn't afraid of anything. In middle school I was a handful, always getting into trouble, sneaking off with boys, driving without a license. In high school my middle name was trouble. Grandpa Jake was sure I'd either be pregnant or in jail by the time I was nineteen. He was right about the former." Her voice softened. "It changed me—marrying, becoming a mother. I knew without a doubt I'd finally found what I did best. I nourish people, REEF," she said fervently. "I feed their stomachs and I fill them up with love and make them strong, and I feel as if I've accomplished something. I don't need a college degree for that. I like being the one in this crazy world everyone can depend on, the heart of the home, the one who's always there...always...no matter what. I like who I am now...but I don't want to lose who I used to be, either."

She stood there, thinking hard, wrestling with her indecision. For a hopeful moment he thought she'd say yes; then she bent over and kissed him on the lips. "I need to go bang some pans in the kitchen," she mumbled and fled.

Bang pans? Sadie lifted her head, her sleepy eyes slits as she pondered her mistress's hasty departure. "Well, she didn't say no," he told the little dog.

Dare he hope Evie would make the journey with him? He didn't want to make it without her. After so many years of a solitary existence, he could no longer abide by it. He wasn't meant to be alone.

More accurately, he wasn't meant to be without Evie.

———————

In the intense heat of a July afternoon, the Jasper family gathered around REEF's spaceship, preparing to say "bon voyage."

Ellen walked around the outside of it, touching the hull with longing caresses, letting her fingers drag over the sunbaked fuselage. "This metal has touched space," she said. "It's visited other worlds."

"You'll have your chance someday," Cavin assured her.

Evie knew by the expression on her daughter's face that she wanted that chance now.

You have that chance now, Evie—take it!

She'd been so close to changing her mind and leaving with REEF that she'd even packed a suitcase. Second thoughts had her pushing the case back under the bed. There it sat, a testament to her fear.

The *whop-whop* sound of a helicopter approached. "Are we expecting someone?" she asked her sister.

"Not that I know of." Jana lifted her eyes to Cavin, who replied, "Beats me." He'd gotten a much better handle on Earth slang than REEF, but REEF was fast catching up.

The landing helicopter kicked up a storm of dead oak leaves and made the dried grasses of the pasture billow.

The whine of blades subsided. The door opened and Colonel Connick jumped out. He turned to someone sitting in the backseat, helping her down with care. A small woman with a shining smile blinked in the sunshine. Evie couldn't get a true feel for her age, but she looked to be in her seventies or eighties. She wore a crisp cotton dress and sensible shoes. Frizzy graying auburn hair was pulled back from her face in a bun. Freckles speckled her pale skin, and her brown eyes twinkled impishly. "There's my REEF."

Surprise and affection played over REEF's face. "The Gatekeeper." It was the government agent who'd hidden and guarded the Roswell saucer all these years, and who'd cared for REEF with equal care for months.

Jana and Cavin looked shocked. "Gatekeeper, you haven't left the farmhouse since the nineteen fifties," Jana said.

"Fifty-three to be exact," the old woman replied. "That's when I retrieved *him* and brought him back."

Him?

"Tom?" the woman prompted.

"Help me with this container," Connick called to REEF.

"Cargo?" REEF asked, scrutinizing the rectangular box.

"Precious cargo."

"Yes." The Gatekeeper's eyes gleamed. "The remains of the pilot of our Roswell saucer. Or what was left of him after the autopsy. May he rest in peace."

Mama crossed herself, murmuring in Russian.

"Uncle Magnus?" REEF dropped to his knees, pressing a hand in wonder on the long metal box.

"Yes, it is."

"You told me there was no body."

"I am a liar, young man." She didn't look sorry about it, either. "I've lied to every U.S. president since Eisenhower, and scores of generals. I've hidden your Uncle Magnus all these years and no one knew, not even my own husband. I did it because I wanted to give your uncle the one thing history denied him. Respect."

In silence they pondered the makeshift casket.

"I felt his remains deserved to rest undisturbed at the very least. Now he has the chance to go home. I waited until the last minute to make sure no one intercepted him before he got to where he needed to go."

"Home," REEF said, his voice gruff. "There he will be laid to rest."

There was hardly a dry eye left.

They loaded the box into the cargo hold.

REEF returned to her. "Come with me, Evie," he said. "I want you to meet my parents."

"On Earth that's what you say when it's getting serious."

His amazing eyes studied her. "Won't it?" he asked. "Isn't it?"

Before she could answer, he brought his lips to her ear. "I believe you feel the same."

I love you. Her secret almost spilled out, but she bit back the words she knew he'd want to hear. He was at a turning point in his life, returning home at long last. He needed to be free to make important choices—where he wanted to live, whom he might want to be with. If she admitted her feelings, he might feel obligated to her, the way Pierce had felt obligated, until it finally became too suffocating and he'd fled. Her breath caught with an echo of the old heartache and humiliation. She never wanted to feel that way again.

She turned away. REEF caught her shoulder and spun her back to him. Her hair whipped around her face, and he brushed it out of the way. His gaze was gentle as he brought a hand to her cheek. "My goddess," he whispered. "Have faith in me."

She pulled him down to her lips and kissed him soundly.

The Gatekeeper grinned, nodding her approval.

REEF climbed up to the hatch that opened to the cockpit, stopping there to gaze at her one last time. He was going home. Home. She shivered with an odd sense of destiny. She remembered the baby birds she'd set free when she was a young girl. After a few tries, they'd flutter and fly away. And then they were gone. She'd done the same for REEF, nursing him back to health, being there while he fought to regain his life.

Unlike those baby birds, REEF didn't want to fly off alone. He wanted her there with him as he took to the air for the first time. He wanted *her* to fly.

By God, she did too. Hadn't she always felt that her wings were clipped?

What was she so scared about? It was just a two-week trip. His ship was as safe—or safer—than any Earthbound airliner. The war was over; there was no threat to their safety. As a mom she had little reason to worry. Her parents would be here to watch the kids. What was she waiting for?

She spun around, finding John standing close. She searched her son's face. *It's your turn now,* he seemed to say with twinkling eyes and a lopsided grin.

"I'm going," she whispered, liking the way the words made her feel. Then, louder, "I'm going." She spun, looking for her daughter. "Wait—where's Ellen?" She couldn't leave without saying goodbye. "She won't want to miss the launch." Hurriedly, she texted her the change in plans.

The reply was instant. *Mom I want you to go with REEF. Please do it.*

Where are you sweetie?

I'm fine. Go Mom. I want you to.

She turned to the rest of her family. "REEF, don't leave. I'm coming with you."

His smile was brilliant and heart-stopping.

"I have to get my clothes."

"Already took care of that," Jana said. "Your suitcase is in the ship."

"How—?"

"We might be different in a lot of ways, but we've always known each other better than anyone else," her sister said.

Evie hugged Jana close, soaking in the years of love. "Thank you," she whispered. She found her son again and dragged a trembling hand down his cheek. "I think I'll be out of cell coverage for a while." She smiled tearfully. "I love you. Tell Ellen too."

He nodded, grinning, and hugged her again in that awkward way of teenaged boys.

She said good-bye to each member of her family. Her heart wrenched when she realized Ellen still hadn't shown up by the time she climbed into the ship.

REEF strapped her into a comfortable seat that molded around her. His hands on the harness, he kissed her. His mouth was warm and wet and delicious. "Zero-G," she reminded him.

His eyes darkened. "I haven't forgotten."

He left her to close up the ship. The hatch sealed, making her ears pop. Her heart pounded wildly. Evie Holloway was going into space. Who would have ever dreamed it?

She was about to fly.

REEF was calm, confident and capable as he readied the ship. It put her at ease. The engine started, rumbling. The vibration made her teeth chatter. She gripped the armrests as the ship lifted vertically off the ground. It hovered there. Below she saw her family waving, their clothing and hair whipping in the wind. "What do you think, Evie?" REEF asked.

"Juice it."

He grinned. "Hold on." He moved the throttle forward. She whooped in delight as the ship's nose pointed at the sky. Gravity pressed her into the seat. She felt vaguely nauseated as the sky turned from sky to indigo and finally to starry black.

"Look," REEF said a few moments later, pointing outside. His arm bobbed slightly as if underwater. "Earth."

Her hair floated around her head as she peered in wonder at the delicate blue ball decorated with wisps of clouds. "Omigod. It's beautiful." She knew that soon many people would be seeing such sights. Space travel would become commonplace.

REEF threw off his straps and floated free. She unhooked her harnesses too. She laughed. "I'm in space. Floating! This is incredible."

He took her by the hips and pulled her close. With her thighs, she anchored herself to him. As they spun slowly, his gaze dropped to her mouth then lifted to her eyes. The heat in his gaze took her breath away. "Your turn to be the virgin, yes?"

Dear Lord.

Her belly pulled tight as he lowered his mouth to hers—

"Mom?"

They froze at the sound of a girl's voice.

"Don't be mad."

TWENTY-ONE

"You stowed away?" Evie gaped at her daughter, half-horrified by and half marveling at the girl's audacity that made her own high school antics pale in comparison.

It was a family confrontation out of the *Jetsons*: the three of them bobbing like beach balls; teenage Ellen equal parts sheepish and unrepentant; Evie the mom, furious, and REEF in the father role looking mildly amused.

Then reality sank in, cold and hard. "The custody arrangement stipulates that I have your father's permission before taking you out of state." She threw a hand at the porthole framing a nice view of a rapidly shrinking planet Earth. "Think we've pushed the boundaries a little?"

Ellen tried to shuffle her feet. The motion sent her spinning. She grabbed the back of the chair. "Cool."

Evie groaned. "Ellen, sweetie, you've put me in an awkward spot."

"I'll call the ranch."

"I don't think our data plan reaches this far."

"Mom, I'll use the comm. Whatever it takes. They'll put me through to Dad."

"And if he demands you come back right away?"

"Radio problems." Ellen lifted her hands and shrugged.

Pretty damn clever. Evie rolled her eyes. "This is my flesh and blood."

"Is it so surprising?" REEF smiled.

She elbowed him, sending her floating off in the opposite direction. She grabbed hold of a computer panel and hoped she didn't break a vital piece of equipment in her clumsiness.

"You shouldn't have popped your head out so soon, Ellen," she scolded. "You should have waited past the point of no return. Then there'd be no turning around. The pressure of letting you stay or not wouldn't be all on me."

"That was the plan, Mom. But then you and REEF..." She waggled her eyebrows. "It was either hide and listen, or let you know I was here."

Evie traded a loaded glance with REEF. "Good choice."

"We will soon proceed to the jump node—from where we will enter faster-than-light speed," he said quietly. "Any changes in travel plans should be made prior to the point."

By now, Earth had shrunken to the size of a marble. The forward window displayed nothing but empty space. "Then we have to turn this ship around."

"No." Ellen tempered the harshness of her response almost immediately. "Please." Her eyes shimmered with tears she refused to let fall. Her ponytail floated in zero gravity as she beseeched Evie and REEF in turn. "Don't make me go back. This is my dream."

Dreams... Evie was chasing hers now—a six-foot-plus former assassin who'd turned her world upside down, shaken her awake and pulled her out of her safe shell.

REEF also regarded Ellen, rubbing a contemplative finger under his chin. Maybe he was thinking of dreams, the ones he held close now and all those shattered in his past.

Neither of them had the best of luck when it came to dreams. Who were they to deny someone else theirs?

He turned to her. "I have come to care a great deal for your children. I would welcome Ellen on our journey."

She searched his face for the truth and found it. He really did care for her children.

Knowing this, she fell in love a little bit more. "Well, then." She clapped her hands. "What are we waiting for? Let's take you home, Eriff of Sandreem."

The second day into the journey, REEF checked coordinates on the star map. The three-dimensional, full-color display shimmered in front of him. They were about to enter the last in a series of wormholes that served as shortcuts through space. It would drop them off a short distance, astronomically speaking, from Sandreem.

REEF struggled to stay ahead of all the data streaming from the ship's sensors, a task that used to be easy. Evie, fighting mild space sickness, was sleeping in the bunkroom, while Ellen napped, curled up in the copilot chair she refused to leave.

He studied the girl as she slept. Protectiveness washed

over him. And worry. With his bio-threads severed, he'd lost his heightened senses, stamina and accelerated healing, not to mention his powers of concentration. As much as he despised his REEF characteristics, he'd come to rely on them. Oh, they'd regenerate, requiring either more surgery or a more permanent solution, but for now, he was merely human.

Selfishly, perhaps, he'd urged Evie to accompany him, wanting her to experience his return home with him. It was normal, *human,* this need to share with loved ones, was it not? Then her daughter had appeared, an unexpected addition.

Responsibility.

He jerked his attention from the star map back to Ellen. Her ponytail swayed in the air with her quiet breathing. A beaded necklace drifted under her chin. In one curled arm was a small, stuffed dog, a vestige of younger days that she'd been loath to leave behind even on this grand adventure. Such innocence, such vulnerability. The desire to keep the child safe struck a chord on a different, more basic level than what he felt with Evie.

Each day had brought new revelations on the complicated journey to becoming fully human. Now there was one more discovery to ponder: his fierce, unquestioning, unconditional drive to keep Ellen safe from harm. He had the feeling he'd just gotten a taste of parenthood.

REEF went very still. Him? A parent?

Until that moment, he'd never contemplated children of his own. It had been the furthest thing from his mind. He didn't know what toll his bioengineering had taken on his ability to father a child, but the possibility shed new light on his relationship with Evie.

He wasn't sure what served as birth prevention on Earth but he was fairly certain they hadn't used any. What if he had gotten her pregnant? The thought brought him to his knees, emotionally...her belly rounded and full, new life growing in her womb. A future. Their future.

The thought overwhelmed him. Was it normal to feel so utterly unprepared at the prospect?

He forced his attention back to the starship's imminent entry into the wormhole. First things first—his impending arrival on a planet whose inhabitants most likely thought him long dead.

TWENTY-TWO

Sandreem

Miles after miles of pristine forest rolled underneath the star-craft as it streaked down through Sandreem's atmosphere. Lakes, dark and deep, were scattered like gemstones amidst the trees. Mist hung in the river valleys, twisting and turning like the streams they followed.

"The ring," Ellen cried out. "I see it!" A bright band across the sky, the remains of Sandreem's moon glowed. The sash of the goddess.

Evie sighed in awe. "It looks like a shattered rainbow. Look at it."

"Wait until you see it at night." Pride glowed in him like a banked fire. They too found his world a thing of beauty.

The horizon opened up before them, shimmering in the late spring sunshine. "There it is!" He couldn't help crying out. "The sea." He pointed to the starboard side as memories overwhelmed him. The great inland sea of his childhood spread out before them, welcoming him home.

He swallowed, gripping the control stick in his hand, part of him longing for the composure of his REEF days, while in truth he was glad he could feel.

"What's going through your mind, babe?" Evie's voice was soft in the private channel in his headset. "What are you feeling right now? Are you excited?"

"Excited. Nervous too," he added truthfully. His home village had appeared on the radar but he'd not yet acquired it visually. "Unsure..."

"Why?"

He hesitated, trying to make sense of the fear underlying the thrill of his return. "It has been so long, Evie. I was a small boy when I left. What if they don't remember me?"

Evie's voice was gentle, sure. "A mother never forgets."

He scraped an unsteady hand over his hair and nodded at Ellen. Her copilot duties included working the communications. She was doing an admirable job.

She recited what she'd spent a day memorizing, reading from a piece of notepaper torn from her journal. The Queen's tongue. No English was spoken here. REEF knew her words translated to: "Planetary Watch, this is Reunion One. Request permission for entry."

Until now only silence had met their requests. This time a burst of static came in response. Then a faint sound.

"It sounds like a person this time, REEF," Ellen said with excitement. "A man. Are the radios hand-cranked or what?"

REEF chuckled. "In a way it's comforting to know little

about my home has changed. Unfortunately, it means communications are no better now than they were then."

Beyond wooded hills a sprawling village appeared, small homes scattered over the hills. "Behold, the capital of Sandreem." Was it always this small? "I don't remember it looking quite so...backward."

You're an off-worlder now.

In many ways, he was. Would his people, his family, see him the same way?

"Planetary Watch, this is Reunion One," Ellen said again. "Request permission for entry."

More garbled transmissions.

He rolled his eyes. They were going to have to replace that comm equipment! "We'll find our own place to land." Banking steeply, he found a suitable meadow. With a rumble of the star-drive engine that probably echoed like thunder in these quiet hills, the ship descended.

Once they'd settled to the ground, he shut down the engine. The silence was immediate and overwhelming.

Hastily, he climbed to the hatch and shoved it open. He jumped out onto the hull of the craft and spread his arms wide. Reborn in the bracing air and clear sunshine, he breathed deep. Eriff of Sandreem had arrived home.

His eyes match the sky here, was Evie's first thought seeing REEF standing on his home turf. He turned in a full circle, taking in the view. Then he threw back his head and laughed. The sound was rich and triumphant.

She walked across the spongy turf to stand with him. He took her hand in his. "The colors here are so pure and bright. It almost hurts to look at them."

"Our star's light is more violet than your sun. That's what you detect."

The idea was more than a little disorienting. She looped her arm over Ellen's slim shoulders. "We're the aliens here, kiddo."

A woman's voice rang out in the distance. "Hai-ho!"

They spun around. Three people made their way toward them. Their clothing was functional and struck her as vaguely Mongolian in style—leathers, loose trousers, muted colors, tall, pointy boots. She adored those boots, decided immediately that she wasn't leaving without a pair.

"Hai-ho!" REEF called back. "It's a Sandreemer greeting," he explained out the corner of his mouth.

Ellen waved excitedly. "Hai-ho!"

"Hey-ho, hey-ho, it's off to work we go," Evie couldn't help humming under her breath. Though the arriving trio looked nothing like Snow White's dwarves. There was a tall woman armed with archery gear who seemed to be the leader. Also armed with various weapons, two equally tall men followed her. One of them was young, not much older than John.

"It's the Planetary Watch," REEF told them. "It's an honor to be chosen as a member of the Watch, and very difficult. My father was one of them. When news comes of an arriving starship—very rare—an alarm goes out mobilizing them. Another group bearing gifts will be along soon."

They'd brought gifts of their own from Earth for the Sandreemers, from generators to books to chocolate.

REEF raised his hand, fingers splayed, then brought his fist down over his chest. The group slowed. He smiled. "I've confused them. They're wondering how an off-worlder knows how to make a Sandreem greeting."

The youngest man's gaze had focused on Ellen. He was handsome in a wholesome way, already broad in the shoulders. Seventeen, maybe? In the corner of Evie's eye she noticed her daughter's hands dart up to smooth her ponytail. Uh-oh.

The woman leading the group suddenly pulled up short. Her waist-length dark braid swung. Her chest began to rise and fall rapidly. The older of the two men grabbed her arm, but she shook free, running now to hurry up the hill where they stood close to the still-steaming starship.

Sudden goose bumps tingled up and down Evie's arms. The woman looked like REEF.

She turned to him. He'd already noticed what she had.

By the time the woman reached him, her blue eyes were full of tears. "Eriff? Is that you? Or do the goddesses deceive me?"

Evie didn't understand what the woman asked, but "Eriff" was unmistakable.

"They don't—" REEF's voice caught "—they don't deceive you."

The woman brought a shaking hand to her chest. "I'm Karah. Your sister."

A wrenching sob came from deep within REEF's chest. "My little sister," he managed to translate for Evie. "Karah."

He took a few shy steps toward her before Karah flew into his arms.

Weeping softly, Evie drew Ellen close and watched the beautiful, long-awaited reunion.

REEF's grip on Evie's hand was firm as they were swept along to the village in an ever-increasing crowd. Evie had never seen so many happy, healthy people. They didn't live in primitive conditions—she saw electric, or some sort of artificial lighting—but it was definitely rustic. The streets were dirt. There were puddles from a recent shower. The sun was pleasant but the air had a chilly bite. She and Ellen weren't dressed warm enough, they soon found out. Sandreemers came out of nowhere to drape hardy knitted sweaters over their thin hoodies. Soon, REEF sported a rugged leather duster.

The crowd opened up to allow more people through. A woman's shriek rang out. "Eriff!"

She was pretty, plump and blond. The handsome man with her was an older version of REEF. The expression on his face upon seeing REEF was heartbreaking.

"My father and mother," REEF said huskily.

They came together in a crash of tears and embracing.

Again, Evie was moved to tears, clutching her daughter close as another passionate, poignant reunion unfolded.

When the trio finally moved apart, REEF's mother's shining gaze found Evie and Ellen. She smiled and said something, but Evie shook her head.

REEF translated. "She wanted to know if you were my wife, and Ellen my daughter."

"I hope it wasn't too hard to explain."

"Not in the least." His smile widened. "I told her I wasn't yet ready to give up hope on that."

The heat of a full-on blush flooded her cheeks as he turned away for more reunions—a younger brother he'd never met, his sister Sayree, her husband and their children—REEF had nieces and nephews.

"I told her I wasn't yet ready to give up hope on that." A silly smile curved Evie's mouth as she watched the scene unfold.

The party went late into the night. It was difficult listening to REEF tell the horrifying story of his capture and of the years since. Although Evie couldn't understand the words, she didn't need to. The shock and anger and grief in his family's faces were all the translation she needed.

They could care less that he still had the vestiges of hardware in his body, that even as they sat there, it was regenerating. To them he was their beloved Eriff.

The celebration took place in and around the cottage where REEF grew up. Evie imagined him as a little boy sitting at the rough-hewn wooden table. How horrible it must have been for his family the day he went missing, seeing his empty chair that night and all the nights afterward. What pain his mother must have felt.

Suddenly missing her own child, she glanced around,

hunting for Ellen, and found her clutching a mug of hot ebbe-apple tea, her smile soft as she listened to a young man try to overcome the language barrier. It was the good-looking cadet from the Planetary Watch. Finnen was his name, she'd learned. Ellen's expression looked dreamy.

"Don't go falling in love with a Sandreemer," Evie said under her breath.

REEF's hand slid in a soft caress over her shoulder. "And why not?"

"Because—" she turned in his arms "—once you start, you just can't stop."

His hands framed her face, his thumbs tracing over her cheekbones, her jawline, her lips. Then, with a bent finger, he tipped her chin up. "I can't wait to get you alone."

She almost moaned. He hadn't done anything but look at her, and already she was putty.

Molten putty, she thought a few hours later when in the privacy of their cottage bedroom she stripped off his coat and was halfway through the buttons on his shirt when he tugged her sweater over her head. Their kiss was feverish, greedy, as the rest of their clothes fell away. This was no slow seduction. This was hunger—*need*—pure and simple.

He hoisted her off her feet, plunging into her before they ever made it to the bed. Legs wrapped around his hips as they fell to the mattress, she half laughed, half moaned at their urgency as he took her hard and hot.

"What did you say about loving a Sandreemer?" he demanded, slowing as she approached her peak.

"REEF, don't stop," she pleaded.

"Eriff," he said.

"Eriff..." She smiled, then bit back a cry as his deepened his thrusts. The slow, deliberate motion restoked the fire inside her.

Again he brought her almost to orgasm before backing off. Her cry was hoarser now. "Eriff..." His control over her was complete, breathtaking, and she loved it. She grabbed his hair and pulled him down to her. "Please."

His kissed her, their tongues tangling, and it pulled her over the edge. She exploded, taking him with her, their orgasms quaking on and on, until they sagged, sated, in each other's arms.

Afterward, perched on an elbow, he smoothed her damp bangs off her forehead. "Tell me again about loving Sandreemers, Evie."

"Once you start," she traced the outline of his mouth, "you can't stop."

"I'll love you for a lifetime if you give me the chance."

She froze. He wanted her. He loved her. He didn't want to hold his options open for a Sandreemer.

She came first with him. She *was* his first.

"Will you, sweet goddess?" He held her gaze. "Will you give me the chance?"

"I will. I love you. I do." And as she gazed into those sky-blue eyes, honest, intense and dark with passion, she decided she just might find her happy ending after all.

It was amazing to Eriff, the difference that his and Evie's open declaration of love had made. Not only were they giddy about it, the feeling had spread to everyone around them.

Happily, the day would be one of relaxation. After all, they hadn't had a chance to recover from their long trip from Earth. Goddess knew, Eriff needed the time to rest. He felt the loss of his REEF abilities far more when he was fatigued.

After breakfast, Evie had disappeared into the kitchen with his mother, his sister Sayree and several other women. Not Karah; his middle sister had grown up to prefer weaponry to cooking. Apparently, Evie's pleas to learn Sandreemer baking was to be all too happily indulged.

Thwack. "Missed again!" Ellen frowned at the tree branch upon which she and Eriff had lined up several cups for target practice.

He took the slingshot from her. "It takes practice. Here." He placed a rock in the sling and took aim at a young green ebbe-apple. Firing as if it hadn't been over two decades since the last time he was deep in these woods, he let the rock fly.

He didn't want to think of the last day he was here. The terrifying day was over and gone, and now it was his goal to forget it. The latent anger would never go away completely, not as long as the men who took him lived, but vengeance was not his desire. There had been too much death in his life. He wanted no more part of it.

The rock snapped the twig holding the apple. It dropped into one of the cups. Ellen shrieked when the cup wobbled but did not fall.

He grinned. "It takes a delicate touch."

"Let me try." Squinting, she aimed the slingshot and fired. Her rock arced into the tree.

"Perhaps next time," he started to say, thinking the rock was lost, when a little unripe apple plunged down to the cups, knocking one to the ground.

He laughed heartily. "That's pretty good for an off-worlder."

Her eyes twinkled with pride. "I won't be like an off-worlder for long."

Twigs snapped. A group of teenagers appeared, boys and girls. They were holding spears and nets. Ellen's face lit up at the sight of young Finnen, who held out a spear for her.

The boy was lost. Eriff knew the look. It was the charm of Holloway women.

Eriff considered warning Finnen but decided to let the boy figure it out for himself. As long as he didn't act too forward with Ellen, he thought, protective instincts bristling.

"Hei-ho," Ellen called to them.

Finnen issued an invitation from the group. "They want to know if you're interested in helping catch eel for dinner," Eriff translated.

"Heck, yeah!" She wedged her slingshot in Eriff's back pocket and was off, scampering into the deep forest with new friends.

Much like he used to do, he thought, although his adventures were mostly solitary. Smiling, lost in memories of his childhood, Eriff wandered deeper into the woods. It was hushed and fragrant amongst the trees. Above, the trees laced together, muting the sunlight. He was happy, content. He'd found love, and he'd come home.

It did not get any better than this, he decided.

He walked for some time along a narrow trail. A flash

appeared in the corner of his vision, followed by a hiss. He spun around, grasping for data, having to rely on his human senses to find it.

Not twenty steps away, a quivering arrow sank into the trunk of a tree. Eriff's gaze tracked backward and found only shadows.

"Up here."

Eriff jerked his gaze higher. Up in the trees, well above the forest floor, a man stood half-hidden in the branches. He wore a uniform. A Coalition uniform.

"Tsk tsk, Oh-One. You're not armed are you?"

The man drew back on the bowstring. A red laser light coursed over the ground and up Eriff's leg, stopping over his hammering heart. The man took a step sideways, into the open.

Orange hair...light eyes.

"Oh-One," he'd called him. It stood for REEF 01-A, his former model designation. Eriff sifted through memories of the staff of the REEF Academy. The Captain was the Headmaster.

They were one and the same.

The Captain smiled, a triumphant smile, his voice soft. "Run, little rimmer."

TWENTY-THREE

Think. Without streams of helpful data to guide him, Eriff was forced to sort through a jumble of information in his head. He cast his gaze around, looking high and low, remembering the forest he used to know like the back of his hand.

"So much talent, wasted," the Captain said. "Had you still been a REEF I'd be dead already. Instead—" he let the arrow fly "—you're a laughably easy target."

Eriff whipped his body out of the way. Not fast enough. Pain roared through his midsection. The arrow had lodged in the flesh of his hip. Growling in pain, he tugged it out.

He didn't know how the captain had found him here. He didn't know what the man intended, or why he'd returned for him. One thing was certain—if Eriff stayed where he was, he was dead.

While the Captain reloaded, Eriff bolted into the brush. He found a dangling vine and hoisted his body into the trees, feet high, using momentum and his still-powerful arms to vault to a branch. He straddled the branch, woozy with pain.

An arrow whizzed past his head. Goddess, the man was out to kill him.

Fury vibrated through Eriff, not fear. Hatred. This man had conscripted him, using him to help start his school. He'd turned him into a monster.

A monster no more!

Eriff crouched down, his pants soaked with blood. Thank the goddess his remaining nanomeds were swarming to the sight of injury, repairing the wound. It didn't much help the pain—the wound was too deep—but it had slowed the flow of blood.

He jumped to the next tree, and then the next, to put distance between himself and his attacker. Movement in the trees told of the Captain's approach. How? The man was older, and unfamiliar with the landscape.

An arrow came from an unexpected direction, narrowly missing him. How?

"After so long watching the miracle of my creations, did you think I would not sample the wares myself?"

Goddess be. The captain had bio-implants? To what extent?

Enough to keep Eriff on the run.

"It's not fun being a mere human, is it, Oh-One? Being weak."

"I prefer human to monster!"

"Monster, bah! You were a thing of beauty. The closest thing to a deity in human form. Come back home, Oh-One. I'll take care of you. I'll heal you."

"Go to hell!"

"As you wish, Oh-One. But I'm taking you with me."

Evie was having the time of her life. It was pure heaven: cooking with ingredients she'd never seen, delicious smells, the happy chatter of Eriff's family, even though she had no idea what they were saying.

They'd given her a pile of tiny red berries to chop for a sort of pastry. The fruit was a cross between raspberries and cherries. She used a heavy knife to slice off the thorny stems. Laughter rang out, distracting her, and the unwieldy knife sliced into the soft pad of her index finger.

"Ow." Blood welled out of the cut.

Sayree took a look at her bleeding finger, frowned, and found her a Sandreem version of a Band-Aid. Evie stuck her fingertip in her mouth to clean the wound and wrapped it in the bandage.

Evie went back to sorting through a fresh pile of berries while Eriff's mother prepared the dough. After a while, wet, the bandage slipped off her finger. She jerked her hand back, anticipating the sting of acidic fruit juice on the wound, but there was no cut. For a second she thought she'd wrapped the wrong finger. A closer look revealed a cut that was halfway healed. The line was there; the skin had fused. Whatever microscopic healing bots Eriff had swimming in his blood-stream had gotten into *her*.

Ellen came into the kitchen. "Hey, Mom."

Quickly, she hid her hand. "Hey, sweetie."

"Do you know where REEF—I mean, Eriff, went?"

"I thought he was in the woods with you."

"He was. Then I went eel spearing. I caught one! But we're done. I want to finish my slingshot lessons. I'll see if I can find him." Grinning, Ellen ran off.

———

Eriff had neither the agility of a six-year-old nor the bioengineered advantages of a robotic combatant. It seemed to be what the man wanted to prove: his humanity was a liability.

"What happened to you?" the Captain called out. "Was it a malfunction? When you first disappeared, they told me you may have been forced to activate your self-destruct device. Every REEF has such a suicide device, but I never made a single one operational."

The man's laughter echoed in the hush of the woods. "If the Coalition ever finds out, I'll be executed for treason. But what they'd asked of me was far worse, Oh-One. Ah, yes. How could they have expected me to provide my precious treasures the means with which to destroy yourselves after I gave you life?"

The Captain actually believed he gave Eriff and the other REEFs *life?* He leaned his head back against the tree and laughed hollowly.

"Instead, the self-destruct cap bears the exact time and day of the insertion of your command hardware, and my name. Thus each of my rare and wonderful REEFs remain irrevocably tethered to me. My precious children."

"You're mad," Eriff shouted. A pause. Then an arrow hissed past.

He ducked back behind the tree, his heart racing. Sweat trickled down his face as he contemplated his next perch.

"And you, Oh-One? You are perfection. The models prior to you proved unstable, but you grew into my best. Come with me, Oh-One. I'll make you better—better than you ever were!"

Eriff leaped silently to the next tree.

"We have so much history together. I'll never forget the little wild thing you were before I crafted you into a magnificent combatant. There hasn't been another one like you since." The Captain's voice echoed in the forest. "The closest was a recruit brought in some years ago. He was a spirited little boy, much like you were. I had high hopes for him once he was brought under control. But then there was a malfunction of the brain implant. It caused a stroke. He never recovered and had to be put down."

Eriff swallowed against a gag reflex.

"Eriff! Eriff!"

Evie's daughter. His blood turned to ice. "Run, Ellen!" he shouted.

The girl walked into view and squinted up at him. "What are you doing up in the tree?"

The Captain landed behind her. She spun around, sucking in a startled breath as the unstable officer pressed a knife to her throat.

TWENTY-FOUR

Eriff stood out in the open, no longer caring what happened to him. The color had drained from Ellen's face. Eyes opened wide with fear, she glued her gaze on Eriff's, holding it there as if he were her anchor. She was depending on him to save her.

"I believe the current situation demonstrates yet another disadvantage to being human," the Captain said.

"Don't hurt her," Eriff demanded.

"Empathy..."

"I'll...do anything."

"Caring for the welfare of another is the greatest human weakness of all. It makes you hesitate. Hesitation will get you killed." He pressed the knife into Ellen's throat far enough to break the skin. Ellen winced but she didn't cry out.

"I'll go with you! I'll go," Eriff said in misery. "Just don't hurt her. Please."

"See how he begs, child? See how you have made him weak?"

Ellen's rapid, shaky breaths belied her terror. Still her eyes remained fixed on Eriff. *She trusts you to save her. She's waiting for your lead.*

Goddess be, he felt unworthy.

He felt *human.*

He backed up against the tree. Something pressed into his ass. The slingshot Ellen had stuck in his pocket.

He slipped his right hand behind his back.

"You see how emotions are a handicap, Oh-One. We are better off without them."

He must overcome his emotions, then, to save her.

"I said I'll go with you," Eriff stalled, his mind racing, looking at all the possible shots he could make, the possible consequences of each as the child of the woman he loved stood trembling in the grip of a sadistic killer. If he moved too soon, he'd lose her. The right shot at the right time would save her.

"*Let me say this. It seems the goddess gifted you with infinite patience. With life so slow on this backwater planet, it'll serve you well, I think.*" His father's words echoed down the years, never as appropriate as now.

"Me, back in your care, Headmaster. Under your guidance. Isn't that what you want?" Eriff moved back until a leafy branch shaded him, hiding the fact he plucked off a couple of last season's ackor-nuts. "To make me well?" He held eye contact with Ellen, willing her to stay still.

Then, suddenly, Eriff grimaced, falling to one knee. "The pain—goddess, the pain. Make it stop!"

"Oh-One!" the Captain cried out.

In one swift move Eriff whipped out the slingshot, loaded the nut and fired. The nut impacted the Captain in the center of his forehead. The next shot caught him in the left eye. The man roared in agony and surprise. As he fell, he took a wild swipe at the fleeing girl. She went down.

"No!" Eriff leaped out of the tree. He wanted to go to Ellen but he had to take care of the captain first. He fell onto the Captain's unconscious body and closed his hands around his throat. *Kill.*

It was not an order commanded by a piece of hardware, but one driven by grief and terror and urgency—everything that was human, nothing that was machine.

He straddled the captain's twitching body, his hands crushing the windpipe until the pulse became thready, faint and finally died.

He fell back, gasping, and crawled to the girl. "Ellen." He turned her over. Blood...there was blood everywhere. He found the deep gash on her neck.

Picking up the Captain's knife, he slit his wrist and brought the pumping blood to the girl's wound, holding the contact and willing the part of him that wasn't human to heal what was.

TWENTY-FIVE

Only a few million of the billions of nanomeds sharing Eriff's bloodstream with his human cells had flowed into Ellen's body, providing enough initial healing to get her safely to the village physician. The scar was barely visible now.

A week later, Sandreemers gathered for the burial of one of their own. Long-lost Magnus Slipstream had finally come home.

The sun was setting, lighting the Sash of the Goddess afire. Eriff stood flanked by Evie and her daughter. As Sandreem's high priestess began the funeral, Ellen squeezed Eriff's hand.

He smiled down at the teen. They shared more than their love of Evie and a friendship that transcended age and origin; they now shared their blood.

As did Evie, from what they'd learned. The part of him that he'd long despised had been a gift in the end. A gift of life.

Eriff reached for Evie and drew her close as Sandreem's high priestess oversaw the lowering of his great-uncle's body into the dirt. Long ago Uncle Magnus had traveled to Earth, never knowing where his mission would lead. By colliding with a weather balloon over New Mexico, the Sandreemer pilot of the "Roswell saucer" had unwittingly set off a chain of events that saved the galaxy, generations later, bringing lasting peace.

In life as in the game of Sech, the lowliest pawn can topple an empire.

TWENTY-SIX

Pierce was waiting with Evie's family when they landed back at the ranch right on schedule. "Oh, no, what's he doing here?" Evie slurred, dry-mouthed, as REEF helped her climb out of the hatch. The fresh air cleared her head and made her stomach feel marginally better. Space sickness was a bitch.

It also put her in one hell of a foul mood. She ignored that mood while she tearfully greeted John, her parents, and Jana and Cavin.

Pierce marched up to her. "You've gone too far this time, Evie. Here's the court order."

She took the paper, held it in front of him, paused, and ripped it down the middle. She folded it in half, tearing it again. Then she let the pieces fall. Carried away in the wind of the dying engine, the scraps took to the sky like she had in this very spot two weeks ago. It was liberating to watch. She felt lighter than air.

Then she smiled sweetly at her ex. "Bite me."

He drew back in shock.

Yipping, tail whipping wildly, Sadie bounded across the meadow, excitedly licking her, Eriff and Ellen. Finally, she scampered over to Pierce. Evie turned, unable to bear the sight of the little dog fawning over a man who paid her no attention.

Then the sound of water spilling dragged her attention back to her ex-husband and Sadie, who squatted on the toe of his beige Italian leather moccasin, peeing.

***

"This time you handled Pierce," Eriff said later that day as they relaxed poolside, side by side in chaises. "I plan to take care of you for the rest of our lives so next time allow me to handle him."

"Deal." She smiled her best damsel smile at her knight and took another sip of iced tea. "Here we are talking about lifetimes when it used to be seven days."

Eriff pulled her hand onto his chest, placing it over his heart. "Let's make seven days into seven decades. Ten decades. Fifteen!"

She laughed. "Summers in Sandreem, the rest of the year here. At least until John and Ellen are out of the nest. Is that going to work for you? Be sure, baby."

"I am sure. My home is with you. Wherever you are, that's where I want to be."

"Good, because—" she pulled her hand back, bringing his with it, placing his palm over her stomach "—it wasn't space sickness."

For a fraction of a second he looked confused. The sheer panic that appeared next was obliterated almost immediately by pure joy. "You're with child, Evie?"

"*We* are. I'm two weeks late. I'm like clockwork, so...I think it's pretty much a done deal."

He was kissing her before she got the last few words out. "I guess you'll have to make me a legal woman now," she mumbled against his mouth.

"I plan to do more than that. I'm going to make you the happiest woman in the galaxy."

If they talked about anything else after that, she didn't remember. Eriff of Sandreem was better than chocolate...

Did you enjoy Cyborg and the Single Mom? Please leave a review. :)

While there, check out other Susan Grant books and start reading today!!

SUSAN GRANT KINDLE BOOKS

The next episode of the saga begun in the OtherWorldly Men series is here...

WARLEADER
book #1 in the Borderlands Series

Now that the galaxy has been united, dark forces seek to tear it apart...

Welcome to the Borderlands, where rules are meant to be broken

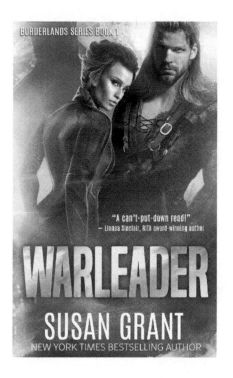

Admiral Brit Bandar is the Coalition's greatest starship commander. The outlaw known as the Scourge of the Borderlands taunted her in a galactic game of cat and mouse for years, but she never caught him. Now they're supposed to make peace *and* serve together on the same starship? Not so easy to do when her sworn enemy turns out to be the only man who can make her remember what it is to feel.

Warleader and space pirate Finn Rorkken doesn't care how many medals "Stone-Heart" Bandar has. He's going to show her what it's like to be pursued and caught by a master. Intergalactic peace is on the line, and if she wants his cooperation, she'll have to surrender her heart. Challenge accepted, Admiral.

"One of my favorite science fiction romances. Action-packed, a strong heroine, and a sexy hero—a guaranteed great read." —Anna Hackett, *USA Today* bestselling author

---

Click to Read WARLEADER today!

The Borderlands Series:
- Book #1 WARLEADER
- Book #2 HUNTING THE WARLORD'S DAUGHTER
- Book #3 RAIDER BORN

Three Borderlands prequels: (**The Otherworldly Men Series**):
- Book #1 GUARDIAN ALIEN
- Book #2 ROYAL RECRUIT
- Book #3 CYBORG AND THE SINGLE MOM

FROM THE AUTHOR

Susan's childhood dreams of becoming a space explorer fizzled when she found out calculus was involved. Luckily, she didn't need math skills to fly jets—or to create space stories in her head, first for herself, then for friends, and now for readers everywhere.

A *New York Times/USA Today* bestselling author and a military veteran, Susan won the prestigious RITA® Award for her book *Contact,* a sci-fi aviation-thriller romance.

Want to know about my next release? Sign up for my newsletter and receive a free book! (I'll never share your email address—ever.)

Follow me on Facebook, Twitter, and Bookbub.

Until next time... Fly high!

Susan

facebook.com/author.susan.grant

twitter.com/flyerdreamer

bookbub.com/authors/susan-grant

goodreads.com/susangrant

amazon.com/author/susangrant

Also by Susan Grant

New York Times & *USA Today* Bestselling Author

RITA Award Winner

Star Series

Star King (RITA finalist)

Star Prince

Star Rogue

Star Champion

Star Hero

Puppy

Star Raider (prequel)

Star Series—4 book boxed set

Star Heroes—2 book boxed set

2176 Freedom Series

The Legend of Banzai Maguire

The Scarlet Empress

2176 Freedom Series—2 book boxed set

Stand-alone Books

Contact (RITA winner)

Once A Pirate

The Day Her Heart Stood Still

The Lost Colony Series
The Last Warrior

The Borderlands Series
Warleader (RITA *finalist*)

Hunting the Warlord's Daughter

Raider Born

Otherworldly Men Series
Guardian Alien

Royal Recruit

Cyborg and the Single Mom

Anthologies
Mission: Christmas (featuring "Snowbound with a Prince")

Mysteria (featuring "Mortal in Mysteria")

Mysteria Lane (featuring "The Nanny from Hell")

Mysteria Nights (combines the *Mysteria* and *Mysteria Lane* anthologies)